CRIMEUCOPIA

The 's Have It

A Murderous Ink Press Anthology

****

I0733145

CRIMEUCOPIA

The 👁's Have It

First published by

Murderous-Ink Press

Crowland

LINCOLNSHIRE

England

www.murderousinkpress.co.uk

Paperback Edition ISBN: 9781909498327

eBook Edition ISBN: 9781909498334

Acknowledgements

To those writers and artists who helped make this anthology what it is, I can only say a heartfelt Thank You!

And to Den, as always.

Contents

*Triangles has appeared in *The Eyes of Texas: Private Eyes from the Panhandle to the Piney Woods* (Down & Out Press Oct, 2019)

It Was 3:15 in the A.M...
(An Editorial of Sorts)

Investigators and investigations are the mainstay of most Crime fiction sub-genres. Everything from the original Golden Age of country houses and the amateur sleuth, through to the high tech ultra-modern 21st Century – a place where the cyber investigators sometimes appear to be baffled by old-fashioned motivations of power and greed, and human foibles such as love and revenge.

So is there any real difference between the Private and the Public Sector? Not much, if writers are to be believed, and the two can often be found straddling both sides of the 'what's legal procedure?' fence.

Apart from **John M. Floyd** – who takes us back to the era of the early Private Eyes in his **Triangles** – the remaining writers are all new voices to Crimeucopia.

This time round **Mike Job** opens with his **Just Deserts** – a nice main course rather than just an amuse-bouche – closely followed by **Jill Hand** and **A Goddess, Enraged** which moves us into the edges of Urban Fantasy.

Joe Giordano sort of brings us back on track with his **Prophetic Justice**, and **Michael Thomét** introduces us to his two long-running, multi-story adventurers in ***Bear and Bird at Clairmont Circle***.

From there we hopscotch between the 'Cosy'-ness of ***Michele Bazan Reed's The Coveted Coverlet***, and the much harder edged ***The Knockoff King*** from ***Paul R. Paradise***.

There is that classic line that *snitches get stiches*, but does that apply to wildlife? Namely ***The Tell-Tale Armadillo*** from ***Mike Tuggle***? And after pondering that question, ***Edward Lodi*** then transports us into a Fredric Brown-esque world of humour and observation with his ***Death on a Pedestal***.

Lynn Hesse moves us from the Private to the Public side of investigators with her ***Bitter Love***, then ***Conestoga Number Four*** from ***Kelly Zimmer*** turns us almost full circle with a visit to American Cosy country.

And after ***John M. Floyd***'s ***Triangles***, what better way to close this collection than with ***Shannon Lawrence*** and her ***Alligator in a Sweatsuit***. Please note, no fictional alligators were harmed in the creation of this short story.

As with all of these anthologies, we hope you'll find something that you immediately like, as well as something that takes you out of your comfort zone – and puts you into a new one.

In other words, in the spirit of the *Murderous Ink Press* motto:

You never know what you like until you read it.

Just Deserts

Mike Job

Thursday November 20th 1969

Thursday November 20th 1969

East London, South Africa

At the outset, I suspected the salad. There were vegetables and leaves in there I couldn't identify, certainly not after the heat and the bugs had taken their toll. After the meal, the poor woman had managed to get to her bedroom and onto the bed to writhe around in what appeared to be prolonged death agonies, judging by the state of the bedclothes. Beverley Madison had died a hard death.

The body had been taken away, so with all the windows wide open, at least the stench in the room was abating. She may have been pretty at some stage, but she didn't look much better than the salad did after two weeks. Yooth came back in from outside, where he'd been recovering from his first experience of a bloater. His hair was damp with sweat and he was pale, but putting a brave face on it.

"Sorry about the puking, Sarge – I couldn't help it. Should I go down and apologise to the people downstairs?"

"What? All three floors? Naah, I need you here. Here, take some pics. Make yourself useful."

I was looking at the bathroom medicine chest, open to

expose the few things it contained. A bottle of liver salts, broken on the tiles, had reacted to a now-dry puddle of water from the shattered tumbler beside it.

"Good thinking, Beverley. But it wasn't indigestion was it? None like you've ever had, anyway. Hey Strip!! C'mere!"

"Yes, Sarge?" He poked his head in the door, camera in hand, eyes fearful in case I had some new horror to inflict on him. Nice kid, Strip. Anyone with a name like Yooth could expect some wag in the department to come up with a nickname like Strip – short for Stripling. "Pic of the stuff on the floor, take a sample, then bag all this stuff in the cabinet. Might be interesting."

I took my time on the scene. Her diary was interesting, but not startling. Nothing racy, no smutty letters in her drawers, mind-altering substances or kinky underwear. No pictures of family. The canary on its back on the cage-floor had stopped smelling - mummified by the afternoon sun. I wondered how long the empty plastic seed and water dishes had sustained it, and whether it had sung until the end came.

The caretaker arrived, a small, dull man with a big, shiny bunch of keys. He stood outside on the landing, looking like he was composing an alibi. All I wanted was the front door key – and assurance that there were no other copies.

Strange that there'd been no keys in her bag. Stranger perhaps, that she'd lain there for two weeks with the front door unlocked, nobody any the wiser or trying to enter. Until the woman across the hall knocked on the door to complain about the smell, and then tried the handle. By now she should be getting some sort of chemical support at Casualty with Jugs Wilson, our only policewoman, standing by to take a statement.

I turned to the refrigerator, humming quietly to itself in the little kitchen. Mineral water, half a bottle of semi-sweet wine, cheese turning green, celery and lettuce wilted despite the cold, broccoli brown and starting to seed, odds and ends of left-overs. The little ice-box was icing over and empty. There was a small piece of cardboard stuck to the side – a fold-in tag off the end of an ice cream carton. *Dreyer's Polar Moonballs.*

Back to the kitchen sink, where two unwashed bowls contained shreds of blackened lettuce and cress and two forks and two spoons. From the rock-hard, yellowing deposit on the sides and a dessert spoon, another bowl must have contained ice-cream, and there were two used coffee-mugs in there, too. I scraped a finger-nail across the bottom of each and carefully tasted the dried residues. One sugared and one not. There was still sugar in the sugar-bowl, although a column of ants was hard at work.

I left the stuff where it was. It could wait for the outcome of the post mortem. People die in the strangest circumstances and you don't rush everything to the lab. Scenes would come and dust for prints.

I locked the front door and pocketed the key, Strip a thankful pace ahead of me. He was quiet on the way back to the office and I let him be. As I say, he was a good youngster, dead keen and willing.

*****

Doc Parker was never at his most affable in the morning. Not in the afternoon either, nor at night when he got called out. Maybe when he was asleep things improved. He ignored me, standing there with my clipboard, waiting for him to begin. Strip was nowhere to be seen. Doc Parker deliberately started on the body next to mine – a road accident. Traffic never showed up on time so I took the blood sample bottle he handed me, although it wasn't my case, and held it out while he syringed a test sample out of the femoral artery. Then I screwed the top back on and gently shook the liquid back and forth to dissolve the anti-coagulant.

"Don't brutalise it, boy, you're not making a fucking margarita!!" he growled, only marginally appreciative of my help. He took his time, made his notes, tossed all the leftovers and dissected bits back into the thoracic cavity and signalled to Amos to stitch up.

The old mortuary attendant shuffled forward, threading a sail needle with coarse twine. Doc Parker paused to rinse his gloved hands before packing and lighting his foul smelling pipe. I stepped back discreetly and it wasn't because of my own decomposing cadaver. The pipe was legendary.

Parker ignored me and set to work. At her advanced stage, there was no longer viable blood to recover, so he'd have to look for other signs of alcohol or poison. About thirty minutes later, he held out his palm. In the goo and slime there were glints of some small metallic things. I put my hands in my pockets in case he expected me to take them from him, but he switched on the sluice hose and gently washed them clean. Six or seven four inch lengths of what looked like thin, stainless steel wire.

"Peritonitis, I'll bet." growled Parker around the stem of his pipe. "But how the hell could someone swallow stuff like this? Voluntarily?" I cleared my throat but said nothing. Parker's questions were always rhetorical. He dropped the things into a specimen bottle and went back to work.

I peered through the glass at the wire. At this range, the ends looked as if they'd been sharpened. I went back to watching Doc Parker. In another few minutes, he grunted and held out another object, misshapen but strangely familiar, no bigger than my fist.

"There y'go, Mister Plod , another piece of your puzzle. She was pregnant. I'm done. *You* work it out."

And he was gone. In a cloud of evil-smelling smoke to the next of his silent, uncomplaining patients as Amos began his perfunctory restoration of the damage left by post mortems the world over.

I left the foetus where it was in the formaldehyde jar, picked up my exhibit and left, glad to be in the open air again. Parker would fax his smudged post mortem findings in due course, but his verdict seemed logical. Bad way to go, peritonitis. Infection swarming in through a punctured stomach lining will do it every time. But to do that to yourself deliberately?

Strip was filling out forms when I got back, tongue protruding and intent on his neat block letters. He looked up at me expectantly. "Peritonitis. And she was pregnant."

"Who?"

"Enough of the owl impressions. Get me coffee." Rank has its privileges.

When he returned, I had the pieces of wire out on the blotter,

"What's that, Sarge? Looks like light gauge fishing trace wire." But he didn't move to touch the things.

"Course it is. I know that." Although I didn't. "Each piece has been sharpened at either end. Wonder why?"

Strip studied the wires, poking them about with his pen. "They're quite bent, Sarge."

"Like most of the people we deal with – is that a criticism or a useful observation?"

"I reckon I know how it happened." He'd picked up one of the wires, gingerly, but suddenly dead excited.

"See?" Now he'd wound the wire around his little finger, in two small, neat circles. "Like the Eskimos did it, y'know? Well used to...when they killed a polar bear – before guns!"

"Have you been at the exhibits, Yooth? I swear if that bag of weed is..." I started.

"No, no Sarge! They used whale-bone, only bigger, bent like this in a circle and frozen into a ball of seal blubber. The bear..."

I'd heard enough. "Get out of my office! And take your bloody nature study lecture with you!" I roared.

The look Strip gave me was pure hurt, but he dropped the wire back with the others, gathered his forms and stalked out, ears crimson. I sat there after he'd gone, staring at the wires, then wound one round my little finger as Strip had done, released it and watched it spring almost straight again, Then did it a few more times, thinking.

Pregnant. Flat keys missing. The items in the sink. Nothing interesting in the bin. Lethal items ingested, Impossible in their present form. The scrap of cardboard on the wall of the ice-box.

I reached for the phone and dialled the pathology lab from memory. "Trevor...s'me. Will you check the stomach contents of SDD 37/2 for any signs of gelatine – like in medication capsules. Yeah? Mazeltov! Push it ahead of the queue for typing, would you. I owe you!"

"*YOOTH!!*" I bellowed, and his head popped round the door. "Bring me the 'phone book!"

*****

At Arctic Frozen Foods, the owner came out of his office when he saw us. He didn't ask many questions himself when I asked about freezing techniques. Thirty minutes later I knew a lot more about blast freezing and seen it in use. Beats waiting for the 'fridge to cool your beer. Just zap it in the old blast freeze. Nearly instant.

They take your prints even for driving over the limit, and when those from my crime scene turned up, I had a suspect. A few other frozen food suppliers used the blast freeze technique and at *Gibson's Goodies*, I had that feeling. The one that only policemen know.

Brett Gibson was good-looking in a sleazy sort of way. Somehow, it made his discomfort seem more obvious. He was used to being admired by women, not stared at by hard-faced veteran detectives. The photos on his desk were of a pleasant faced woman and two kids, so I guessed he was fertile. Pictures on the wall showed him grinning in parkas and snow-gear on various ships or against bleak white backgrounds with Eskimo hunters. For someone in the refrigeration business, he sweated a lot.

He sweated a lot more when I asked if he knew a Beverley Madison and I thought he was going to cry when I tipped the specimen bottle out onto his desk. He sat there, staring numbly at the wires gleaming under the desk-lamp. When I took out the half medicine capsule from which I had cut the ends to form a little tube, then showed him how one of the wires could be held together in two or three tight little circles to be blast-frozen in a ball of ice-cream – like *Dreyer's Polar Moonballs* – he really did cry.

I could hear Strip breathing through his mouth close beside me.

"Could I have Beverley's keys back, Brett?" I asked quite gently. "I need to return them to the landlord."

He reached for the drawer without thinking.

A Goddess, Enraged
Jill Hand

The client seated himself in the chair across from my desk. Lighting a cigarette, he said, "It's my wife."

In my business, the business of private investigation, the three little words heard most often aren't 'I love you,' but 'It's my wife.' Sometimes clients say, 'It's my husband,' but no matter which of the pair is stepping out on the other, that despairing, angry tone of voice is the same. Their mister or missus has done them wrong, and they're honked off about it. Honked off enough to take serious measures.

The client, a guy named Mitch, a long-haul trucker by profession, took a deep drag from his cigarette and looked at me with haunted, bloodshot eyes. "You know what I'm saying?" he asked.

"I think I do," I said. "You wife has become interested in someone else."

Mitch took another drag from his cancer stick and laughed. It was the hollow laugh of a man who's had the emotional rug pulled out from under his feet. What once was sweet has turned sour, and now he's hurting. And vengeful.

By the look of things Mitch had decided to make me the instrument of his revenge. I can do that, for a price. I'd follow furtive couples to a hot-sheet motel, parking outside and watching them go in, arms around each other. Click would go the shutter of my camera as they smooched and one of them (the guy, usually) unlocked the door to their temporary love nest. I'd wait, drinking coffee and eating a sandwich, taking note of the time until they came out, hair mussed, clothes rumpled. Oh, yeah. I did that, provided evidence of hanky-panky. For a price. It's not nice, but there are worse ways to make a living.

"She's more than interested in him. Jack, that's his name. She's moved him into our goddamn house," he said.

That was different. Generally, ladies don't boldly bring their side pieces home to live with them and their husband. Threesomes happen, sure they do, but usually it's a one-night-only thing. Not always, but usually.

"So, it was acceptable to you, at first? The three of you being, um, together?"

Mitch smashed out his cigarette in the ashtray on my desk with an angry, corkscrew motion. "Hell no! I didn't want him there. I didn't want anything to do with him," he said indignantly. "Diana insisted. She claimed she needed company while I was on the road."

He shook his head, fighting back tears. It's hard to see a grown man cry. I've witnessed it plenty of times, and it never gets any easier. That injured pride, that grief. It's not pleasant to see, but I watched, sympathetic and professionally distant, like a shrink hearing a client profess a penchant for sniffing his mother-in-law's dirty undies, or for setting fires.

"All those nights I spent at truck stops, sacked out all alone. I could have invited a lot lizard to come in and warm my bed, but I never did. I only wanted Diana. And then she went and did this," he said.

He lit another cigarette, sucked in smoke and blew it out. Thank heaven for nicotine. Its soothing properties are a boon to the sick at heart.

"He sleeps with her. On my side of the bed, when I'm not there. She swears he doesn't, but I can smell him on the sheets and in the blankets," he said.

"I'm sorry," I said. "What would you like me to do?"

I was expecting him to ask for the usual: pictures documenting his wife's infidelity, to be used as evidence in a divorce. What he said shocked me, and I'm not easily shocked.

"I want you to take him for a ride."

"A ride?"

"Yeah, you know. Take him for a ride. Take him somewhere 'way out in the country where there's nobody around, and then…you know."

He named a price for me to take Jack for a ride. I accepted. Like I said, sometimes I have to do things that aren't nice, not if I want to keep paying the rent on my apartment and on this crummy office in a building downtown where the landlord doesn't care if my clients smoke or that the "doctor" on the second floor never even set foot in a medical school, let alone graduated from one. Laissez faire best describes the attitude of Jay, my landlord. Phony sawbones, prostitutes masquerading as massage therapists, shifty psychics, all are welcome under his roof, as long as the rent gets paid.

My partner, Morris Archer, had retired and moved to Florida. Now it was just me, Sam Nisnoff, running Archer and

Nisnoff Private Investigations LLC. I was the only one keeping the wolf from the door, metaphorically speaking. I couldn't afford to turn down an offer of work.

Mitch held out his phone to show me a picture of Jack. I gasped.

"Yeah, I know. He's a big mofo, ain't he?" Mitch said.

Big wasn't the word. Jack was huge. His head was enormous, with a massive jaw that looked as though it could bite through a steel cable. Heavily muscled, dark and arrogant, Jack was clearly a force to be reckoned with.

"I don't think I can handle him, alone," I said, studying the picture uneasily. "I guess I could if he were unconscious. Then maybe I could drag him out to my car and get him into the trunk, although my trunk's not that big." I pondered the problem, thinking of a way to make this work. "He'd fit in the back seat, I guess, but then if he woke up and went after me…"

Mitch held up his hand. "That won't be necessary. He'll go with you voluntarily. See, Jack loves hamburgers, and going for rides in the car. Offer him a hamburger and a ride in the car and he'll be putty in your hands. He won't suspect a thing, until it's too late."

"Not the sharpest needle on the cactus, is he?" I said, thinking of dim, friendly Lenny in "Of Mice and Men."

Mitch nodded. "He's dumb as they come. He won't give you a problem, I promise."

He was right. When I went to the address he gave me, Jack presented no problem at all. He was sprawled on the living room sofa when I let myself in the front door with Mitch's spare key. He looked up questioningly at the presence of a stranger, and then his eyes went to the paper bag I held in one hand. He grinned, a big, sloppy grin.

I grinned back. "Hey, Jack! How you doing, buddy? I brought you some hamburgers. What do you say we go for a ride in the car?"

Jack rolled off the sofa and accompanied me to my car, gentle as a lamb, his eyes locked on the bag of burgers. I opened the back door and he hopped in. *This is going to be a piece of cake,* I thought.

I was wrong.

A car pulled into the driveway behind me, blocking the only path of escape. The driver's side door flew open and a woman leaped out.

"You're stealing my dog," she yelled.

"No, I'm not," I said. "Your husband asked me to come over and bring Jack some hamburgers. I thought it would be nice to take him for a little ride, that's all."

"Bullshit," she said. "My husband hates Jack. You're stealing him."

With that she went around to the trunk of her car. I got a good view of her derriere as she leaned into the trunk to fetch something. It was an enjoyable view (the lady was stunning: fully six feet tall, slim, lissome as a young birch tree, her long flowing hair the color between red and yellow that's known in art circles as titian.) My enjoyment was cut short by what she held in her hands as she straightened up. A bow, a big one, too. She leaned into the trunk again and came up with a quiver of arrows. She slung it over one shoulder and nocked an arrow. Sighting down at me she drew back the bow string.

Mitch had mentioned that she taught gym at the local high school. Apparently one of the classes was archery. Diana seemed superbly at home with a bow and arrow, to the point where I had no doubt that if she let one fly in my direction my goose would be cooked.

Jack watched all this with interest from the back seat of my car.

"Hold on. I can explain," I said.

Diana raised a skeptical eyebrow. "Go ahead," she said.

I explained about her husband coming to me and expressing his jealousy of Jack, the Rottweiler/German Shepherd mix, asking me to take him for a ride in the country and drop him off somewhere far from home.

"He said Jack was too stupid to find his way home again," I said.

Diana lowered the bow. Adjusting the silver ornament she wore on her headband, an ornament shaped like a sickle moon, the horns pointing upward, she said, "Mitch is the stupid one. Jack would always find his way home to me, wouldn't you, sweetheart?"

That last remark was addressed to the dog. He wagged his plume-like tail, his brown eyes soft with adoration for his mistress.

"I should never have married him," Diana said, sounding disgusted. "We met on a cruise, in the Mediterranean. It was so romantic, with the balmy breezes, dancing under the stars, the ship rocking gently on the waves. I guess I got swept away. The captain married us. They really can do that, you know."

I nodded. I knew. I'd married two of my former wives on

cruise ships. There's something about being on a cruise that puts folks in the mood to tie the knot.

"I'm sorry," I said. "I'll be going now, if you don't mind."

"You don't have to go," she said, surprising me. She pointed her chin at the bag of hamburgers in my hand. "Come on inside. Let's have lunch. I've got soda, or wine, whichever you prefer. I have a proposition for you."

One month later Diana appeared at my office. Jack, who was curled up in the beat-up leather chair in the corner woofed happily and went to her. She hugged him and stroked his massive head.

"I missed you, sweetie," she cooed, speaking to the dog, not to me. She'd barely glanced at me. I was only the dog-sitter. I'd kept Jack for a month while Diana laid her plans. Jay, my easy-going landlord, didn't mind my having a dog in the office. Hell, he wouldn't have minded my keeping a herd of bison in there, as long as the rent was paid on time.

Seating herself in the chair where Mitch had sat a month previously, she drew a fat envelope from her purse and pushed it across the desk to me.

"Ten thousand dollars," she said. "You can count it if you want."

Mitch had paid me two thousand to take Jack for a one-way ride. He didn't know that Diana had given the dog over to my custody, temporarily. He thought Jack was gone for good.

Mitch's two thousand, and Diana's ten thousand for thirty days of dog-sitting and for keeping my mouth shut about her plans for Mitch wasn't bad pay. Sometimes Dame Fortune smiles upon you. When she does, it's in your best interest to smile back and say thank you, ma'am.

"No need to count it," I told her. "Thanks."

"Mitch's life insurance policy paid out yesterday. He was insured for five hundred thousand dollars."

"That's good," I said, adding, belatedly, "I'm sorry for your loss."

She waved a casual hand as if pushing that remark away. "It was bound to happen, sooner or later. He was careless with his cigarettes. I told him countless times to watch out when he was working in the garage around the gas can for the rider mower. I said if he wasn't careful, he'd knock it over and start a fire. That's exactly what happened."

"I'm sorry," I said again.

"It's all right. I have Jack to keep me company. I'm going to get more dogs. I'm always happiest around dogs." She surveyed me with those keen grey eyes, the eyes of a huntress, and rose. Walking to the door with Jack padding along at her side she spoke over her shoulder. "Thank you, Mr. Nisnoff. I don't suppose we'll be seeing each other again."

"Probably not," I said. I wasn't regretful. A woman like Diana spells trouble for men. She always has and she always will.

Prophetic Justice
Joe Giordano

Will my entire life be awash with scumbags?

I'm sitting inside a gray interrogation room that smells of stress sweat and vomit, staring across the table at dead eyes and a three-day beard.

"I have all day," I say, "but you stand a better chance of getting a deal from the D.A. if you cooperate."

In response, the prick parodies me. "You have the right to remain silent…"

I stop him in mid-sentence. "I already Mirandized you. You don't need to acknowledge the warning. Everything's on the video recording."

"You've really lost it," he says leaning back, unbuttoning his jacket to reveal a gold detective's shield.

Holy shit. I'm the suspect.

That's when I wake up. My name is Bragg, and I'm a gold-shield detective in Brooklyn South.

*****

Officer Jill Mancuso slalomed the multi-colored sidewalk tents, careful not to step in scattered mounds of human excrement, when she spotted a regular resident of Brooklyn South's homeless community wearing a black ski cap and tattered overcoat sitting on a bench next to her shopping cart trying to jam on Jimmy Choo red stiletto pumps. She was having as much success as Cinderella's ugly sisters had donning the glass slippers.

"Hi Dolly," Jill said, "where did you get those?"

Dolly clutched the shoes to her chest. "I bought 'em," she said defensively.

Jill smirked. "From where, Midnight Mary's Shoe Store? They cost six hundred bucks."

"They're mine."

"Those shoes are about as practical for you getting around as they would be for me." Jill put a hand on her hip. "You stole them?"

Dolly's voice rose. "I bought 'em."

"Sure." Jill sighed with a tinge of exasperation. "Last chance. Tell me where you got them, or I'm rousting you for shoplifting."

Scowling, Dolly made a final attempt to cram a shoe onto her foot without success. She huffed and extended the pumps toward the cop with two hands. "Take 'em."

Jill observed that the name, "Talisa Knox," was neatly taped inside each shoe.

"I don't suppose you know who Talisa Knox is, Dolly?"

Dolly shook her head.

"Where did you find these?"

Dolly looked away before answering. "In a dumpster, next

to a bar."

"The bar got a name?"

"I forgot."

"Show me."

Dolly crossed her arms.

Jill fished a sawbuck from her pants. "Show me and you get this."

Dolly's squinted at the money, then rose from her bench. "Follow me."

Dolly led Jill to the alley next to Gus's Saloon. They arrived just as a refuse truck was about to empty the dumpster. Jill halted the collection and after a quick glance inside, recovered a yellow hardhat with "Cagle" stenciled on the brim. The garbage stank, but not from a dead body. No Talisa Knox.

"When you grabbed the shoes," Jill asked Dolly, "did you see the hardhat as well?"

"Sure," Dolly said shrugging, "but what good is that to me?"

*****

Around four a.m. the night before Jill Mancuso recovered Talisa Knox's Jimmy Choo pumps and discovered the hardhat, two Brooklyn cops found Moose Cagle sleeping in the front seat of his red Dodge Charger a block from Gus's Saloon. Cagle looked like an evil Mr. Clean. A muscular skin head with a scorpion tattoo on his neck, six-three, he weighed in at about two-sixty. The loud rap of a flashlight on the windshield opened his eyes and the Brooklyn cops ordered him out of the car. Apparently cranky from loss of beauty sleep, he exploded from the vehicle, swinging. Fortunately, a second squad car was passing because four cops were required to wrestle Cagle to the ground and cuff him before hauling him to central holding.

*****

My boss, Lieutenant Dixon, an African American with salt-and-pepper hair, called me into his office. "Remember Dirk Mancuso?"

"Sure," I said. "Retired a couple of years ago."

Dixon nodded. "His daughter, Jill, is a cop. Pretty sharp. She came upon a missing person situation, Talisa Knox. She consulted with her father, and he called me. They both suspect the woman was murdered."

"But no body?"

"Right. I've wrangled getting Jill assigned to work with you for a day or two. Good training for her."

"Dirk has ambitions for his daughter and you're doing him a favor."

Dixon's eyebrows rose. "You have a problem with that?"

"It's not like I have nothing to do."

"Mancuso specifically asked for you. Apparently, he thinks you know what the hell you're doing." Dixon smirked. "Maybe his judgement isn't as good as I thought."

"I'm a babysitter."

"You mentored Casey London and she's now one of the brass."

"Female cops have become my specialty. Is that it?"

Dixon blew out a long breath. "Pick Jill up at the reception desk on your way out."

Dixon dismissed me with the wave of his hand, and as I left, he said to my back, "I want to hear good reports."

I spotted Jill's serious looking face as she paced nervously awaiting my arrival. I gauged how old I'd become by how young recent academy graduates looked. Wisps of honey-blonde hair were visible under her cap. She was attractive but had taken care to appear professional. Even so, her intensity couldn't hide that under the baggy blue uniform, she had the figure of a Zumba instructor. Youth, I thought to myself. Even with years on the job, she probably still thought life was fair.

I extended my hand.

"Detective Bragg," she said shaking mine, "it's an honor to be working with you."

"No need to butter me up. Your father was a great detective. Give him my regards."

She relaxed a bit. "I will."

"What have you got?"

She handed me a photocopy of Talisa Knox's DMV record, which included a photo,

I observed, "Early thirties, a looker. Lives in a good neighborhood." My glance rose. "Why do you think she's been murdered rather than just wandered or run off?"

She related the story of the homeless woman finding the stilettos ending with, "Nobody throws away Jimmy Choo pumps."

"Expensive?"

"Off the charts."

"Prints or blood on the shoes?" I asked.

"Dolly smudged up most everything. Forensics found no

blood trace."

"Okay. I'm still wondering if she could be hitchhiking to Florida rather than dead."

She referenced a small spiral notebook. "Talisa is married. Her husband reported her missing."

"They live together, yet she dolls herself up and goes out without him?"

"Open marriage?" Jill speculated.

"Sounds like motive. Let's start with him."

She turned a page. "I spoke to the owner of Gus's Saloon. He told me he knew her only as a customer, but his manner suggested he lied."

"Everybody is a suspect. Liars especially. What else?"

"Saloon Gus said Talisa was in the bar earlier that evening and very chummy with Moose Cagle. I found his hardhat in the same dumpster where the pumps were taken."

"A guy picks up a woman wearing a hardhat? What is he, a member of the Village People?"

Jill gave me a blank stare.

"Sorry, musical group before you were born. 'Y.M.C.A.'"

"Oh," Jill responded politely to my irrelevant comment. "Saloon Gus didn't see Cagle and Talisa leave together." She gave me the background on the cops' violent arrest of Cagle ending with, "He's being held on assault."

"And Talisa?"

"Forensics found no trace of her in Cagle's Charger."

"Nonetheless, he's still a suspect."

I let her drive. On the way over to Lester and Talisa Knox's apartment, we spoke about her goals. "You're bucking to become a detective?"

"A homicide cop, like my dad." Her eyes smiled. "And you."

"What's your plan?"

"I've been on the job five years and made it known I want to be a detective. I'm trying to distinguish myself." She glanced at me. "You're agreeing to take me along on this case will help, big time. Thanks for that."

I nodded, thinking that Jill was a sincere kid trying to get ahead. Was I different at her age?

She continued. "My dad tells me there's a strong element of politics about who gets ahead. He's coaching me on that."

"Lieutenant Dixon is a good guy to have on your side."

"I expect I'll need to be a general-assignment detective for some years before I can apply to homicide."

"That sounds right." We'd almost arrived at the Knox's building. "Back to the case, you'll lead the suspect interviews. I'll jump in at the end or if there's an element I want to explore."

Her grip on the steering wheel tightened. "Any advice?"

"We all love our intuition, but don't let that get in the way of evidence."

"Means, motive, and opportunity."

"The fundamentals are always good to keep in mind."

*****

Lester and Talisa Knox lived in one of those high-rise Brooklyn apartment buildings that provide refrigerators for delivered groceries while you work.

When he invited us into his modern motif living room, Lester Knox was fidgety and a bit distracted. Could've been worry about his wife or could've been guilt.

He offered us something to drink, which we refused, and we sat around a glass cocktail table.

Jill produced a Bic ballpoint and her spiral notebook. I saw her questions were already written. "Mr. Knox," she asked, "when did you see your wife last?"

"Saturday evening around eight, before she went out."

"Do you know where she was headed?"

Knox slowly shook his head. "Not exactly."

"I see. What was she wearing?"

"A black sheath dress and those damn Jimmy Choo stilettos."

"What do you mean?"

He blew out a breath. "Whenever she put on those shoes, it was like they cast a spell over her. She'd be off, and I wouldn't see her again until dawn."

"She'd gone out alone like this before. How often?"

He shrugged. "Maybe once a month. Whenever her hormones were up."

Jill glanced at me before she continued. "You didn't know where she was going but you knew why she went out?"

Knox ran his hands through his hair. "The prospect of sex with a stranger turned her on."

"Might there have been someone in particular?"

"She discouraged complications."

"Did you learn any of their names?"

"No," he said quietly.

"For all you know, she might've met someone specific that Saturday?"

He shifted uncomfortably. "I suppose."

Jill scribbled something before she asked, "Have you checked if Talisa is with friends or family?"

"Her parents are deceased and she's an only child. She doesn't have close friends and they haven't heard from her at work."

"What does she do?"

"Works on Wall Street. She's a Vice President at Bogle and Banks."

"Do you work there as well?"

Knox looked away. "I was furloughed months ago."

"How would you describe your relationship with your wife?"

"I know what you're thinking."

"What is that?"

"Her cheating on me was a motive."

"Isn't it?"

"I didn't like it. We argued, but I didn't hurt her. Check. She didn't file any domestic violence reports."

"Some women never do, then it's too late."

"Ask at work if she ever walked in with a black eye or

bruises."

"We will," Jill said. "Let's move on. Did the fact that she was the only earner create tension in your marriage?"

"Have you ever been laid off? It hurts. But I cooked and took care of the apartment, so she didn't need to worry about stuff like that."

"How would you describe your financial situation?"

"Talisa earns a good living but most of our money went into buying this apartment. Units like this cost a small fortune."

"Can you think of any enemies, a disgruntled client, anyone she fought with lately or might wish her harm for any reason?"

"No," he said in a forlorn tone.

"Does she have a passport?"

Knox rose and retrieved the document from a desk drawer, which he handed to Jill. She made note of the details before returning it to him.

Jill sat back, which I took as my cue to jump in. "Mr. Knox," I began, "I can imagine that having your wife step out on you must've been painful."

His eyes turned to me, but he didn't respond.

"Perhaps," I continued, "she also lorded over you that she was the bread winner."

He stared back at me blankly.

"Under all that stress and anger, if you snapped, nobody would blame you."

Knox cleared his throat before responding. "Detective Bragg, you may not understand it, but I love Talisa. I did her no harm. Please focus on getting her back to me."

"Did Talisa have a life insurance policy?"

Knox broke eye contact. "One million dollars. A key-executive policy taken out by her company." His gaze returned to me. "And, yes, I'm the beneficiary."

"Without proof she's deceased, they won't pay."

"Just find Talisa, alive," he said in a curt tone.

Jill requested and Knox gave us a better photo of Talisa, and we left his apartment.

When we were back in the car, she asked, "Did you believe him?"

I took a beat before answering. "I enjoy watching actors in a good movie especially because I'm reminded how convincingly people can lie. He could've followed Talisa, spied on her tryst, then killed her. Considering how he feels about the shoes, his tossing the Jimmy Choo pumps into a dumpster before disposing his wife's body, would fit."

"Wouldn't he have made her easy to find, so he could collect the insurance?"

I shrugged. "Fear of getting caught may have trumped greed. We still might find her. In any case, Knox remains on our suspect list."

"Nobody is off until only one person is on," Jill noted with spot-on perception.

"We'll get a warrant to search the apartment. Maybe forensics will get lucky and find cleaned up blood."

"You're not optimistic."

"We know Talisa made it to Gus's Saloon. Would Knox have waited for her to come home to kill her, then drop off the shoes in the bar's dumpster? More likely he killed her near the saloon and tossed her shoes. Still, we need to cross the Ts."

Our next stop was Gus's Saloon. A neighborhood joint with a long oak bar and a few tables in the rear.

Gus Lambert, the bartender and saloon owner was slim, in his forties wearing a newsboy cap and a rolled-up sleeve white shirt under his black apron.

He remembered Jill, and I introduced myself.

Jill said, "If you don't mind, I'd like to go over some of the things we discussed previously for the benefit of Detective Bragg."

Gus nodded without enthusiasm.

Jill opened her notebook. "Tell us about Talisa Knox."

"Attractive. Thirties. She dropped in occasionally. Drank Cosmos. Never paid for a drink."

"Popular?" Jill asked.

"Like bees to honey. But never the same guy."

"Oh. How did that go?"

"If someone she'd been friendly with on a previous evening approached, she'd make clear she wasn't interested in an encore."

"That could've become tense."

Gus nodded. "Especially if someone else was chatting her up."

"Any fights?"

Gus wiped a glass with a towel. "I'd anticipate what was happening and step in quickly to defuse the situation with a free drink. On occasion, I had to threaten to call the cops."

"She made friends as well as enemies."

Gus shrugged. "I suppose."

"We'd like the names and addresses if you have them of your customers who took an interest in Talisa, particularly those who were spurned when they made a second advance."

Gus hesitated and Jill added, "There's no bartender-client privilege."

Gus nodded agreement.

"Tell us about the last night you saw her," she said.

"Saturday a week ago. A skin head, Moose Cagle took a turn. Big dude. Nobody tried to cut in during their conversation."

"Was he wearing a yellow hardhat?"

"Yeah." Gus snickered. "Like one of the friggen Village People."

Jill glanced at me. I gave her a "see, I told you" look.

She refocused on Gus. "Did Talisa and Cagle leave together?"

"I don't know. I don't think so."

"How did their liaison end?"

Gus shifted on his feet before answering. "Like the others."

"Tell me."

"Sex with a stranger." He shrugged. "Some women get off on that. As the evening progressed, they'd sit closer and nuzzle each other before the affectionate couple would disappear into the men's room for a quickie. The guy would re-appear first, hot and sweaty like he'd been working out, if you know what I mean."

Jill just stared at him.

He grimaced, then continued. "Talisa would return flushed, but like nothing happened, sometimes leaving straight away, sometimes finishing her drink."

"Was Cagle or any of her other 'dates' upset that she didn't want a relationship?"

Gus scoffed. "Hey, this is 2020. Hookups are common. Relationships aren't."

Jill gave me the glance indicating that it was my turn to ask questions.

I asked in an innocent tone, "Did Talisa ever drop into the saloon on a less crowded night?"

Gus reflected a moment before answering. "I suppose."

I leaned forward. "Were you ever interested in taking your turn?"

Gus stiffened. "What are you implying?"

"You kept pretty close tabs on her. She's attractive. Are you telling me you never took her into the men's room yourself?"

Gus was indignant. "I knew you'd go there as soon as I told you what she did."

"Congratulations on your police acumen," I said with a sarcastic tone. "I think the academy is accepting applications."

He held up his left hand to reveal a silver band. "I'm married."

"That's not a denial. Are you sure no one will tell us that they saw you and Talisa getting together?"

Gus's eyes darted.

"Better," I said, "you don't lie to the police."

"Hypothetically," Gus responded, "let's say my appetites got the better of me, but I'm not admitting anything that could get back to my wife."

"That's why you killed Talisa? She threatened to expose the two of you had sex to your wife?"

Gus sputtered. "I didn't kill anyone."

"Can someone testify that you never left the bar and went straight home Saturday evening?"

His voice rose. "People come in and out."

"That's a 'no,'" I said. "Stay available, we'll talk again."

I nodded to Jill, and we left the saloon.

Outside, she asked, "Would he kill Talisa and throw her shoes into the dumpster next to his bar?"

"Unlikely but not impossible. We can't always imagine what people under stress will do. We'll get a warrant and search the bar and his car for any traces of Talisa."

"Do you think we'll find something?"

"I imagine the men's room will have her DNA. As for his vehicle, we need to cross that possibility off our list."

Inside the car, Jill asked, "Time to interrogate Cagle?"

"Absolutely."

"Not something I'm looking forward to," she said with a frown.

A real test for her nerve. "You'll be fine."

*****

Cagle had been Mirandized by the officers arresting him for assault, but they hadn't questioned him, and he didn't request an attorney. I decided we'd have a go, hoping he'd spill something before he lawyered up. Frankly, I thought Jill's presence would keep him talking. In the interrogation room, he was handcuffed to the same sort of metal table I'd envisioned in my reoccurring dream. He reeked of body odor. As we walked in, he spotted Jill and half rose from his chair. "Hello, baby. Come to papa." He made mock kissing sounds.

I punch-shoved his shoulder and he fell back into his chair.

"Hey," he said. "That's police brutality."

We ignored his comment and sat. Jill, grim faced, opened a folder on the desk.

"Mr. Cagle," she began, "you're divorced and, according to your wife, always late with child support."

"Yeah. So?"

"You assaulted four police officers."

Cagle had a surly expression. "The pricks woke me up."

"You've been picked up numerous times for violence. Says here, you're a laborer at the docks and according to your employers, you fight with coworkers as well. Cost you a few jobs, hasn't it?"

"Hey, honey," Cagle said leering, "why don't we get rid of your friend and we can do it on this table."

I wanted to punch the punk in the face.

Jill's eyes rose to his, and her tone was stone cold. "Mr. Cagle, are you under the illusion that I can't make your stay with us a living hell?"

All right, Jill.

Cagle sulked.

She continued. "Tell me about Talisa Knox."

"Who?"

Jill huffed. "The woman you were with in Gus's saloon the evening the police arrested you."

"What about her?"

"Did you know her before you met in Gus's saloon."

"Nope."

"What happened?"

"She wanted to get laid. I accommodated her." He flashed his ogling smile. "I accommodate women a lot."

Jill ignored that. "You left together?"

"Nope."

"Why not?"

He swaggered in his chair. "I'd shot my load and left the men's room. When I looked up, she was gone."

"You didn't pursue her?"

"Women chase me."

"Why were you sleeping in your car?"

"I'd done a double shift at the Brooklyn Pier and after a night of drinking and screwing, I collapsed in the car and passed out."

"Why did you attack the police?"

"Told you. They woke me."

"Did you get mad that Talisa walked out on you? Maybe she wasn't satisfied and insulted you?"

Cagle muttered, "She was satisfied."

"Did you murder Talisa Knox?"

Cagle's eyes widened. "What?"

Jill said, "You're a suspect in a murder investigation."

Cagle shifted nervously. "I didn't kill her."

"Did you imagine the police were about to arrest you for murder? Is that why you attacked them?"

His voice rose. "I didn't murder anyone."

"Where did you dispose of Talisa's body?"

"You're not listening."

Jill paused, seemingly for effect. "What happened to your hardhat?"

Cagle's eyes darted. "What do you mean?"

"Did it fall off when you threw Talisa's shoes into the dumpster?"

Cagle blinked a few times before he said. "I'm done talking. I want a lawyer."

"Do you have an alibi for where you were after you left Gus's saloon?"

Cagle crossed his arms and turned away.

Jill glanced at me. I said, "Mr. Cagle, you have a better chance of getting a deal from the D.A. if you cooperate. Tell us what happened and maybe we can get the charges reduced to manslaughter, rather than murder."

Cagle spit out the word. "Lawyer."

Jill closed the folder and we left.

We walked over and sat in my office.

"You did well," I said.

"Thanks." She thought for a moment before asking, "Cagle certainly seems capable of murder, but do you think he did it?"

"Every fiber in my body wants him to be guilty."

A female officer stuck her head in my office. "You have a visitor, Jan Hoff. Claims he has information about Talisa Knox's murder."

Jill and I exchanged glances before I said, "Please show him in."

The officer escorted a burly man with a high forehead, bushy gray hair, and horn-rimmed glasses into my office. We introduced ourselves.

"Mr. Hoff, you have information on a case for us?" I asked.

Hoff settled comfortably in a chair and said matter-of-factly, "You're investigating the disappearance of Talisa Knox."

Jill looked surprised, but I realized he could've read that in the papers. "We are," I said.

He gave me a small smile. "Detective Bragg, I sense that you're suspicious, especially with people you don't know very well."

"Sounds like my job description."

Hoff nodded. "I'm a psychic, and I often see images that are a bit unclear and which might indicate more to others than to me. If you're willing to help, perhaps we can together uncover their meaning."

"You're asking that I consult with you as a psychic?"

Hoff cleared his throat, then turned toward Jill and said, "The charm bracelet you're wearing."

She instinctively fingered the piece.

"Your father gave that to you in commemoration of your

graduation from the police academy."

Jill's mouth gaped. "How did you know that?"

Hoff smiled benignly before continuing. "Mostly, Officer Mancuso, you're shy and quiet, but when the mood strikes you, you can become the center of attention."

Jill's eyes widened and she looked at me before returning her gaze to Hoff. "That's true"

Hoff gave me a self-satisfied smile.

My sense of amazement was well under control. I said, "Nice parlor tricks, Mr. Hoff. What do you wish to tell us?"

Hoff's brow furrowed. "I'm afraid Ms. Knox is deceased. In my mind, I see her floating in water."

"Bathtub or ocean?" I asked not hiding my skepticism.

"This is one of those images I hoped you'd help with."

"Mr. Hoff, if you wish to claim that you assisted the Brooklyn police in their investigation, which no doubt you'd use as an endorsement to sell your psychic schtick to others, you can't get away with giving me some vague reference and ask me to fill in the blanks. I'll need you to provide the equivalent of an 8 by 10 glossy image of where we can find the body."

Hoff grimaced before he said, "You'll find her floating in Sheepshead Bay."

"Anybody could guess that."

Hoff let out a long, frustrated breath before he said, "You'll also find that she's pregnant."

I sat up. Hoff had gone out on a limb. "Care to tell us who the father is?"

"Isn't that why DNA and paternity tests were invented?" he replied in a snide tone.

"Anything else?"

Hoff stood. "Not right now."

Before he saw himself out, I asked if Jill could snap his picture.

He bristled. "What for?"

"We who are less gifted," I said with a straight face, "need more tangible images to guide us."

He permitted Jill to take the photo, then saw himself out.

When he was gone, Jill turned to me. "What was that?"

"Charlatans turn up every so often."

"Are you sure? What he knew about me was eerie."

"As you're not married and I don't detect you have a serious boyfriend, who else but a proud father would give you an expensive bracelet?"

"Okay."

"And, even if we think ourselves modest, aren't we all sometimes the center of attention?"

"I suppose."

"Standard ploys of the psychic trade."

"And saying Talisa was pregnant?"

"Trickier, I agree."

*****

As if on cue, later that evening, Talisa Knox's body was discovered by a couple of amateur fishermen on Sheepshead Bay. She'd been wrapped inside a tarp and weighed down, which was the reason she hadn't come to the surface earlier.

The coroner's autopsy determined death was caused by strangulation. There were no defensive wounds or signs that she struggled with her assailant. The bay washed away any forensic traces on the body. A blood analysis revealed she'd been given a roofie, likely slipped into her drink at Gus's Saloon as her stomach contents had only her dinner at home. As Hoff predicted, she was pregnant. The fetus's DNA indicated that neither her husband, Gus, nor Cagle were the father.

"Should we conclude the baby didn't figure into motive?" Jill asked.

I thought a bit before responding. "Hard to say. Perhaps only Talisa knew about her condition. On the other hand, maybe she confronted the father and they fought. Alternatively, if she revealed the pregnancy to her husband, he might've been tipped over the edge."

"Gus had obvious access to drug her drink."

"Gus didn't say Talisa seemed drowsy when she and Cagle went into the men's room. While they were inside, anyone could've spiked whatever remained of her Cosmo, and since Cagle was the first to emerge, he also had access."

"Roofies are a scary thought for the next time I order a drink at a bar."

Jill and I did the death notification with Lester Knox. His eyes welled at the news, but I couldn't shove aside my cynicism and eliminate him as a suspect.

"Did you know she was pregnant?" I asked.

He shook his head then wiped his eyes.

"Knowing must make you angry, though."

"Hurt heaped upon devastation," he said rising from the sofa. "I don't feel like answering any more of your questions."

*****

Jill and I were discussing next steps when our conversation was interrupted by Jan Hoff arriving at my office door, puffed up with ego.

"Will you tell the press that I predicted Talisa Knox would be found in Sheepshead Bay and that she was pregnant?" he asked.

"You're the psychic," I responded wryly. "You should know the answer to your question."

Hoff tilted his head. "You still don't believe in me?"

I crossed my arms.

He stared at me a moment before he said, "You have a reoccurring dream. Don't you, Detective Bragg."

I straightened in my chair.

"In your nightmare, you're the murder suspect."

A chill went up my spine, and I couldn't speak.

Hoff nodded in satisfaction, turned on his heel, and strode off.

"Whew," Jill said. "What was that?"

I took a few diaphragmatic breaths to ease the angst that Hoff's revelation had caused.

Jill must've sensed my distress because she said, "Everyone has reoccurring dreams."

I nodded.

"As you told me, Hoff is clever. Isn't that the sort of nightmare a homicide detective *would* have?"

I appreciated her concern but didn't buy her explanation. Nonetheless, I turned my detective brain back on. "Perhaps Mr. Hoff's interest in this case is too intense and his knowledge too exact?"

"What are you thinking?"

"Hoff is large enough to have strangled Talisa and carted her body away, particularly if he'd drugged her beforehand."

Jill rose. "We're headed for Gus's Saloon."

"Great minds think alike." I followed her to our car.

*****

The forensic search of Gus's vehicle and the saloon had turned up nothing incriminating, so we focused our questioning on Hoff. Jill showed him the psychic's picture.

"A regular," Gus said. "Likes to entertain drinkers by guessing stuff. He's surprisingly good at it."

Jill asked, "Was he here the night Talisa hooked up with Cagle?"

"Yes. Definitely. He was talking to her when Cagle butted in." Gus chuckled. "He just slunk away."

"Had he talked with Talisa on previous occasions?"

Gus paused. "Sure. A time or two."

"Did you ever hear Talisa tell Hoff that she was pregnant?" Jill asked.

Gus's eyes widened. "First I've heard about it."

I anticipated Gus's answer, but I had to ask. "Had Talisa ever taken a turn with Hoff?"

"Oh. He would've loved that, but no, not her type."

"Might he have been obsessed with her?" I asked.

"Could be," Gus said, "but that didn't get him to first base."

*****

Back in my office, I received a call from a newspaper editor. I put him on speaker so Jill could hear.

"Detective Bragg, would you like to comment on Jan Hoff's claim that his psychic powers provided Brooklyn PD with crucial information that led to the discovery of Talisa Knox's body and also that she was pregnant at the time of her death?"

"Mr. Hoff overstates his contribution."

I heard the editor scribbling a bit before he continued. "Mr. Hoff has provided us with a sketch he claims represents a vision he received. Shows the killer as a husky skin head with his hands around Talisa Knox's throat. What do you say to that?"

Jill and I exchanged glances before I said, "No comment."

*****

Jill's sergeant insisted that he needed her back.

I asked her, "Would you like me to have Lieutenant Dixon intercede?"

Jill thought for a long moment before she said, "I hate to leave the case but ..."

"Better to keep your sergeant sweet," I said finishing her sentence. "You've been a huge help and I'll make sure that's noted in your personnel file."

"Thank you, Detective Bragg. I learned more from you in a few days than my entire six months at the police academy."

"My pleasure," I said and sincerely meant it. "Before you go, let's review our list of suspects." We sat in my office and she pulled out her notebook.

"Talisa's husband Lester," she began, "was angry she stepped out on him and probably resented that she made all the money. He's the beneficiary of her million-dollar insurance policy. If he learned she was pregnant by another man, that could've triggered his killing her."

"What's on the other side of the ledger?" I asked.

"He wasn't seen in the saloon, so he couldn't have spiked her drink. If he wanted to kill her, he could've found someplace more private rather than ambushing her outside a bar."

"Agreed. Next?"

"Gus the saloon keeper," she said. "Talisa was a threat to tell his wife that they had sex, and he could easily have slipped something into her drink."

"Thin, wouldn't you say?"

She nodded. "And Talisa left the bar before closing, which would've been the only time he could've killed her and not risked being missed."

"Okay."

"Jan Hoff," she continued, "knew details of the case, which he claims arose from his psychic powers. He released to the press a drawing of Talisa being strangled by one of the key suspects, Cagle. Hoff saw Cagle and Talisa together and probably was jealous. By pointing toward Cagle, he deflected away from himself as the murderer."

"But, he's not your prime suspect?" I asked.

"We still don't know the father of Talisa's child. In addition, she had numerous liaisons with different men at Gus's Saloon, and any of them could've become jealous of her other lovers and ended her."

"Mudding the waters and requiring further investigation," I said.

"Then there's Moose Cagle," Jill said. "Violence is his first instinct. The morning after the murder, he fought with the cops who woke him in his car a block away from the bar. I discovered his hardhat in the same dumpster where Dolly found Talisa's red pumps. He'd gone to Gus's Saloon straight from work, still wearing the hardhat. He'd never throw it away and when we questioned him, he didn't say it had been lost or stolen. Could've fallen off accidentally when he threw Talisa's shoes into the dumpster. He was drunk and might not have realized it. They had sex in the bar's men's room. Maybe he wanted a second go or a service she refused. He could've slipped her a roofie in the drink she'd left sitting on the bar."

I nodded. "Is that enough to take to the D.A. and recommend charging Cagle with the murder?"

Jill's face clouded with doubt. "There was no trace of Talisa in his car and he seemed genuinely surprised when we told him she was murdered."

"Cagle," I said, "could've wrapped her in the tarp before stuffing her into his trunk and forensics wouldn't find any of her fibers or hair. He worked the docks and knew where a body could be dumped surreptitiously."

"But why would he drive his car back to the bar?" she asked. "We still have no direct connection with him to Talisa's murder. It's all circumstantial."

"Sometimes we must go with the evidence we have," I said, "not the evidence we wish existed."

Jill said, "I want Cagle to be guilty because he's a creep."

"How else did Cagle's hardhat get into the dumpster?" I asked.

"That seems to be the crucial question. You don't put any credence in Hoff's depiction of Cagle as the murderer?"

"None at all."

"What will you do?" she asked, obviously in a quandary.

I blew out a long breath and tipped my chair back. "Jill, we make our best case and the D.A. decides if there's enough evidence to charge a crime. Cagle's ultimate guilt or innocence will be determined by a jury. His defense attorney may very well ask the same questions that you've raised."

Jill shifted uncomfortably in her chair. "So, you're ready to charge him with Talisa's murder?"

"I'm going to let the world turn," I said kneading my chin, "while I follow up on Talisa's other lovers and try to find out who is the father of her child. Maybe I'll catch a break and come up with a concrete piece of additional evidence."

"And if nothing new pops up?"

"I'll take my findings to the D.A. and my guess is that he'll see enough evidence to charge Cagle."

She made no effort to hide the troubled look on her face when we shook hands, but she thanked me again before she left.

I was sorry to see her go. If she'd been a little naïve when we first met, that had been scuffed off.

The first name on the list of Talisa's liaisons Gus had given me was Bruce Walsh. I found him standing in front of the Deep Dive Bar checking IDs and collecting the cover charge. I flashed my shield as I asked, "Do you know Talisa Knox?"

He frowned at my credentials like I was an underage teenager attempting to crash the bar. "Who?"

"A woman you met at Gus's Saloon."

He shrugged and continued to vet the line of kids wanting to enter the bar. Each had money in their fists, and for some he made change.

I showed him Talisa's picture. "Does this jog your memory?"

He gave the photo half a glance. "Maybe."

Whenever I'd shown a murderer a picture of the person they'd slain, some stared, reliving and relishing the moment when the light left their victim's eyes, others turned away, trying to push their savagery out of their head. Never had they acted bored. Still, that little voice reminding me how well people can lie played in my skull, so I blocked the next patron in line, a guy with black stud earrings, raised my badge and announced loudly, "Police business. You'll have to wait."

Walsh's face screwed into a pissed-off frown, but I took his elbow and led him away from the crowd into the alley alongside the club.

"Now that I have your undivided attention," I said, "tell me about Talisa Knox."

He blew out a frustrated breath. "There's not much to tell."

"You had sex with her?"

"Yeah. So? Months ago. Is she filing some sort of

complaint?"

I ignored his question. "How many times?"

"Just once." He smirked. "In the men's room."

"Ever try for an encore?"

He spit the words. "The bitch spurned me the next time I saw her."

"Made you angry?"

He raised his palms. "I didn't do anything about it, if that's what you're asking."

"I'd like you to give me a DNA sample."

He stiffened. "What the hell for?"

"I want to eliminate you as a suspect."

"For what?"

I eyed him closely as I said, "The murder of Talisa Knox."

His voice rose. "Are you crazy? I didn't lay a hand on her."

"You screwed her."

"Other than that. Hey look, I didn't kill her and I'm not giving you a DNA sample."

"Innocent people have nothing to hide."

"You can't make me give you shit."

I puffed out a breath. "Then you remain on my suspect list."

I asked for his alibi for the night Talisa was killed.

"Like most evenings," he said in a snide tone, "I was here, checking IDs for a bunch of social media junkies who'll post that they had the time of their lives trying to make all their Facebook friends jealous."

"Your boss will vouch for you?"

"He pays me for days I'm here." He crossed his arms. "That it? Am I under arrest?"

I slowly shook my head.

"Then I'm getting back to work."

I allowed him to return to his post.

Over the next three weeks, I went through the list of names Gus had given me, interviewing all of Talisa's lovers and checking their alibis. Most wouldn't volunteer a DNA sample, and I didn't discover the father of Talisa's baby. Jill would contact me periodically, asking how the case was going. I enjoyed hearing from her and gave her updates, even though they were frustratingly sparse of new evidence.

I despaired that I'd find case-cracking proof of Talisa's murderer and resigned myself to approach the D.A.'s office to make my case against Cagle when I received another call from Jill, speaking excitedly. She'd found a YouTube clip posted by a young woman as she and her boyfriend drove past Gus's Saloon the night of Talisa's murder. Three seconds of the video, enhanced by the police lab, caught a glimpse of Jan Hoff approaching the dumpster with red pumps in his left and Moose Cagle's yellow hardhat in his right hand.

There is a God.

"Great work, detective," I said to Jill.

I could feel her smile on the other end of the phone.

After I spoke to the D.A., and we presented the evidence, a judge signed the warrant to arrest Jan Hoff. When I slapped the cuffs on him, he looked surprised. So much for his being a psychic.

Bear and Bird at Clairmont Circle
Michael Thomét

"Zachary, you've got to be feeling pretty good about yourself!" Andrew Bear sat at the steering wheel of his maroon, 2010 Malibu, guiding the car through rush-hour traffic in downtown Allston. The sun, low on the horizon, shone down the six-lanes of black asphalt filled with cars. The copper glow of the October sunset reddened the man's normally cream-colored face, cut off just below the eyes by the help of the visor, allowing Andrew to see at least a little of the car in front of him.

Zachary Bird, in the passenger seat, held a hand up over his eyes. The visor on his side of the car was of no use to someone of his short stature. The direct light betrayed the slightest tinge of brown in his irises, which normally looked pitch black. The sun washed all the tawny brown out of his face, replacing it with the copper hue of the sunset. Against hope, he squinted down at a phone settled against the knee of his faded denim jeans. A dim map displayed on the screen, the details nearly washed out by the oncoming evening. "Someone died and that entire production is in turmoil. How can I feel good about that?"

"But Zachary!" Andrew put on his turn signal and wedged the car into the right lane. "They wrote about you in the Allston Tribune! We're bound to start getting some proper clients soon. And they get the Tribune in Wexwood, don't they?"

Zachary hunched down, trying to hide his head below the dash. His fine, brown hair fell into his eyes. Sweeping it back to the side, he was momentarily exposed to direct sunlight. "I'm not popular in Wexwood after Nina's diner closed. I doubt it'll endear me to their hearts to see that I'm doing alright in the big city." He shielded the map and his eyes from the sun again. "I think it's straight here and then a right on... Fairfield?" Zachary turned his head to look at Andrew. "And I'll believe the clients when they start asking about cases and not about photo sets. Real cases, Andrew, not scandals."

Andrew looked at the man through the corner of his hazel eyes. "Hey, that was a real case! Sure... it may have started out looking for scandals. Hell, I'm surprised that a murder was the only thing we found!" Andrew turned his eyes back to the car in front of him. "And you caught the perp! Would have gone unsolved without you, I'd say."

"Maybe if this were fifty years ago," Zachary said, turning his head forward to watch the traffic. "Give the police a little more credit. I know that they've seen a lot of changes since the last election, but they still know how to investigate a crime scene." He watched as they passed under a set of streetlights. "Oh, that was Fairfield. You were supposed to turn there, right?"

Andrew turned onto the next side street. "I guess I'll just take this here, and we'll loop around to it. It's a bit down Fairfield, yeah?"

A row of houses blocked the sunset, causing Zachary to blink and lower his hand. In the absence of the light, everything looked dark as night. When his vision returned, he checked for a new route. "You'll pass a cul-de-sac on your left and then there's another street, and it's on the corner of Fairfield and the street after that." He looked up, out the window. "Oh, there's the cul-de-sac now it–" He paused for a moment. "Looks like something's happening over there."

Andrew slowed the car as they passed the entrance to the small circle of road. A black-and-white police SUV was parked out front of one of the four houses, and a black uniformed woman stood beside it directing a handful of beige-shirted officers. "Oh," Zachary said as he pointed at the woman. "Isn't that detective Perez?"

The car slowed to a stop at the side of the road, just out of sight. "You think we should go see what's up?"

"I think they can handle it, Andrew." Zachary put his phone into his pocket. "And you know she won't even talk to you about it anyway. Shouldn't we just get on with our plans?"

"But there's no harm in trying, is there? Where's your sense of adventure?" Andrew had already released his seat belt and opened the door. Reluctantly, Zachary followed suit and they walked past the low, cinder-block wall beside the sidewalk that prevented people from peering into a back yard. Andrew's height was just about level with the wall. If he'd wanted, he could have peeked over it. The wall gave way to a yard filled with small, red rocks in front of the first house on the right of the cul-de-sac. A sign at the end of the yard where the sidewalk turned in pronounced the street "Clairmont Cir".

Clairmont Circle was small, even for cul-de-sacs. It housed four, two-story houses, each with a modest yard and driveway. The house with the red rocks on the right side had the police

SUV parked in front. The house was long with white stucco that had collected grime over the years. The red rocks were a dull, earthy color, and they formed a mound in the front, as though the yard were a massive red desert with a sand dune looming over it. The drive led up to a garage on the opposite side of the house.

The other houses also had messy stucco with brush-like strokes left by the trowel. The stucco on the house next to the white one was brown and the other two houses were beige. Otherwise, the houses were practically cookie-cutter, though the white house with the red rocks had a more confident, taller roof with an attic window, making the others look like poor imitations. The beige houses both bore white rocks for yards, the one on the far left more pristine than the other. It also featured a neat patch of verdant green with sapling planted in the center. Every house had a small, wooden gate on either side, some unlatched and rattling in the wind. Andrew noted that this was a neighborhood that likely did not lock its doors.

The brown house had not followed its neighbors in replacing its yard with low-maintenance rocks, though that didn't mean that they put effort into what was left of the yellowing crabgrass. A pit sat in the center of the yard, mounds of loose soil piled up next to it. A shovel stuck out of the dirt.

Andrew and Zachary marched across the dull, red rocks, angling towards Detective Lucy Perez. She had brought along two officers and was talking with a young boy who was still in high school, by Andrew's estimation. After only a few feet, the two stopped as the black-shirted police detective turned and spotted them. "No, no, no, no!" She bounded across the rocks and shooed the pair back onto the sidewalk. "Andrew Bear.

You're not getting anywhere near this house." She turned her head to look at Zachary. "Bird, right? Got yourself mixed up with this troublemaker?"

"I'm afraid so, Detective Perez." Zachary shied away from the woman's stern gaze. "Zach Bird. We work together now."

"Lucy, Lucy, we were just passing by on our way to dinner, honest!" Andrew had known Lucy Perez for years. She was a tough cop who had embraced the recent reforms. She came from an immigrant family who had spent a lot of their lives in fear of being sent back home. Andrew suspected that Lucy had joined the force specifically to help protect people like her family. With the recent changes and oversight going on, it seemed to be working, at least that's how it looked from the outside. Andrew had occasionally popped up in the middle of Lucy's investigations, sometimes as a witness, sometimes as a person of interest. Almost never as a friend, but Andrew hoped they had built at least an appreciation for one another.

Detective Perez waved one of the two officers over and looked between the two trespassers. "You're quite the pair! Zach, I read about you in the paper." She gave the shorter man a slight smile. "You know we're capable of doing our jobs, though, right?"

Zachary turned to Andrew and gestured. "See, that's what I told you! They'd have gotten it with or without us."

"Still," Lucy continued, "saved us some time and resources. It was good work, I hear."

Andrew broke into a grin and took the opportunity. "So, Lucy, what's going on here?"

The officer arrived and stood next to the detective. He wore the beige shirt and pants of a lower officer. By the look of him, he was probably a recruit along for the day on training. Lucy squinted at Andrew with a sly grin. "Officer, we're not cooperating with these investigators. Make sure these two don't go anywhere near the house. They're not to talk to Mr. Parks, unless he initiates it, of course." She leaned in closer to look Andrew right in the eye, her height rivaling the man's own. "If you do find them on the property, feel free to arrest Mr. Bear here." She turned on the spot, whipping Andrew in the face with a high, black ponytail. "Zach's alright, though. You can let him off with a warning."

Left with only the beige-shirted officer, Andrew gave the man a smile. "So, what have we got here? Kidnapping? Homicide?" The officer grunted a reply and looked off into the distance, ignoring the request. He followed the two as Andrew led Zachary down the sidewalk. "Ok, Zachary, so something's happened here, and Lucy and our bodyguard here aren't saying what. But there's nothing they can do about us asking the locals." The officer left them at the edge of the yard as they crossed over to the other side of the cul-de-sac. "We need them to trust us enough to tell us what's going on. Spin them a little tale. Go along with me here."

A couple, both with amber complexions and straight, black hair, stood chatting with the group. The woman had long, black hair draped over one shoulder, and she stopped in mid-sentence as the investigators approached. The man, probably her husband given the rings, was gesturing wildly to another woman in the group. She had a dark brown tone to her cheeks that matched her eyes. Her wild, black hair had been tamed by a tie at the back. The three of them looked to all be in their forties. A pasty-skinned man, with white hair behind a blue bandanna, placed himself between the newcomers and the group. He had kept an eye on Andrew and Zachary as they approached.

"Heyo," Andrew started and glanced around at the crowd. "My partner and I moved in a few streets down and were out for a walk. Anything wrong here? We'd heard this was a safe neighborhood."

The woman with the tied-up hair glanced between Zachary and Andrew, a suspicious smile alighting her dark features. The group's eyes drifted over to the white-haired man who addressed them. "You two move in over on Edison?"

Andrew squinted his eyes and turned to his fellow investigator. "Is that the street Zach?"

Zachary stood there, his mouth slightly open, coal-black eyes filed to points staring back at Andrew. "Uh, no, uh."

Andrew gave the group a grin. "Get's so nervous in front of strangers. Adorable, isn't it?"

Zachary put his head down and studied his shoes as he mumbled, "It's Denton..." His face flushed as he added, "...dear."

"Over on Denton," Andrew announced. He put an arm around Zachary's shoulder and held the man up. He could feel Zachary's body tense as strong as steel under the gaze of the crowd. "Zach's not used to being so out in the open as I am, if you catch my meaning." Smiles began forming on the faces of the residents. Andrew jerked a thumb at himself. "Andrew, by the way. Andrew Bear."

The older man relaxed slightly and extended a hand. His

hand felt calloused and strong as Andrew shook. "Welcome to the neighborhood, Andrew and Zach. Name's Hap. This is Sharon and John Xing, and that's Jenny Parks." Andrew proceeded to shake their hands down the line.

Jenny, the woman with the wild hair, stepped forward and gently patted Zachary on the arm. Andrew could feel a jump from Zachary with each pat. "No need to worry, hun. You must not be from Allston if you're so nervous about that."

"Wexwood, ma'am." Zachary's voice quivered the whole while as he tried his best to shrink into Andrew's shadow.

"Wexwood's not so far away," John Xing said. It was the first time he'd spoken. His voice had a cheerful, clear tone to it. "Didn't think they were so behind the times over there."

Jenny pointed over Zachary's shoulder and Andrew steered the quaking man to look. At the end of the point was the kid talking with Detective Perez. The third officer, not the rookie, had disappeared. "That's my boy Kiante. It's no secret around the neighborhood that he's madly in love with Jin, Sharon and John's oldest boy."

"Can't keep them apart, except when Jin's in school or at practice," Sharon added. She took on a feigned air of superiority and said, "Jenny's boy graduated early this year."

Zachary lifted his head and took a deep breath that did nothing to steady himself. "Impressive. I hear the Allston schools are tough." Everyone leaned in to hear him, but his voice fell away on the wind.

"So, tell me," Andrew segued, "what's the deal here? Nothing serious, I hope?"

Hap cleared his throat. "Hope so too." He nodded in the

direction of the white house with the red rocks. "That house belongs to Thompson Chesterfield. He's got to be 80 by now. Was here when I moved in thirty years ago and lived alone the whole time."

Jenny scrunched up the side of her mouth. "Mr. Chesterfield's not all there these days. We take turns checking in on him, making sure he's eating, you know."

Wringing his hands, John said, "Kiante's been doing it a lot lately, since he's home more. During the day, I'm busy at the school, and Sharon's got her practice-"

"Veterinary," Sharon interrupted. "Do you two have any pets?"

"No," Zachary said just as Andrew said, "Yes."

"Zach's not used to Chloe," Andrew said. "Never had a pet growing up, did you?" He smiled and turned to his partner.

"We couldn't with mother," Zachary said and didn't explain further.

Hap continued Sharon's train of thought. "I work in corporate landscaping, so I'm usually up early and home around five. And Jenny's a nurse at Allston Memorial."

Andrew leaned in. "Oh, wow, are you alright? I'd heard about what happened."

"I wasn't working at the time," she said. The others murmured questions. "Really, I don't know anything about it. Most people don't even know anything happened."

Sensing that Jenny was uncomfortable with the subject, Andrew returned to the topic that most interested him. "So, Mr. Chesterfield?"

Jenny cleared her throat. "Uh, yes, so, Kiante went to check on him this afternoon and he wasn't home."

"Did he go out somewhere?" Zachary ventured a question, finding enough of a voice to be heard this time.

"He's not supposed to," John said. "He gets lost easily. We usually keep his door locked so he remembers to stay put before he unlocks it. But every once in a while..."

"You're not out looking for him?" Zachary turned to take in the whole neighborhood, looking for a clue to the man's whereabouts.

"Don't need to," Sharon said. "Last time this happened, Kiante got a tracker from the police department and put it in Thompson's shoe."

"Oh," Andrew said, a bit quietly. "I suppose everything's under control then."

Zachary pointed at the hole in the middle of the grassy yard. "What's going on with the hole?"

Hap let out a long sigh. "Jenny's tree rotted away last year, and we cut it down. Finally getting round to digging out the stump. Planted that tree right when I moved in. Sad to see it go."

"Thanks so much for your help, Hap." Jenny looked away at her yard. "As you can see, I don't really have a lot of time for yard work."

"It's been dry a lot, Jenny." Sharon patted the other woman on her arm. "And you've been swamped at the hospital for a while now.

With a voice that was just barely audible, John muttered, "Now, perhaps your son might put as much focus into the yardwork as he did his schoolwork..."

Jenny sucked in air through her teeth as she turned back to see the rest of them. "Oh!" She pointed. "Looks like we found our missing octogenarian."

One of the officers gently guided an old man down the sidewalk at the side of the house. The man held a bewildered look as he glanced all around the cul-de-sac. Hollow, greying eyes peered out of his face. He had a sallow, almost jaundiced, look to him. The officer led Mr. Chesterfield around the rocks and up to the high schooler, where the old man reached his hands out to trace the kid's bushy, black hair. A grin broke through the confusion on the man's face, and he grabbed onto the boy's shoulder. Blinking wildly, the man looked all about and eventually found the group standing on the other side of the circle. A hoarse voice escaped his lips. "John, Hap–" A fit of coughing cut him off from any further words. Jenny excused herself and rushed over to check on the man.

"Her work is never done," John said.

"How does Mr. Chesterfield support himself?" Zachary asked the question to no one in particular.

"Us, mostly," Sharon said. "He gets disability and SSI, of course, but it's a big house. We all chip in."

"Sharon, we shouldn't..." John trailed his sentence off.

"Oh, you're right." Sharon reddened. "I wouldn't go spreading that around. And don't tell Jenny, please." They watched as Jenny and her son led the old man back inside. Just before he went in, the man cocked his neck staring off into the distance towards Jenny's house, and then back looking directly at Andrew. It was a haunting look, his soulless, empty eyes had just enough sharpness to feel the gaze, somewhere deep inside. Detective Perez got into her SUV with her officers and gave a curt wave back to Andrew before driving around and out of the street.

"Well, now that he's back, guess I better get back to work." Hap nodded to the others and started off towards Jenny's yard.

Excusing themselves, Andrew and Zachary made their way back to the car. As soon as they were out of sight, Zachary let out a long, heavy breath and turned beat red. "I cannot believe you put me through that. Is that how you operate? You lie and pretend to be someone you're not just to get them to talk to you?"

Andrew slapped the shorter man on the back. "You should see your face. I'm sorry about that. It wasn't all lies. I mean we are partners." He laughed out loud. "You're the one who made it a romantic partnership, Zachary!"

Zachary narrowed his eyes at his business partner. "You know that's not how they would have taken it! And if they'd asked you to clarify?"

"I might have kissed you on the cheek!"

As they drove off, Zachary turned an even deeper red and sat stewing in silence on the remainder of the drive to the restaurant.

*****

A couple hours later, darkness had fallen. Clouds gathered in the night sky, lit in clumps by the low-hanging crescent moon. Andrew and Zachary sat at a small, dimly lit table next to a window looking out onto Fairfield. Plates had long since been cleared away, with only a cooling teapot and a pair of cups still there. The restaurant, more a café than anything, definitely catered to a lunch crowd, as only a few tables remained filled so late into the evening.

The two had talked at length about their plans for the future, celebrating the good press Zachary, and the duo by extension, had gotten. Andrew had been used to working behind the scenes, making sure nobody noticed his efforts. Discretion was the hallmark of a good blackmailer, and Andrew had certainly been that. He looked across the table at the man who had pulled him out of that life.

Zachary, 33, was a short, roundish sort of man. Almost every part of him was soft in some way, except for his eyes. They were large black discs that could pinpoint something out of place across a room, if he were looking for it. Two years older than Andrew, Zachary looked perpetually young in comparison. Andrew had never shied away from the rougher parts of life, and Zachary definitely had. Perhaps, Andrew mused to himself as the two talked, growing up in a small town had sheltered Zachary. The range of things that the man did and did not know felt disparate and odd to someone who grew up with a phone practically in his hand at any moment. It was a surreal experience having to teach a 33-year-old man how to send a text message.

Zachary's parentage had some mixture to it that Andrew hadn't yet figured out and that Zachary hadn't been forthcoming about. His complexion had that soft, washed-out tan to it of someone who had only one parent of color. Of course, it didn't matter, really, but Zachary had been so quiet about his parents, even to the point of changing the subject if Andrew ever asked about them. Andrew's mind had been poisoned by his former profession, spinning stories about what dark secret Zachary's family tree might hold. Was it an affair? Was it a fling? Had he only known his mother? Had one of his parents been in prison? Did they get sent to a rehabilitation center after the county prison closed? Andrew just couldn't help himself playing with all the scenarios in his head.

"Hey, I think they're closing." Zachary broke the silence while looking around the room. He swept his hair out of his eyes and hid a goofy smile with his hand. True enough, servers were busying themselves with stacking chairs on the tables in the center of the restaurant.

"What's got you so smiley?" Andrew proceeded to get up from the table. Their bill had been paid ages ago. He gave a cheerful smile and waved to their waiter who nodded in the duo's direction.

Zachary reddened a bit and said, "Oh nothing." The two proceeded out the door and into the windy night air. After they were outside, he added, "You get quiet sometimes, you know?"

"Huh?" Andrew blinked at his fellow investigator. "Oh, I guess I do, sometimes."

They made their way to Andrew's car, an old Malibu with peeling, maroon paint. As they climbed into the car. Zachary scrunched up his face. When asked about it, he said, "Isn't it strange how that old man looked at you, earlier?"

Andrew shook his head. "Earlier?" He searched his thoughts. "You mean Mr. Chesterfield? What about it?"

"Well, I don't know." Zachary held a hand up in the air as if they were back in the moment. "He looked over to the house in the middle, and then back over to us. Not to any of the residents. Specifically to us."

"Now that you mention it," Andrew said while tilting his head, "that does seem rather odd. But then again the two of us were rather odd."

"Maybe it's nothing." Zachary propped his elbow up against the door and shifted in his seat. "I just wonder if there's something up there?"

"Well, it's dark enough." Andrew jerked a thumb towards the trunk. "I've got my camera with me. Wanna snoop around a little bit?"

Zachary's eyes grew wide. "Not if you put it like that," he said, "but I don't think it would hurt to check in on him or at least take a look."

Andrew cackled as the car roared to life. He jostled Zachary on the shoulder and then put the car into gear and made way for Clairmont Circle.

*****

Andrew parked the car opposite to the cul-de-sac, in a pocket of shadow between the streetlamps. The circle bore just enough light from a singular lamp placed between the brown and white houses, Jenny's and Mr. Chesterfield's, as Andrew recalled. Illumination came, too, from behind closed curtains in several of the houses, and a few dots of lights in upper rooms poked out into the night. Only Mr. Chesterfield's house was completely dark. Being so late, that didn't seem very unusual to Andrew.

Even still he motioned to the house and said, "You want to take a look around the house with me?"

"Uh," Zachary stammered and fumbled with his hands. "I– We can't go inside. You weren't thinking of...?"

Andrew ruffled the man's hair and grinned. "You're too easy!" Zachary jerked away, flattening his hair. "Just teasing, of course. But maybe we can peek in the backyard or maybe even hop the wall and look in through the windows."

"I suppose looking into the yard wouldn't be a bad thing." Even in the darkness, the color draining from Zachary's face was practically shining through his voice.

Nevertheless, the two quietly exited the car. Andrew retrieved his travel case from the trunk and expertly attached a lens to the camera stored inside. He used this lens when doing low-light work. It helped, but taking photos in near total darkness still took a lot of skill and a very steady hand. The camera flared to life as he adjusted the ISO, aperture, and shutter speed to better suit dark conditions. When he was done, he put the camera in standby and nodded toward the cinderblock wall that surrounded Mr. Chesterfield's backyard.

The two crept over. Zachary stood up as far as he could and pulled at the top of the wall, but even still could not see over the wall. Andrew motioned to the windows poking up over the wall and to his eyes. Zachary, taking the hint, stepped a bit out into the road and watched for signs of life within the upper floor of the house.

Andrew, nearly half a foot taller than Zachary, could see just over the wall if he stood on the balls of his feet. The backyard was dimly lit under the clouded sky, the only light spilling in from the lonely streetlamp in the circle. About a third of the backyard was illuminated, the house blocking the rest of the light. In the yellow glow, a small, white shed hid away in the back corner of the yard. The doorway stood agape, an empty hollow amidst the white aluminum siding.

The rest of the yard that was visible looked to be hard-packed earth, not a single scrap of grass or a bush about. It spoke to years of neglect and sun-beaten summers with little shade. Towards the house, a small overhang stuck out over the door that led inside. There was just enough space there for a round, metal table and a chair to match. Too dark to see, a shape rested on the table, perhaps a box, by Andrew's guess.

Andrew lifted the camera over the wall and tried to hold his hands steady enough to take a few pictures of the yard. After a moment he whispered, "Hey, Zach, can you steady my arms?"

The shorter man reached over and braced the photographer's arms with his hands, ending up back against the wall for support. Had anyone approached the two while in this position, they'd have gotten some fairly weird looks.

Andrew nodded and let his elbows rest on the shorter man's hands. This relaxed Andrew's muscles well enough that he could steady the shot. It was one thing to take a shot from your chest and quite another to take one from over your head. As he stopped taking pictures, a small flash of light emanated from the confines of the shed, and Andrew zipped the camera out of sight. A figure emerged from the shed, dressed all in black, but clearly visible under the yellow light of the streetlamp. Mr. Chesterfield.

Not altogether surprised to find the man tooling about in his own tool shed, Andrew watched as the elderly man pulled something from the shed, hidden in the shadow of his own body, along with a small flashlight in hand. He then moved over to the table and chair. The shaded area proved too dark to see much detail, but the light of the man's flashlight fell across the shape resting on the table. It was a thick, hardcover book. Mr. Chesterfield sat down in the metal chair and proceeded to read by flashlight.

As the elderly man's back was to Andrew, he risked taking another photo, aiming for the curious sight of an old man sitting in the dark, reading a book by the feeble light of a small flashlight. Occasionally, Mr. Chesterfield stopped to shine the flashlight upon a small wristwatch, and then he went back to his reading.

It was just then that the rain started coming in. First one drop, then two, but they were great massive drops of rain that felt like marbles when they pelted the top of one's head. In the yard, Mr. Chesterfield glanced nervously up as the rain began picking up, and a great grumbling voice came from the yard. "Not now, of all–" He silenced himself with his hand, and then he gathered the book, flashlight, and the unidentified object and ferried them inside.

Andrew stepped away from the wall and motioned for Zachary to follow him, sheltering his camera with his shirt. Within moments, the two quietly clamored into Andrew's car and shut the doors.

"So?" Zachary ruffled the water out of his hair. "What did you see?"

Andrew shrugged. "Nothing much, really. He got something out of his shed, and he was reading with a flashlight. Quirky, but nothing too far out of the ordinary."

"He seemed a bit upset about the rain, didn't he?" Zachary stared out the window at the rain, which was slowly becoming a downpour.

Andrew nodded. "Yeah, that's true. Maybe he's waiting for

something? Kept checking his watch."

Zachary turned to look the man in the eye. "You think it's something?"

Andrew mulled it over for a while. "I don't know. I don't think anything's wrong here, like there's no crime probably, but something just doesn't feel right."

"So, is there anything to do?" Zachary pulled out his phone and checked the time. "It's almost ten."

Andrew sighed and rocked left and right in his seat. After a few moments, he said, "Maybe it won't hurt too much to keep a watch for a while. My gut tells me something's going to happen tonight, and we want to be here for it."

"We open at nine tomorrow morning," Zachary said, counting points off on his fingers. "There's a client for shooting in at 9:30, and there's a pickup at one that isn't printed yet."

Andrew cast the man a sidelong smile, mostly lost in the darkness of their parking spot. "Who owns the studio, me or you? Besides, that's just photo stuff. We can handle it. We'll take shifts watching and sleeping, and if it gets to three, then we'll just go sleep it off in the studio or something. You think you can sleep in the car ok?"

Zachary shrugged and yawned. "This seat goes back, doesn't it?" He adjusted the seat to comfortably lay back. "Wake me up when you need a break." The slightest of smiles was visible on the man's face in the darkness as he closed his eyes and settled in. Andrew punched Zachary in the shoulder and turned to look out into the drizzle of the evening.

*****

"Zach! Wake up!" Andrew's voice was a hiss. He shook the man next to him, without taking his eyes from the drizzle-soaked circle. It was about midnight, and all the lights had disappeared from the houses. Only the yellow light from the single streetlamp remained. The rain made it hard to see and Andrew had given up trying to get a recognizable shot with the camera. In front of Jenny's house, in the very center of the circle, a figure huddled over the hole in the yard.

"Huh?" Zachary lumbered from his sleep and blinked around in the darkness of the car. "Did something happen?"

"Look! Over there!" Andrew pointed in the direction of the figure.

Zachary squinted, rubbed his eyes, then leaned over to get a closer look. "I don't see anything in this rain, and my eyes are tired." He blinked a few times and then opened his eyes as wide as they could go. "Is that a person?"

"There was a big torrent of rain, so I couldn't see for a bit, but then there was someone there, hanging about the hole in Jenny's yard." He leaned closer to the glass and stared at the figure, hoping to find some detail that would help identification. "I don't know who it is. I think it's one of the guys, but who knows?"

"It might be Hap," Zachary said, "he was working on the yard. Maybe he found something? I don't really know much about John."

"Mr. Chesterfield was waiting for something," Andrew added. "But would he be outside on a night like this?"

"He's old, and didn't Jenny say that he wasn't all there?" Zachary leaned away from the window to give Andrew more space. "I don't know if he's got the faculties to secretly go digging in the middle of the night."

"I don't know if he's really that far gone," Andrew said. "We haven't met him." Just then the rain intensified and blotted out the view. It remained that way for several minutes, Andrew pressed against the window trying to make out what was happening. When the rain subsided again, the figure had disappeared. "He's disappeared!"

"That didn't take long." Zachary pulled his chair up into the upright position. "So, something happened tonight. What now?"

Andrew turned his head away from the glass, a fire in his eyes. "Want to go digging for buried treasure?"

Zachary sat there, jaw open, as Andrew opened the door to the car and stepped out into the rain. A quick jaunt to the trunk produced a hand trowel that Andrew kept for occasions where the dirt had been literally buried. Zachary joined him moments later. The rain soaked the two almost immediately as they gingerly stepped across the asphalt to the hole in Jenny's yard.

"This is ridiculous," Zachary whispered as they approached the hole. "There's only one trowel, what am I even doing here?"

Andrew pointed. "Hey, there's another over there you can use. I'd have thought Hap was more protective of his tools." Reluctantly, Zachary grabbed the indicated trowel from the side of the hole and picked his way down into the mass of mud and old roots.

Hap had mostly cut away the roots, and the stump had been

discarded on the lawn, ready to be mulched away. The pit was rather well lit from the proximity to the streetlamp, and the two had little trouble identifying where the figure had been digging. The rain couldn't do much to penetrate the packed ground, but some sections of earth had been worked well enough to create patches of slick mud and clay. It was inevitable that the two soon had dirt and grime up to their knees and elbows and smeared across their formerly clean clothes.

After several minutes of digging, Zachary unearthed a large metal tin, about one foot on each side and four inches deep. The metal had nearly been eaten through by rust. Several strips of old duct tape hung loosely about the tin. The lid moved easily, as if recently opened, and the inside was host to mildew and silt from years of rain. A glass mason jar sat inside, unsealed. The jar housed a nearly intact, small, stuffed rabbit. A second jar, completely broken, housed the remains of some papers, long since eaten away by water and time.

Not long after this discovery, Andrew dug up a single discarded shoe, completely ruined from the dirt and wet. It was a brown loafer with a thick, hollow sole, which had been nearly torn off. It was newer than the tin. The two men dug around in the mud for at least an hour but found nothing else. The rain eventually subsided, and with it the two extracted themselves and their finds from the hole, did their best to clean themselves off, and then took the car back to Andrew's photography studio.

The grime of the evening followed them in and up the stairs and stopped only after the two took turns using the shower curiously included in the studio's only bathroom. Their clothes still ruined with dirt, the two decided to call it a night, go home, change, and deal with the situation the next day.

*****

Around six in the evening the next day, the two found themselves, much cleaner, in front of Jenny's door. They had brought their finds with them, cleaned as well as could be hoped, as well as prints from Andrew's camera. Despite having taken three showers that day, Andrew still felt the gritty mud between his toes and under his nails, and anywhere else mud might have gotten trapped.

Jenny and her son answered the knock, Jenny's eyes a bit narrow at the two of them carrying such an assortment of things. "Oh, it's Andrew and Zach, isn't it? From yesterday?" She turned to her son and nodded. "You remember seeing them last night, right?"

The boy nodded but didn't say anything.

"Sorry to bother you Jenny," Andrew said and flashed a smile. "Truth is, we're not sure quite what we should be doing about this." He looked around at the yard and back to the woman in the doorway.

"There's no crime," Zachary added, "but Andrew thought it best to tell you since it happened in your yard."

"A crime?" Jenny folded her arms. "What are you talking about? Nothing ever happens on this street."

"Well, you see," Andrew said. "That's just it. Something did happen here last night."

Kiante spoke up. "During the rain?" He scrunched his eyebrows together as he stared at the two men.

"In the rain, yeah." Andrew pointed at the hole in the yard.

"Around midnight, we saw someone digging around in your yard there."

Jenny cocked her head and squinted her eyes further. "And just what were you doing watching my yard at midnight?"

Zachary cleared his throat and tried not to look sheepish. "We're private investigators, ma'am."

"Oh, that explains it," she said, rolling her eyes. "I'm guessing you aren't a cute couple who moved in down the street, huh?"

Andrew shrugged, gave the woman an apologetic grin, and pushed the conversation along. "After the person left, we went and investigated, and found these things." He indicated the tin and the shoe. "We think that someone was looking for something buried in your yard."

"Ok. And?" Jenny squared her shoulders and stared at the two like they had just told her they were aliens.

"So, like we said, we don't think it's a crime," Andrew reminded her. "But we do think that it was Mr. Chesterfield." He pointed at the shoe. "This is his shoe, right?"

The two in the doorway squinted at the somewhat cleaned up shoe. Kiante spoke up. "That the right one?" Zachary looked at the shoe and verified it. The boy continued, "And you didn't find a tab in the heel? They gonna have my head for losing that thing."

"Jenny! Jenny!" A hoarse voice called from the street and the group all turned to look. Mr. Chesterfield stood there only in his stockings, hands behind his back. The man lumbered up the path to the door. "Jenny, have you seen my shoes? I lost– I lost..." He trailed off as he approached the group. His eyes went from Andrew to Zachary to the things that they held.

"Good afternoon Mr. Chesterfield," Jenny said in a soft, kind voice. "I think these two gentlemen found one of your shoes." She stressed the word 'gentlemen' as if convincing herself to believe it. "But you can't wear this one, it's broken."

"Oh!" The old man stared blankly off into space before he brought his hands around to the front, producing an old, rust-lidded mason jar. "Oh! I found these in the attic today." He held the jar out to Jenny, and then down to Kiante. "They're some old baseball cards. You're into baseball, aren't you?"

"Uh, yeah," Kiante said and took the jar from the elderly man after some insistence.

"Mr. Chesterfield, this is Andrew and Zach. They're private investigators."

"And photographers!" Andrew pointed at the photographs as if it proved the point.

"Oh?" The old man loosely offered a hand to the both of them. "Such a dirty job," he commented, "don't you think?"

The group stood in awkward silence for a few moments before Kiante piped up. "Hey old man, do you know what you've got here? Some of these cards are supposed to be lost." He squeezed past the two investigators and dragged Mr. Chesterfield down the path to discuss the cards.

"Ok, look," Jenny said. "I don't know what you were trying to do here, but I think whatever it is, it's over."

Andrew shrugged. "Honestly, I'm not sure myself. Truth of it is, we saw Mr. Chesterfield preparing for something, going to dig in your yard, and here he is now suddenly with baseball cards sealed away in a jar much like this one." Andrew pulled out the jar with the stuffed rabbit in it.

"It doesn't seem like the kind of thing someone who 'gets lost' would do," Zachary said.

Jenny slumped her shoulders and sighed. "Oh, I get it. You're thinking it's an act."

Andrew tilted his head to the side. "Well, maybe, yeah we do."

Jenny let out a howl of laughter and waved her son away when he turned back to look at them. "Took you all of a day to figure that out? He had some of us going for years!"

Zachary frowned. "So, you–"

"Yeah, we know." She caught her breath from laughing. "We've known for a long time. He's harmless, and his disability is really the only thing he's got to survive on. I don't even know how he manages with just that! We just play along when he gets lost, we go check in on him. It's him who's fooled." She cleared her throat. "You two are sharp, though. And he's not as put together as he thinks he is."

Andrew looked deflated. "Ok, so I guess things are all settled here? Do you want these?" He offered the tin and the shoe.

"God no! You're not bringing those filthy things past this doorway." She planted herself squarely in the door frame. "Though, I guess, I should thank you for not going right to the police about this. Mr. Chesterfield would lose his disability, and I don't know what would happen to him then." She tapped a finger to her lips. "You know, he always did say he had a treasure somewhere. We all thought it was part of the act!" She laughed and shooed the investigators away.

On his way back to the car, Andrew offered the jar with the rabbit to the old man. He looked at it, blinked a few times and then returned to his discussion of the cards.

Back in the car, Zachary said, "So, was that a case?"

"Zachary, that was us putting our nose in where it didn't belong." Andrew indicated the tin. "This is a case."

Zachary winced. "I guess they can't all be worthy of celebration."

"Let's hope this one doesn't make the paper."

The two drove off into the oncoming night.

The Coveted Coverlet
Michele Bazan Reed

"Ouch!" Putting up the quilt square she'd been embroidering with bunnies for her grandson's crib, Freida Brice dabbed at her thumb, where the needle pricked it when the phone startled her.

"Hello?" She winced, and not just from the sting of the pinprick. She knew she sounded annoyed, and she didn't want her caller to think she was rude. Forty-five years of answering the phone at the Perth Police Department, with all sorts of troubled or angry people on the other end of the line, and she was well known for keeping her cool. Why should retirement change that?

"Hey, Freida, you busy?" Officer Joe Alfred always started his calls that way.

"Hi, Alf, nothing I can't stop for you." A smile lit up her face. The young officer was like a little brother to Freida. She'd taken him under her wing when he joined the force, and they'd become friends.

"Geez, don't let the guys hear you call me that!" Freida had christened him Alf after the 1980s TV alien. The creature's auburn hair matched Joe's, even down to the way it stood up straight no matter how many times he'd pat it down. Although he complained loudly every time she said it, his lips twitched in a barely concealed grin.

"So what's up?" She carefully set the tiny cotton square aside in her basket.

"There's been a theft at Sonya's Quilt Shop," Alf said. "I figured with your expertise in needlework – not to mention your crime-solving instincts – you might be able to help us out."

Freida grinned to herself. Ever since her husband, Bill, died, Alf was always calling her to help on his cases. It wasn't only to get her out of the house. She'd helped him solve more than one mystery, and even earned herself a nickname. The local newspaper, *The Perth Prattler,* had dubbed her the Granny Gumshoe.

"You know that antique quilt Sonya's been displaying in the window of her shop? The one they're gonna raffle off for the town's Sequicent… Seski-bi-cent… oh, you know, the 150th? It's gone."

Freida nodded, although Alf couldn't see it. She'd been down to look at the artfully embroidered piece of town history several times with its huge centerpiece of the town founders' von Stratford mansion, studying it with an eye to designing a project of her own.

"I'll meet you at the shop," Freida said, grabbing a jacket and heading out the door.

*****

Parking her aging Toyota near the shop, Freida looked around for Alf's tell-tale shock of auburn hair. She could still recall that first time he walked into the station, to apply for the patrolman's job, with his round, smiling face and the way he kept patting down that unruly coiffure. Other than a few more laugh lines around his eyes and mouth, Alf was still that fresh-faced kid all these years later.

"This morning, while Sonya was in the back room teaching a class, someone made off with the quilt," Alf explained, as he and Freida entered the shop together.

"Yeah, I can see how that's possible. I've been to Sonya's classes, there are about ten, maybe a dozen people, all running sewing machines, chatting, asking advice. It's no wonder she never heard anything," Freida said, glancing at the plate glass window, empty except for a sign advertising the quilt raffle to be drawn in just a week. "But you would think someone would have heard the bell on the front door ring. It's loud on purpose." She paused, as she realized she hadn't heard the familiar ding when Alf pulled the door open. Looking up, she grimaced.

"Look," she said, pointing. "The thief muffled the bell using a handful of quilt batting from that roll right there." Sure enough, there was a hand-sized gouge missing from a roll of polyester padding on a shelf just inches from the door.

"Everyone's here, Officer Alfred." A tiny woman with frizzy brown hair, wearing an oversized sweater and a chatelaine – a kind of patchwork scarf holding scissors, a needle case and pin cushion – around her neck, was just coming out of the back room. Sonya was wringing her hands and looking nervous, probably thinking she'd be blamed for losing the precious artifact.

Alf turned to the six women gathered around the shop,

some leaning against shelves full of cloth, others perched on the benches Sonya kept around the edges of the shop for weary husbands or antsy children. Quilters were known to enter another time dimension in a fabric shop, awed by the array of colors and patterns of bolt upon bolt of gingham, floral and geometric cottons. Anyone accompanying them could wait for hours while they fingered the fabric and made their choices.

Bargain fabric was piled high in wicker baskets in the center of the shop, and the new cottons were artfully arranged by color on plain pine shelves stretching floor to ceiling along the outer walls.

"You ladies were all here for the class this morning?" Alf pulled a notebook out of his hip pocket. Heads nodded in unison. "Did you hear or see anything unusual?"

A large woman with her hair pulled back in a ponytail and a sweatshirt decorated with cats spoke up first. "We were just sewing in the back room. Are we in some kind of trouble?"

"And I want to know what they're going to do now that the quilt's been stolen. I had five dollars' worth of tickets!" This from a white-haired woman holding a canvas bag with "She who dies with the most fabric wins" stenciled on the front.

"Eleanor!" Another woman snapped at her. "What's more important, your five bucks or a priceless piece of Perth County history?"

The scowl Eleanor gave her made the answer obvious.

"She left the room halfway through and came back a few minutes later." A sharp-faced woman looked over half glasses at one of her companions and nodded.

"I went out into the shop to get a spool of thread – Sonya

lets us pay for any supplies we use at the end of class. I thought I saw a suspicious character skulking past the window." The speaker was a tall, thin woman with her hair in a fashionable bun and bright red lipstick. She wore a cashmere sweater over leggings. She kept glancing over Alf's shoulder toward the store's window.

"Do you know what time that was?" asked Alf.

"Well, it was while I was working on the binding for my project, so it would have to be in the last third of the class, maybe 10:30 or 11 o'clock?"

"Can you describe this 'suspicious character,' and what did you say your name was?" Alf chewed his lower lip as he scribbled her testimony in his notebook.

"Sandy. I mean, that's my name, not that the person was sandy." Here she erupted into nervous giggles. To hide her embarrassment, she bent down to shove the quilt squares she'd been piecing into a tote bag at her feet.

"The suspicious person?" Alf prompted.

"Right. Well, it must have been a woman, because who else would steal a quilt?" She raised her eyes to the ceiling. "And she was wearing a big coat, I think grey. She was wearing a hat so I couldn't really see her face and she was carrying a canvas bag, like a reusable grocery bag. She kept staring at the quilt in the window, and only turned and pretended to walk away when she saw me looking at her. I bet when I went back into the classroom, she snuck in, muffled the bell with batting, and stole the quilt." She nodded at Alf, waiting for his thanks.

"Thank you all, ladies. You can go back to your quilting now," said Alf.

The officer turned to Freida, shrugging his shoulders with a look of consternation on his face.

Just then the sixth quilter, who had been silent during the interrogation, came out from the classroom, calling over her shoulder. "Sonya, I'm going to pick up a bit of binding. Be right back." She sidled over to the young cop and said, in a low voice, "I didn't want to say anything in front of the others. But I've always wondered about Sonya. She's only been in town a short time, and they say she used to sell antique quilts on the Internet. Even wrote a magazine article about evaluating them. If anyone would know what that quilt was worth and how to sell it, I'll bet it's her!" She reached for a package of pink ribbon and with a wink, returned to the back room.

"Well, I guess all we've got to go on are Sonya's side business or this 'mysterious person' Sandy seems to have seen. But if you ask me, they all seem innocent enough, if a little dotty."

"Oh, Alf." Freida shook her head. "Your suspect is right here. And it's not Sonya or a mysterious stranger."

She looked back at the classroom door and frowned. "It makes me crazy the way people in this town won't accept an outsider – even one who's been here for years, like Sonya. Why would Sonya steal something from her own store window? At least in broad daylight? She could just sneak it out the back door after the shop was closed and fake a break-in, smash a window in the door or something. Then she could claim insurance money in addition to making a pretty penny off the quilt."

Alf nodded, acknowledging her argument. "OK, then who is it?"

Freida peered out the now-bare window. "That's Sandy's car out front. The silver Audi? She kept glancing at it nervously while you were questioning her. I'll bet if you get her to open the trunk, you'll find the quilt stashed in there."

"But how? And why?" The puzzled young officer stared at his friend.

"Well, I noticed Sandy's tote bag on the floor. It was an expensive model and monogrammed with the initials SvS. That's when I recognized her. Sandra von Stratford. Her family founded the town, so there's your why. The quilt was donated by her cousin Grace, who inherited it. Sandy coveted it and probably couldn't bear the idea of some stranger winning a piece of her family's history in a raffle. I know I wouldn't."

She pointed to the rack of thread, out of sight of the back room. "It was easy enough for her to call out her intentions to get a spool of thread. It would have taken some time to find the exact matching color, so that covers her absence of several minutes." Freida glanced over to see if Alf was listening. "How did she know the bell was muffled with batting, if the thief did it after Sandy returned to the sewing room? Because she did herself. Then she grabbed the precious coverlet and hurried it out into her car, grabbed any old spool of thread and wandered back into class. I noticed the thread in the squares she was piecing didn't match. She'd been sewing with red thread but in the second half of the pattern, she'd changed to blue. It stood out like a sore thumb." She grimaced and stared down at her own throbbing digit.

"But what about the suspicious person she saw skulking around? It could easily have happened the way she said, couldn't it?" Alf looked skeptical.

"Nope, and here's all the proof you need." Freida whipped out her smartphone. "I wanted to make a quilt of police department history as a surprise for the guys at the station and spent some time on Sunday when the shop was closed studying the quilt through the window and taking a few pictures. I thought I might be able to print the squares with town landmarks and use them to design a pattern of my own."

She found her photo of the entire quilt. "See how the quilt filled the whole window? Edge to edge? Even if Sandy was staring out the window instead of searching for the right color thread, she couldn't have seen anyone outside. The quilt blocked the entire view."

"Thanks, Freida. Tomorrow's coffee's on me!" Officer Alfred shook his head in admiration as he started toward the back room to bring Sandy down to the station.

*****

The next day, Freida answered the door to find Alf on the porch. True to his word, he clutched a big cup of Country Café's best coffee and a copy of *The Perth Prattler*. As they settled at her kitchen counter with still-warm slices of Freida's prize homemade coffee cake, he proudly displayed the front page with the banner headline: "Granny Gumshoe Does It Again: Conniving Quilter Confounded in the Case of the Coveted Coverlet."

The Knockoff King
Paul R. Paradise

Theo Jones once waited in line for auditions and casting calls. The acting jobs were scarce and didn't pay the bills, so he tried private investigation and discovered his craft useful for working undercover. He specialized in 'trademark cases,' as they're called in the business. However, instead of the glamorous life portrayed on television and in pulp novels, he often chased street peddlers selling knockoff Rolex watches, fake Louis Vuitton handbags, and counterfeit Calvin Klein designer jeans. Nonetheless, he preferred pursuing these low life groundlings rather than audition and be dismissed by an obnoxious casting director with 'next.'

One day Jones got a tip about a MaMala Fashions knockoff factory in Redhook, Brooklyn.

After getting the go ahead from MaMaLa corporate counsel, Mark Sadler, Jones drove to Red Hook, Brooklyn. He was familiar with the neighborhood, which used to be a bustling waterfront but had become rundown over the years. The drive took an hour from Manhattan. The salty smell from the Gowanus Canal made him wince.

Jones drove down Court Street and parked next to a bodega, located a block from a seemingly abandoned one story brick building.

He walked to the back of the building. His heart beat quickened when he spotted three cars parked next to a loading dock. He was certain there were people inside, as well as an illegal manufacturing operation.

Now came the hard part. The counterfeiters had every reason to mistrust anyone who knocked on the door—especially someone looking to buy counterfeit apparel.

Jones had a number of tricks. He returned to his car, opened the trunk and removed a black tattered Samsonite briefcase with three dozen fake Rolex watches inside.

The briefcase and watches had once belonged to an Asian street peddler who had fled during the seizure and left the briefcase and knockoff watches behind.

Rolex had given Jones permission to use the briefcase and knockoff watches as a ruse for information with the caveat that he never sell any. That was understandable: posing as a peddler selling fake Rolex watches was one thing; selling fake watches was a legal matter that could wind up in court.

Rolex, which had a big counterfeiting problem, was happy with the intelligence Jones supplied. Working undercover as a street peddler, as soon as he opened the briefcase and flashed the knockoff watches, other street peddlers gave him tips on suppliers and other counterfeiters.

Jones walked to the door with the briefcase in hand. He tried the doorknob and discovered it wasn't locked. He entered and was greeted by a dank musty smell. A few feet ahead was a steel door.

The floorboards creaked, as he walked to the door. From inside, he could hear voices.

He knocked. Once, twice.

No answer.

He knocked again, harder.

The door was opened by a Hispanic teenager with acne and long dark hair.

"*¿Qué Pasa?*" The kid looked him over.

"*Hola.*" His street Spanish allowed for a lopsided conversation with the kid, who spoke little English. While they talked, he assessed the operation. There were seven Hispanic men in addition to the kid. Tough odds, especially since he wasn't carrying a gun. He rarely used one in his line of work. Two of the men were older, the others young and tough. He didn't doubt a mistake on his part would result in a severe beating.

Four men were seated behind computerized Brother SE 400 embroidering machines that required marginal sewing skills because the designs were stored in the hard drive. Nearby were two men working a portable shrink wrapper and handing off to another who boxed and loaded onto a flatbed hand truck. Jones counted fifteen boxes waiting to be taken into the next room for shipping.

One of the men, seated behind an embroidery machine, stood up. He had just finished a white polo shirt and, as he handed it for shrink wrapping, Jones spotted the MaMala Double M trademark on the breast of the shirt.

The man, who was swarthy and menacing, walked over and scowled, "Who are you?"

Jones knew it was hit or miss from this point on. "I'm a watch salesman." He smiled. "I was in the neighborhood, thought I'd introduce myself."

A flash of anger darted from the man's eyes. "What the hell? Are you kidding?"

Jones knew he had to do something—fast.

He bent down, dropped to one knee, and opened the briefcase. He turned to the teenager. "*Mira...Reloj de pulsera.*"

The kid's eyes bulged. The metal wrist bands gleamed in the room's faded light.

Jones decided to give the kid a fake watch. He figured there wouldn't be any harm if he gave away a watch. No money changed hands.

The kid pointed to one of the Daytonas.

Jones handed it to him. "Go ahead, it's a present—*presente.*"

"*Gracias.*" The kid was wide-eyed. "*Mira, mira,*" he said to the others and held up the watch.

Jones asked his oppressor if he wanted a watch. Instead, the man grabbed his arm, hauled him to his feet and pushed him towards the door, leaving the open briefcase and watches lying on the floor. "I want you out of here right now!" he said.

Jones offered passive resistance. "Hey, easy...I want my watches."

"John, give him his watches," said an older man sitting behind an embroidery machine.

Suddenly the door in the back opened and everyone froze.

The man who entered was imposing. He was short and heavy set, solid like a side of beef. He was dressed casually in denim jeans and wearing a sweatshirt with the New York

Giants logo on the chest.

"What the hell is going on here?" he growled.

"Frank, this guy barged in here," John said.

"He didn't barge in here," the older man said. "Chico let him in."

"All of youse shut up!" Frank glared at everyone.

An obedient silence filled the room.

Frank walked forward with a shuffling gracefulness. He noticed the open briefcase on the floor. "Who are you?" he asked, almost politely.

"I'm a watch salesman…I was trying to make friends and gave the kid a watch."

He looked at Chico and frowned. "Chico…*Reloj de pulsera.*" Chico walked over and meekly handed it over.

After inspecting it, Frank's face hardened. He smacked the side of Chico's head with the back of his hand.

"*Aieeee,*" Chico cried and backed away.

"What I tell you? Never let anyone inside." He made a threatening move to slap him again.

"Hey, don't hit him!" Jones said.

As Frank turned, his eyes narrowed. "No one tells me what to do."

Now that the heavy man's anger was directed at him, Jones figured his best bet to diffuse the situation was to apologize. "Look, it's my fault. If you want to hit someone, hit me."

"Hit you?" he sneered.

"Go on, hit me." Jones tried to sound defiant.

Frank took a deep breath, looked at the watches on the floor and then back at Jones. Unexpectedly, a smile etched across his face. "So, you sell watches?"

"I hope it was all right to hand out a sample," Jones spoke deferentially.

"I'll let it go but talk to me next time."

A curious silence filled the room. Finally, Frank asked," How much you charge for these watches?"

"Five dollars." This was a fraction of the $70 street price.

The heavy man eyed him suspiciously. "If you don't mind my asking, how much was the wholesale price?"

"That's a secret."

He chuckled, obviously amused by the answer. "No, man, come on. I have contacts that might be useful."

"Really…." Jones continued with the ruse. "All right, since we're friends…Twenty-five cents apiece."

This was a ridiculous fraction of the usual price. Jones knew the wholesale prices better than anyone.

"Twenty-five cents?" Frank was flabbergasted.

"I know a guy who imports from mainland China. I got a deal going with him. He sells me watches cheap. I sell him sweaters cheap."

"Bullshit, this is a Rolex." Frank winked. "A fake Rolex, right?"

"You said it, not me." Jones winked.

Frank stroked his chin. "C'mon, who are you?" he snapped. "How'd you get into this kind of business?"

"Hey, I don't answer questions like that."

Frank's eyes narrowed. He took a menacing step towards Jones, who didn't know what the heavy man planned to do, push him out the door or even strike him.

For several tense seconds they stood staring at each other while standing less than a foot away. Each waited for the other to make a move.

Finally, Frank relented. "C'mon, I like you. I want to know who I'm dealing with, that's all."

Jones nodded. Apparently, his ruse as a watch salesman had won the day. He had been expecting to be thrown out the door.

"Well fine," Jones said. "I have samples for everyone, including you!"

He reached inside the briefcase for a fake Oyster Perpetual and handed it to Frank, who chuckled and held it up for a better look.

"Go ahead, it's free," he said. "A present—*presente.*"

Jones gestured to another man. "Go ahead, take one."

The worker timidly ventured forward. "For me?"

"Sure, man. What's your name?"

"Miguel."

Everyone got a watch, even John, his oppressor, who apologized. The workers looked at their watches and compared them. Jones was nervous about giving out so many.

At this point, Jones decided to risk a move. "What are you guys embroidering? Looks like polo shirts?"

"That's right," Frank said. "It's MaMala Fashions."

Jones feigned surprise "Is that what you guys are up to? Can I take a look?"

Frank said something in Spanish to Chico, who trotted over to a pallet and retrieved a polo shirt with the familiar MaMala Double M trademark on the left breast. He walked back and handed it to him.

Jones inspected the fake. "I've seen these in Macy's in Manhattan. Is that where these are headed?"

"These?" the heavy man chuckled. "No, I work with jobbers and friends."

"They're fake, right?" Jones winked. Everyone chuckled. Even Frank was amused.

He handed back the polo shirt. "Maybe you and I can do business. I could use something to help with my watch business. How about a sample to show people I do business with?"

Jones offered to buy a shirt sample. He sensed the other workers were rooting for him and hoping to get more free watches.

"Oh no, my friend," Frank replied. "Everything I have is on consignment. At another time, maybe."

Jones was disappointed. He thought Frank was won over and would sell him a sample. Only one was needed for the corporate counsel to apply for a court-ordered seizure of counterfeit inventory and equipment. Unfortunately, the judge would not sign a seizure order without a sample.

Nonetheless, he had his hooks into Frank. He asked to be shown the operation.

"Sure...sure," Frank apologized. "Maybe afterwards we go to lunch. What's your name?"

"Everyone calls me Winston," he said using an undercover

name.

"So, you're Winston." The heavy man had a strong handshake and penetrating eyes that bored right through him.

"That's me. I sell apparel—and funny watches," Jones said and winked.

"Funny watches?" Frank chortled. "That's why I like you. You're my best friend."

Jones delivered a prepared spiel about working in the garment district.

"I started with Haines, doing source work for women's underwear. After that, I

was a buyer in training at Gimbels, until Gimbels went under; and then I worked at Alexander's, until Alexander's went under. And then I worked for B. Altman, until B.

Altman went under… Sound familiar?"

Jones was hoping Frank would be sympathetic. New York City's garment district department store shake-up had been ongoing since the late 1980's.

Frank listened and nodded. "Interesting… Sorry, I can't sell you any polo shirts. I only work with people I've done business with."

"Let's do business," Jones said. "I have contacts for just about every knockoff around. See these sunglasses…."

He reached into his pocket for a pair of genuine $100 Carrera sunglasses. "Here, check this out."

Frank inspected the sunglasses. "How much?"

"Ten cents apiece for an order of twenty or more." He opened his pea coat and pointed to the shirt he was wearing.

"This is Chaps. Retails for $10. I can get you wholesale lots, all sizes, for fifty cents a unit MSRP."

He continued to quote ridiculous wholesale prices for his clothes, which were genuine and not counterfeit. It was almost like a game. At one point, he gave a quote for the Calvin Klein jeans he was wearing, as well as his underwear.

"Thirty cents for Hugo Boss underwear…You want to check it out?"

He started to unbutton his pants.

Frank laughed. "No, you don't have to show me!"

There were peals of laughter. One worker whistled and told him to go ahead.

He continued, "I have overseas connections and inside contacts at Bloomingdale's in Manhattan."

Frank was seeing stars, won over by the prospect of doing business abroad or with a major department store. "Really? Who do you know?" he asked.

"Not so fast—not so fast." Jones said. "Before I give names, what can you do for me?"

Frank became silent. "Sure, we're gonna do business…but later on."

Jones closed the Samsonite briefcase and took it with him, as he followed Frank into the next room.

Frank pointed to dozens of cardboard boxes, stacked one atop another, filled with knockoffs ready to be shipped. Off in a corner were hundreds of unfolded cardboard boxes held together in bundles by strips of plastic and stacked to the ceiling. There was little else besides a laptop computer resting on top of a desk, chairs and a filing cabinet.

"The company's named after me, Frank LaScala," he said proudly. "I call the company LaScala's…A long time ago, there was a company that assembled guitars in the other room. The finished guitars were boxed and loaded onto trucks through this grate."

Frank walked to the metal grate located in the middle of the wall. He reached down, grabbed the handle and lifted it up with one hand. A gust of wind greeted them, as the grate slid upwards for a view of the parking area. He pointed outside. "I have two vans for distribution. They park here and load up."

"Where are the vans now?"

"In the field delivering."

Jones did some calculations. Two vans, local delivery. He knew from experience Frank could pull in a thousand dollars a day or about three hundred thousand dollars a year tax free with a minimum investment in equipment and low expenses for labor and rent.

He asked Frank where he bought the computerized embroidery machines. Frank chuckled, guessing what was next. "I should have come to you first…right?"

"Depends… Did you pay more than $200? If you did, I can get used machines like this for under $25."

Frank was stunned. "That's not possible!"

"Next time, call me."

Jones took his briefcase and followed Frank outside.

Frank walked to the back of the factory and got inside a Chevy Camaro. Jones sat next to him in the passenger seat. As he drove, Frank told him how he got into the knockoff business.

"Most of my life I see everyone barely making it," he said sadly. "My dad had a button store for thirty years, lost it, took to drink and beat my mother. I think 'there has to be a better way.' I play by the rules, learn a trade but in the end no work, all gone overseas. I think to myself, 'What's happened to this country?'

"I realize I got to get into a business…I get into knockoffs. Now no one can touch me."

Jones nodded. While outwardly sympathetic, he was disgusted by Frank's reasoning, variations of which he had heard many times.

It wasn't about free enterprise; it was about greed. Fast money. Frank was not alone, part of a subculture of urban outlaws operating a business enterprise that existed day to day. Today it was knockoffs of MaMala Fashions, tomorrow Calvin Klein or Ralph Lauren. Each brand having its moment, then dropped in a continuous blur like the fashion advertisements in a woman's magazine. At the slightest hint of trouble, Frank would pack up and move his operation to another neighborhood.

He despised Frank, a crook who took advantage of the legal system. Prosecutors rarely handled trademark counterfeiting cases; when they did, the counterfeiter did light prison time.

Frank took him to a bar called Angus Oggs.

Jones wanted to leave the the briefcase in the car. Much to his dismay, Frank insisted he take it inside.

He couldn't refuse. After all, he was a watch salesman. His

great fear was Frank was going to find people to buy the fake watches.

They went inside. It was a neighborhood bar serving hot food, beer and wine and had stuffed animal heads on the wall.

"Hello Frank." The bartender smiled. He was an older man with white hair.

"Hello Sam…This is my friend, Winston…He's a knockoff king."

"A knockoff king?" Sam's eyes brightened.

"Don't listen to him," Jones chuckled. He sat down on a bar stool, reached over and shook hands.

"Show him your watches," Frank said.

Jones realized his ruse was going overboard. He didn't want to show Sam the watches but couldn't refuse, either. With the utmost trepidation, he set the briefcase on the counter and opened it.

"Wow, they're beautiful!" Sam's eyes feasted on the glittering fake watches.

"Go ahead, pick one," Frank said.

Now things were getting out of control. He protested but Frank waved his hand. "It's all right." Frank pulled out his wallet and removed two one hundred dollar bills. "Here, this is for your watches. All of them."

Jones tried to refuse but Frank set the money down on the counter and gestured to the patrons. "Listen everyone, free watches. Help yourself!"

Instantly everyone in the bar, ten patrons in all, surrounded them.

His ruse as a watch salesman had backfired. He didn't dare to drop his cover. However, if the case went to court, his selling the counterfeit watches would certainly be raised.

As people picked through the watches, he tried to think of something. "Frank, I can't take money from you, we're friends." He slid the money across the bar to Sam and said with a flourish, "Drinks and food for everyone!"

It was the only thing he could think of.

There were cheers all around, as he gave away the watches. People were hugging him and proposing toasts.

Jones, however, found being hailed a 'knockoff king' by these working-class pasty faces in dungarees and cheap shoes on their lunch break revolting. He almost wanted to scream in indignation—but of course he had to keep quiet. He knew they would throw him out of the bar in an instant if they knew his identity.

A young man covered with tattoos wanted to know what other knockoffs he had. Jones felt nauseous at having to expand on his role as a magnanimous 'knockoff king.' He managed a smile as he quoted ridiculous prices for a coterie of brands, while Frank smiled and told the young man about his new friend, 'the knockoff king.' The young man slapped him on the back and wanted to set up an appointment when he got his pay check.

Someone put quarters into the juke box, while a man danced with the waitress, a bleached blonde named Nancy. She laughed and waved a hand in the air. At one point, Frank took out a twenty-dollar bill and shoved it into the fold of her apron and hugged her warmly.

Everyone feasted on pitchers of sangria and hot food. After partying for two hours, they returned to the factory.

Frank parked behind his car and asked him to wait while he went to the trunk and returned with six sample polo shirts bearing the MaMala Double M trademark.

"These samples are for you," he said warmly. "You're my best friend, a real knockoff king. Give me a call and we'll do business."

Jones assured him he would be in touch. He got into his car and headed for Manhattan.

The next day, Jones met with Mark Sadler at MaMala Fashions corporate headquarters located in the heart of New York City's Garment District.

Sadler looked over the fake polo shirts while Jones told him about infiltrating the factory. He told him what had happened at Angus Oggs and expressed concern over handing out so many fake watches.

"This guy Frank sounds like a character." Sadler laughed.

"Oh yeah, he even takes a bath in the morning." Jones felt humiliated, as if his reputation had been tarnished by being christened a 'knockoff king.'

The attorney said not to worry about the watches and said he'd follow up with corporate counsel at Rolex.

While he waited for Sadler to meet in chambers with the judge who would sign the civil seizure order. Jones contemplated his revenge. He would have the sublime pleasure of serving the seizure order on Frank. He couldn't wait to see the look on his face when he realized he had been dealing with an investigator. It was a victory Jones had savored many times, but this time it was personal.

Jones got the go ahead from Sadler a few days later and was instructed to arrange a meeting with Frank who would be in for a surprise. The meeting was a setup for executing the civil seizure. As soon as Sadler hung up, he called Frank.

"Hello Frank. It's Winston. Remember me?"

"Winston, so good to hear from you. What's up?"

"I showed the samples to some people, now I'm ready to roll. I'd like to place an order for one thousand MaMaLa polo shirts. Split evenly between men's and women's and in sizes extra-large to small."

"Ah-ha, I knew you would come up with something good. You're a real knockoff king. I'll dropship but I need a down payment, $1,000 up front, another $1,000 upon delivery. I only deal in cash."

Jones bristled when Frank again referred to him as a 'knockoff king' but tried to sound bemused and asked when he could inspect the order.

"How about this Thursday," Frank said. "I'll be in the factory."

"It's a deal. I'll have the down payment."

Stan Good, one of his investigators, rented a box truck and parked it in front of the detective agency early on Thursday. Sadler arrived at nine o'clock. Two U.S. Marshals arrived a half hour later.

Jones led a tactical planning meeting with the Marshals in the detective agency's main office. Legally the plaintiff, who was the trademark owner, was executing the civil seizure of counterfeits and equipment; the Marshals were on hand to make sure it was executed peacefully. If anyone resisted, they would be arrested and charged with assault.

Jones, who knew the factory's layout, decided the vehicles would park in front of the factory. The seizure team would form a two-tier front with the Marshals and himself forming a row in the lead, Good and the attorney in the rear. After Frank was served with the seizure order, Good would leave with one of the Marshals for security and move the box truck to the back of the building and park by the loading dock. After that, Good and Jones would load the fake apparel and equipment into the truck.

Good drove the box truck, while Jones traveled with Sadler who was driving his own car. The Marshals took up the rear in a Ford Police Interceptor.

The convoy parked in front of the building as planned. Everyone exited and, after a final rundown, they walked into the building with Jones leading the way. He was holding a manila envelope with the seizure order and planned to serve it on Frank the moment he spotted him.

Jones walked to the door and knocked.

Chico answered. His smile turned to horror the instant he spotted the Marshals in blue windbreakers with the words U.S. MARSHALS in white on the back—and armed with Glock pistols holstered at the hip.

"*Caramba!*" He shook his head, trying to figure out what was happening.

Jones pushed past the kid and stormed inside with the rest of the seizure team right behind.

"It's all over!" he yelled.

The workers were stunned.

"Winston…what's all this?" John asked.

Jones walked up to him. "My name's not Winston—I'm an investigator. See those men. They're police. *Policia! Comprende!*"

"Wow." John was stupefied.

"Now all of you get out of here," Jones yelled. The workers froze. They still did not understand.

"You heard me—get out of here!" He roared with a voice that would have made his acting teacher proud.

Now they understood and raced out the door.

He had another counterfeiter to deal with—and he came into the room at just this instant.

Perplexed, Frank stood at the doorway.

Jones walked up to him. "Here, this is for you."

He slapped the manila envelope against Frank's chest and watched it fall to the ground.

"What… what's going on?" Frank asked numbly.

"Inside is a seizure order signed by a judge," Jones said. "I'm a private investigator. Now do you understand?"

Sadler moved forward to stand next to Jones, while the two Marshals took up position, one on either end so that Frank was facing a four-man front. Sadler told him he was corporate council for MaMala Fashions and had a court order to seize his inventory and equipment.

"My God…." Frank was dumbfounded. His eyebrows arched upwards and a pained look swept over him. He turned to Jones. "I—I—I thought you were my friend," he stammered.

"Save it, cockroach," Jones said. "We're taking everything."

Jones walked away, with Sadler right behind, leaving the Marshals to keep watch over Frank who appeared subdued.

Without warning, Frank pulled a gun from his pocket.

The Marshals immediately took out their Glocks and crouched in unison into combat stances, positioning themselves shoulder to shoulder, so that their bodies acted as shields for the civilians in the seizure team.

"Freeze—drop it!" One of the Marshals yelled. Both officers had their guns trained on Frank who appeared to be in a trance. Tears rolled down his checks.

Both Marshals demanded Frank drop his weapon. "Drop the gun. Drop it now!"

"I thought…you were my friend," Frank mumbled, his gun hand trembling.

"Both of you get out of here!" Jones said to Sadler and Good. Good raced out of the room.

"Theo, aren't you coming with us?" Sadler asked.

"No, I'm staying."

"Are you out of your mind?"

"You go, Jim…It's me he's after." Jones walked forward slowly until he was standing behind one of the Marshals. Sadler, however, refused to leave and joined him.

The situation was tense. Clearly, Frank was emotionally distraught and kept pointing with the gun.

"I trusted you…" Frank blubbered.

For the first time in his career Jones felt sorry for a counterfeiter. He felt sympathy for this dumb shit who was about to lose his life. And for what? Some knockoffs? Didn't he realize this was a civil seizure? He had faced no criminal charges until he pulled the gun and could have walked out the door.

Softly and gently, Jones asked Frank to drop the weapon and surrender. "Please Frank…it's not worth it."

"I trusted you…" His hand was shaking like a branch in a hurricane.

"Drop the gun!" One of the Marshals demanded. The other yelled, "Drop it now!"

"Frank—drop—the—gun," Jones said softly.

Sadness swept across Frank's face. He must have realized the hopelessness of the situation and let go of the gun, which dropped to the floor with a clatter.

While one Marshal kept his weapon leveled at Frank, the other forced the heavy man to the ground and handcuffed him. A radio call for backup was made to the 76th Precinct.

"That took guts to talk to him," Sadler said. "You could have been killed."

"Thanks," Jones muttered. He felt no relief, only disgust.

"What was that about trusting you?" Sadler asked.

"Jim, these greedy bastards have the same gripe after they're caught. Frank had his coming for believing I was a 'knockoff king'."

The Tell-Tale Armadillo

M. C. Tuggle

I don't usually talk to dead people. But after long minutes staring at the glowing CT image of Hector Moreno's corpse, I couldn't help but mutter, "What killed you?"

The sound of my own voice startled me. It was 6:35 on a muggy July evening, and I was working late to catch up on my case load. I glanced around. The door to the hallway was open, but the only faces looking back at me were those of my husband and twelve-year-old daughter in the framed photo on my desk.

And of course, there was the digitized image of Mr. Hector Moreno on my computer screen. Though his corpse lay in the cooler downstairs, his digital file enabled me to handle his case, one that should've been routine. Now I wasn't so sure.

My eyes remained fixed on the screen while I toggled between different angles of my subject. The CT imaging software recreated Moreno's features so that he looked like a white marble statue, which highlighted details. Despite the distorted image, the man's angular features radiated dignity and strength.

So much strength, in fact, that he seemed alive, even with his eyes shut.

A tap on the doorway startled me again, and I looked up to see Dr. Kamada.

"Love the way you focus, Treka. Sorry for scaring you."

"It's okay, Haruki."

"Bad news. Thompson has turned in his notice."

I closed my eyes. "Great."

"Now we're down two techs. And I was just on my way to the City Manager's office. Louise said she wanted to discuss ways we can cut the budget even more. Funny, huh?"

I shook my head.

"Treka, if I could, you and I would switch places. I was crazy to go into administration. You get to have all the fun."

"And the fun hours."

Haruki lowered his head. "I know. And you have a family. But every department that doesn't meet its quotas gets even more scrutiny – and you know what that would mean."

"I get it, Haruki. Less straw, more bricks."

"Gilead's like every other city these days. Even the police are facing cuts."

I said nothing.

"I'll salvage what I can. We all have our jobs to do." Haruki raised his eyebrows and shuffled off.

In his own sweet way, the chief coroner had just told me to move the bodies along a little faster.

But sometimes you can't. I cycled through Moreno's CT scans, searching for something I must've missed. Finally, I saw it. An x-ray taken from above the vertex, the top of the head, revealed a pattern wound, a vivid half-rectangle. I clicked on the photo attachments accompanying Moreno's file. They showed a man in his late 60s with a head of thick black hair. That hair hid the wound, which is why the overworked morgue tech who'd conducted the scan did not place red flags in the file. In the CT's x-rays, Moreno appeared bald. The well-defined wound on the vertex did not show up from the front or rear.

But something wasn't right. Mr. Moreno, a CPA, died in a gas explosion in his home office six days earlier. The blast killed Moreno and severely injured a client named Gordon Jackley. Mrs. Moreno was in the detached garage at the time and escaped unharmed.

The problem was that the low-grade explosion left most of the home's walls and roof intact. According to the investigator's preliminary report, the blast originated in a gas fireplace, and the resulting shock wave careened through several rooms before shooting out of the house through skylights, windows, and the back door.

Still captures from the EMTs' body cams showed Moreno slumped in a chair at his desk when they found him. The shock wave blew open double doors and hit him from behind, slamming him into his desk and breaking two ribs. Any flying debris would have struck Moreno's back, but there was no evidence of that. Even more puzzling was that the area over his desk had not been damaged, so a collapsing ceiling couldn't have killed him.

I paged through the series of CT x-rays, peering down into the head all the way to the foramen magnum at the base of the skull. As I stared at the glowing image, my heart started racing. Ring fractures on the occipital bone indicated the skull had been driven down into the spine. Whatever made the rectangular wound on the top of his head struck him directly from above – with deadly force.

And that was a problem.

I took a long sip of cold coffee and sent a priority text to the investigator handling the case. Hector Moreno's house was now a crime scene. I needed to talk to the victim's wife and client, the only other people present at the time of the explosion. One of them was a murderer.

*****

At 10:15 the next morning, I took my seat opposite Mrs. Roberta Moreno in the living room at her temporary lodging at Creighton Arms Extended Stay Suites. We were in the facility's penthouse, which had been professionally decorated. I settled into a parson's seat, and she took the leather-bound Big Kahuna chair. To my right, a magnificent arrangement of pink lilies and orange roses filled the living room with a cloud of spicy sweetness. The instant I realized this was no sympathy bouquet, I found myself in Mrs. Moreno's caustic gaze.

Clearly, she expected me to wither, but I instead answered with a respectful nod. "Mrs. Moreno, I know this is a trying time for you, and I appreciate you seeing me. Your answering service said you could see me for an hour, but I just have a few questions."

Roberta Moreno had auburn hair, the same shade as mine, though styled a tad more elegantly. Probably two hundred dollars more elegantly. She wore a stylish teal top with a long silver necklace, black skinny jeans, and grey boots. She occupied her chair with perfect posture and studied me in a way that made me self-conscious of my plain white blouse and khaki pants.

She held her gaze on me a couple of beats and finally said, "I was supposed to go home today and meet with my attorney and the insurance company representative. I just want to get back to my normal life. But I've been informed my home is now a crime scene, and I'll have to stay here indefinitely." For just an instant, she took her eyes off me to sweep her surroundings. From the pinched look on her face, you'd think she was trapped in a refugee camp. "And I have to drive that miserable rental car. I assume I have you to thank."

"Mrs. Moreno, we have evidence we cannot explain, so we need to protect the scene and investigate further."

"Evidence? What is there to investigate?" Her voice quivered, and the hardness in her eyes vanished. I believe the woman's color changed.

I pulled a small notepad and pen out of my purse. "There are some loose ends I need to look into."

Roberta Moreno took a long breath. "How long will it take?"

"Maybe a couple of days, maybe a few weeks."

Moreno rubbed her temples.

I leaned forward. "We can move things along faster if you can give us the password for the security system."

"I don't have it. Hector put that system in, as well as his ridiculous tornado room. But if the filing cabinet in his office is still there, he kept his passwords in a folder in the back. I think it's in the bottom drawer."

That sounded like an invitation, which I accepted. I tapped

my cell phone. "I'll send you a form giving us permission to search the house. Just sign it and email it back, and we'll get you back in your home as soon as possible."

"Fine."

When I sent the email, I said, "It sounds like your husband was very security conscious. Are there any interior cameras?"

"No. That would be too creepy. He spent enough as it is stocking his tornado room with guns and supplies."

I stifled a frown. Interior videos would've been a big help. "A lot of people have tornado shelters. Missouri gets its share of twisters."

"I suppose."

"One thing we're looking for is a heavy, rectangular object with hard edges. Did he have anything like that in his office?"

"Rectangular …" She stared at the ceiling. "Why do you care?"

"We believe something fitting that description is what killed him."

She raised a finger to her chin. Otherwise, no reaction. "There's a stapler on his desk."

"Not heavy enough."

"There's his old filing cabinet."

Too big and too heavy, but I said, "Okay, we'll take a look. Oh, and before I forget – you were in your car in the detached garage at the time of the blast. What were you doing?"

"I was about to leave when the car shook, and I heard the explosion. I used Siri to call 911."

"What did you do after you called 911?"

"The operator told me to cut the car off and go outside, so I waited in the yard for the ambulance and fire trucks."

I scribbled a note and studied her. "Your husband was with Mr. Gordon Jackley at the time of the explosion. Do you know him?"

Her posture stiffened. "Gordo. That's what Hector called him. They were roommates at Duke University. Hector's handled his accounts for years. He's a frequent visitor."

The tone in her voice suggested Mr. Jackley's visits were not something she looked forward to.

"What sort of business is he in?"

"Good Lord, everything. He has a nasty reputation for bullying people to get his way."

"Including your late husband?"

"No, they had some sort of understanding. Frankly, I don't know how Hector could stand the man. Gordon Jackley fancies himself to be a financial genius, but believe me, he isn't."

"Right. Was anyone else in the house?"

"No."

"Did you smell gas at any time?"

"No. After lunch, I went to the greenhouse. Just before 4:00, I was on my way to teach a class, and went straight to the garage. Needless to say, I didn't make it to my class."

"What kind of class?"

"Ikebana. That's Japanese flower arrangement."

I nodded toward the end table to my right. "Lovely flowers."

"They'll do. I have them delivered every day since I've been here. Normally, I make my own arrangements from the flowers I grow in my greenhouse. It was destroyed in the blast, and it's been a fight convincing the insurance company those flowers are a necessary living expense. But they're paying for them. And they'll pay for everything else I need as well."

The fiery gleam in her eye signaled a victory she was profoundly proud of. No doubt Roberta Moreno was a claims adjuster's nightmare.

I stood. "Thank you for your help. And again, I'm very sorry for your loss."

She gave me a nod.

"Don't forget the form I emailed you."

"I have a yoga class in an hour and then lunch with friends. I'll read it and get back to you."

"Thank you for help, Roberta."

I left the grieving widow and took the stairs. Minutes later, when I got back into my pickup truck, I glanced through my notes and digested the interview. Roberta Moreno had flinched when I mentioned the ongoing investigation. But was it because she might be stuck longer in squalid, temporary housing? Or did she have something to hide?

Either way, my work was cut out for me. Something my boss would not want to hear.

My truck's console clock displayed the time: 10:48 AM. I'd be back at my desk by 11:20, where I could look forward to working through lunch and maybe getting home by 7:30. There's a cost to chasing down mysteries, with no guarantee of getting answers. But I wasn't complaining.

*****

Skype and Zoom can save time, but there's no substitute for interviewing persons of interest on their home turf. So two days later, I took the visitor's seat in Gordon Jackley's home office.

Everything in his house was new and clean and orderly, including his office. Jackley was a large, round man, with a manicured gray beard and big eyes that looked small from squinting. He managed to look comfortable, even dignified, despite the shoulder immobilizer on his right arm. It was one of those sticky Julys that only northern Missouri can spawn, but despite the heat, Jackley wore dress pants, a long-sleeve dress shirt, and tie. When he moved, he left a hint of expensive, tobacco-scented cologne in his wake. His hair, a tangle of frosted brown, was the only thing about him that appeared out of control.

I scooted my chair closer and pulled out pen and notebook. "Good to see you're recuperating. Thank you for seeing me on such short notice."

"Tell me what you need."

"Just some details about the explosion. What time did you arrive at Hector Moreno's house?"

"Around 2:20."

That went into my notebook. "How long have you and Hector known each other?"

"Almost fifty years. We were college roommates."

"What kind of business are you in?"

"I've owned a number of firms over the years, but it's no longer hands on. Now I'm a full-time investor."

"How well do you know Roberta Moreno?"

"Too well." He leaned back, wincing in pain. "Damn shoulder. Excuse me."

I nodded at his shoulder. "How bad is it?"

"Four cracked ribs, broken ulna, and a torn rotator cuff. As soon as I'm up to it, I need to have shoulder surgery."

"Sorry to hear that. I'll be as brief as possible. The reason I asked about your business dealings is that I hear you're – aggressive."

"So you've already talked to Roberta." Jackley nudged a folder until it was parallel to the edge of his desk. "I think – I *thought* the world of Hector, but Roberta has, well, certain expectations. She likes having money but looks down her nose at those who make it. Including her husband."

"Did you ever see any friction between them?"

He shook his head. "Never. Now, that said, I never saw any real affection. Hector made the money and Roberta spent it. It's a division of labor that apparently suited them."

"I see. Tell me what happened just before the explosion."

"Hector and I were reviewing some P & L statements. Pretty dry stuff. It's time for my quarterly payment to the IRS, and I needed to minimize my taxes."

"So you've been in his office a number of times?"

"Of course."

"We're looking for a heavy, rectangular object we believe struck and killed Mr. Moreno. Did you notice anything in his office that fit that description?"

The large brown eyes turned to slits. "You mean like a

book?"

"No, it would have to be something heavy. Maybe a metal inbox?"

He shook his head. "Sorry."

"So the two of you are looking at your P & L statements. What happened next?"

Jackley leaned back and stared at the ceiling. "Hector was working his usual magic, finding exemptions I never would've imagined. I had to go to the bathroom. I was on my way back when everything went dark."

"How long were you out of the office?"

"I'd say five minutes. Maybe seven. These things take longer at my age."

I was too lost in thought to laugh at his little joke. If Gordon Jackley was out of Moreno's office five minutes, Roberta Moreno could have entered the office, whacked her husband on the head, and escaped to the detached garage before igniting the gas.

"Mr. Jackley, can you remember any details about the explosion?"

"All I remember is a tidal wave of heat, a god-awful roar, and waking up in the hospital. Oh, and the doctor was telling me I must've raised my arms up reflexively before I hit the wall. That's what saved my life."

"Did you hear anything unusual before you went to the bathroom, like maybe the sound of someone in the hallway?"

"If there was any unusual noise, I didn't notice it."

"Did you smell gas?"

"God, I wish I had."

"Did you see Roberta Moreno that day?"

"She always keeps her distance when I visit Hector. I just assumed she was busy elsewhere. Maybe in her precious greenhouse."

I exhaled. Not much to go on. "Mr. Jackley, I appreciate your help. Best of luck with the surgery."

"Thank you. Sorry I couldn't be of more help."

Back at my truck, I read a text from Officer Jerry Simms, one of the cops who'd responded to the explosion. He could meet me tomorrow afternoon at the Moreno house.

Good. I was due a break.

*****

I parked on the street behind Simms's patrol car. The Moreno house was a dignified, aging holdout, a sprawling white brick ranch in an old-money section of Gilead. Neighbors on both sides had torn down the original homes and built two- and three-story mansions.

Clutching my crime kit and laptop, I weaved past dirty shards of glass sparkling in the lawn. The black-and-yellow tape circling the house hung limp in the stagnant July air. I ducked under it and climbed the front steps. Chunks of dry wall, some crushed into white powder, littered the steps.

A small sign on the front door read, "VACATE – DO NOT ENTER" in bright red letters. The door creaked open when I nudged it with my elbow, and I called to Officer Simms. Somewhere in the dark interior, he replied, "Hey, Treka, c'mon in. Hang a right."

I stuck my head in the door and peered into the house. The stench of burned plastic and gypsum dust stung my nose. Magazines, bric-a-brac, and mangled furniture covered the floor. Plantation blinds, twisted and askew, drooped over boarded windows. After putting down my laptop and crime kit on a table and slipping a mask over my face, I stepped into the foyer. The lights came on and I crept into the living room.

Hefty footsteps rounded a corner of the hallway, and Officer Jerry Simms lumbered into the junked room. I'm five-ten, but had to bend backward to look him in the eye. Other than the white mask he wore against the contaminants in the air, Simms wore regulation navy blue.

"Okay," he said, revealing deep smile lines around his eyes. "The gas company turned off the gas, and I just threw the main breaker on the power. I can give you the next forty-five minutes."

"Thanks, Jerry. The owner sent me permission to search, so anything you see is fair game."

"So, you think the perp killed Moreno and set off the explosion to cover up evidence?"

"Actually, I try not to have any preconceived notions about a case."

"You're the expert."

"What I mean is that I can't make any assumptions. It's possible the gas leak was accidental, and just happened to ignite after Moreno was murdered."

"If you say so."

"I have to put together a narrative that fits what evidence we have. So we need to find the rest of the evidence. We're looking for a heavy, rectangular object. That's the murder weapon."

"I'll search the office where they found Moreno."

"Good. Since I'm here, I'll start with the fireplace and work my way toward you. Make me happy by handing me the murder weapon when I get back."

Jerry twitched a smile. "Just watch me."

I kneeled in front of the natural stone fireplace, which occupied one end of the living room. It was a wood-burning, vented fireplace converted to gas, complete with ceramic logs. When I shined a light up the chimney, the white beam lit up tattered sheets of burned paper caught in the rough stones. That struck me as odd, considering how nothing else had caught fire in this room, so I took some pictures and stuffed one into an evidence bag.

The fire department's preliminary report identified the fireplace pilot light as the likely ignition point of the explosion, but the gas had pooled in the center of the house around the main furnace line, where the damage was worst. Damage here was minimal. I got up.

Farther down the hall, I found what was left of the furnace. The fire investigator was right. With so much twisted and scorched metal, it would be impossible to determine if it had been sabotaged.

I turned around and tiptoed through the rubble back to Hector Moreno's office. Judging by the jumble of furniture, books, and files on the floor, the shock wave had hit this area harder than the foyer and living room. On the opposite wall, a wide screen TV hung askew, an ice-colored crack stretching across its entire length.

A dozen gold and silver sports trophies littered the floor. The blast had blown them off a table behind Moreno. Clearly, he had treasured these trophies. Some had shattered, a reminder that a human life had also been shattered, and the thought made my heart pound. That shot of adrenaline kept me going, and I dropped to my knees, slipped on nitrile gloves, and examined each trophy.

But none of them matched the rectangular pattern wound on Moreno's head. I stood and surveyed the wreckage again, searching for some kind of clue.

Simms strode from a corner of the room. "I found something, but I don't think this is what you had in mind." He wore white cloth gloves, and in one massive hand, held out a mahogany appointment calendar holder.

The holder, while solid and rectangular, wasn't massive enough to kill. And the shape was wrong.

"You're right," I said, "we need to keep looking."

Without a word, Simms set the calendar holder on the desk, folded his arms together, and continued searching.

I kneeled beside the filing cabinet beside Moreno's desk. It contained client folders, probably for hard-copy backup. Just as Roberta Moreno had said, an unlabeled folder in the back of the bottom drawer contained her husband's passwords. Moreno also kept a client list in that folder. I downloaded the security system's app onto my phone and entered the password.

The security system's motion detector had triggered two videos the day of the blast and stored them in Moreno's cloud drive. One, taken at 2:20, showed Gordon Jackley driving up and getting out of his car.

At 4:00, the camera caught a shimmering, nightmarish flash of light in the first second of the blast. And then darkness.

The videos confirmed Jackley's story. Now there was no doubt only three people were in the house when Gordon Jackley and Hector Moreno were caught in the explosion an hour and forty minutes later.

Simms and I slogged through the debris another thirty minutes and turned up nothing. Meanwhile, back at the morgue, I had a growing backlog and a nice-guy boss under so much pressure, he was losing his niceness fast. And Simms could only spare another twenty minutes.

I had to refocus my efforts. Assuming the explosion was deliberately set to destroy evidence, the question was, what was missing? A forensic accountant could download the accounting files from the cloud backup drive. But if Moreno operated like most CPAs, he kept the juicy stuff in his paper files.

A quick tally of Moreno's client list revealed the folders for both Gordon Jackley and someone named Anna Romero were missing. Jackley's folder was probably on the desk when the blast hit. So where was the Romero file? Were the two files related?

The blast had hit Moreno from the rear, so I focused on the area directly in front of his desk. Sure enough, I found Gordon Jackley's file on the floor a few feet away.

But another twenty minutes of sifting through the rubble failed to turn up the Romero folder. There'd been no fire in

Moreno's office, so Romero's folder should have been near the other items blown from his desk.

Maybe Anna Romero could shed some light. I found her contact info on Moreno's client list.

"Jerry, I'm going to step outside and make a call."

Simms answered with a distracted wave.

The air was just as sticky hot outside as it was in Moreno's wrecked house. I keyed the number into my phone and held my breath. Time to get lucky. I was due.

On the fourth ring, a woman's voice answered. "Gilead Buyer's Agent, Anna Romero here."

"This is Treka Dunn. I'm the Chief Medical Examiner for Gilead County, investigating the death of Hector Moreno. Could you answer a few questions for me?"

"Gladly."

"I believe you were his client, is that correct?"

A long pause. "That's true. He was also my uncle."

"I see. How long were you his client?"

"Uncle Hector helped me get my business off the ground. I own a real estate firm, which I started in 2008. A rotten time to get into the business, with the housing bubble and all, but I hung in there. I couldn't have done it without him."

"Do you know Gordon Jackley?"

Another pause. "Yes. I represented Jackley on an investment property a few months ago."

"Did your uncle refer Mr. Jackley to you?"

"No, Jackley contacted me through a website ad. He had no idea Hector was my uncle, and I wanted to keep it that way. If he had known about our relationship, he wouldn't have…"

"Wouldn't have – what?"

She sighed. "I might as well tell you – Gordon Jackley is a crook. A con man. He bullied me into paying for inspections and improvements to the property I got for him, then he sued me. He said I misrepresented the property, that I failed to point out defects in the wiring and plumbing. I lost money on that deal."

I had to think about that a moment.

"Did your uncle find out what Jackley did to you?"

"Jackley was squeezing me for even more money, so I contacted Uncle Hector and told him what was going on. After I told Uncle Hector what Jackley was up to, he found at least a dozen others that Jackley had scammed. I sent Uncle Hector documents proving what Jackley had done to me, and he dug up even more proof. Hector was going to talk to him, make him pay back the money he scammed."

I closed my eyes. Finally. Finally I had a solid motive.

But something didn't feel right. "Thank you for telling me this, but I don't see why Jackley would bully a few thousand dollars from his realtor."

"Because Gordon Jackley is a fraud. He's declared bankruptcy at least twice. He pretends to be rich, acts like he lives the perfect life, with total control of everything, a man who never makes mistakes."

I recalled the geometric orderliness of Jackley's desk and office, the elegance of his clothing. A case was coming together, and the thought made me a little light-headed.

"Your Aunt Roberta told me—"

"Excuse me, but Roberta is not my aunt."

"You mean not by blood?"

"Right. Uncle Hector's first wife was my mother's sister. They never had any kids, but he always treated me like a daughter. When my aunt died, Hector remarried, but we – that is, my family – we could never understand why he would marry someone like Roberta."

I chewed my lower lip a moment. "What do you mean?"

"She's disgusting. She drinks too much, has to be the center of attention at family get-togethers. Uncle Hector paid to get her DUIs reduced to reckless driving convictions, takes her on expensive vacations, gives her whatever she wants. She even has an answering service, of all things."

I'd dealt with Roberta Moreno's answering service. And it was interesting that Gordon Jackley had also mentioned her lavish lifestyle. My light-headedness vanished.

"Right in front of the family, she repays him by calling him a bookkeeper to his face. And she hates their house, the house he grew up in, says it's old and ugly. Uncle Hector never said anything when she put him down. He just took it and laughed it off."

I took a deep breath. "Anna, I appreciate your help. I hope I can contact you again if I have any other questions."

"Please do."

I tapped my phone. Great. I'd started with two suspects, and after hours of legwork and interviews, I still had two suspects. Both had motive, means, and opportunity. And time was running out.

When I returned to Moreno's wrecked office, Jerry Simms

gave me a sly look.

"You told me to find the murder weapon." He bent low, and when he rose to his feet, he held what looked like a brass football in his huge, gloved hands.

Before I could comment about the shape, he turned it over. The football-sized object was a brass armadillo. It was mounted on a hollow, rectangular base.

A flutter rose in my belly. "That's it, Jerry. The base matches the pattern wound."

He set the armadillo on the desk. "I bet that's where it sat."

"Where did the EMTs find Jackley?"

"Just outside the bathroom. I'll show you."

Jerry led me down the hall. He stopped and pointed.

"This is where we found him."

I kneeled and studied the area Jerry had indicated. "What's this doing here?"

He squinted at the floor in front of me. "What, the TV remote? A lot of stuff got blown where it doesn't belong. There's a TV in the office."

"Right." The remote went into an evidence bag. I peered to the left. "What's this door lead to?"

Jerry nudged the door with his boot and peeked inside. "Hunh. Lots of food and bottled water. Nice shotgun on the wall. Looks like a Mossberg."

"Moreno's wife said he had a tornado room. Hold on. I just got an idea." I headed to the foyer and powered up my laptop. As the video taken from the EMT's bodycam played, Jerry Simms entered the room and stood beside me.

"Jerry, did the fire department hose down this part of the house?"

"Nah. They only had fire around the furnace and kitchen."

I froze the action and tapped the screen. "And yet, the floor of the firebox is clearly wet."

"Uh-huh. So?"

"So I think I need to take our evidence to the lab and check for fingerprints. You free later this week?"

"For what?"

"An arrest."

A wide smile crinkled Jerry Simms's face. "Always got time for an arrest."

*****

Three days later, I shouldered open the door to the community center of the Gilead Unitarian Church, and Officer Jerry Simms strode in behind me with a black evidence bag in his hand. When I asked the gray-haired lady at the reception desk where the class in Japanese floral arrangement was, she stared wide-eyed at me and the giant in navy blue beside me.

Finally, she raised a bony finger. "Classroom 12-A."

"Thank you, ma'am."

We found the room. Eight women of different ages sat at a long table littered with fresh flowers, vases, shears, and clippings. Roberta Moreno stood near the front. The sound in the room ceased when we entered. All eyes turned toward Simms, who stood silent and unsmiling.

I waited a moment. "Roberta Moreno, could I speak to you alone?"

Her eyes blazed at me. "What is this? How did you know—"

"I apologize for barging in, but we're on a very tight schedule. Your answering service told us you'd be here. Now if you could step outside."

Simms opened the door with his free hand and Roberta Moreno stormed past me into the hallway.

The moment Simms shut the door behind him, Moreno jutted her jaw at me and said, "I specifically told my answering service not to tell anyone where I was."

I regarded her a moment. "Don't blame them. They didn't want to tell me, but I informed them this was part of a murder investigation."

"Murder?"

"Officer Simms, could you show Mrs. Moreno the murder weapon?"

Simms placed the evidence bag on the floor, pulled gloves on both hands, and extracted the brass armadillo, which he thrust toward Roberta Moreno's face.

I gauged her reaction. "Have you ever seen this before?"

Moreno gaped at me.

I added, "We found your fingerprints on it."

"How—"

"You were arrested for DUI three years ago, and the prints we took from this matched."

Moreno's jaw turned slack. "Hector's kept that thing for years."

"Where did he keep it?"

"On – on his desk, in his office. If I touched it, it was to straighten it, you know, tidy up his desk. I didn't realize that's what you were looking for."

"I see. To the best of your knowledge, was this object on your husband's desk the day of the explosion?"

"Yes."

Simms and I scrutinized her.

I said, "Thank you. We needed to establish where Hector kept it. Have a good day."

Just before we entered the lobby, I sneaked a glimpse behind me. Roberta Moreno stood where we'd left her.

When we reached the parking lot, Simms pivoted and raised an eyebrow. "You deliberately made her squirm."

I cocked my head. "Did I?"

*****

Gordon Jackley greeted me and Simms at his front door. We followed him into a den lined with shelves stocked with hardbound books lined up in perfect rows. Jackley's arm was still wrapped in the immobilizer, but he moved about with greater ease than the last time I saw him. He wore a gray suit, including the jacket, with a maroon silk tie. Even my unrefined nose could tell he had splashed on some high-end cologne.

We took seats around a coffee table. Officer Simms extracted the brass armadillo from the evidence bag and set it in front of Jackley, who narrowed his eyes at me.

"Again, I appreciate you seeing us on such short notice, Mr. Jackley. As I told you on the phone, I need to nail down some details about the day Hector Moreno died."

"All right."

"What you see in front of you is the murder weapon."

Jackley's eyes widened. "Murder?"

"I examined the CT scans, and this heavy object is what killed him. It left a distinctive pattern wound on the top of Mr. Moreno's head. The shock wave from the explosion hit him from behind, and the roof over him was undamaged. So someone slammed him on the head with this directly from above." I pointed at the armadillo's base. "Remember when I asked you about a rectangular object in Mr. Moreno's office? This is it. And guess whose fingerprints we found on it?"

Gordon Jackley mechanically shook his head.

"Mrs. Moreno's."

"I see." He rubbed his chin.

"What I need from you are the details of the last moment you saw Hector Moreno."

"As I told you the other day, Hector and I were at his desk looking at P & L statements, when I had to go to the bathroom."

"So both of you were in his office from 2:20 until you had to go to the bathroom?"

"That's right."

"How long were you gone?"

"I'd say five, maybe seven minutes."

Staring into space, I said, "That would have given Roberta Moreno time to enter the room and commit the crime." I fixed my eyes on Jackley. "On your way back, did you see Hector Moreno's corpse before the explosion?"

"No. I was in the hall, coming out of the bathroom when the explosion hit."

"Thank you, Mr. Jackley. That statement will help us make an arrest."

Jackley gave me a weak smile. "Glad to help."

I returned the smile. With my eyes still fixed on Jackley, I said, "Officer Simms, could you show us the other evidence?"

Jerry reached into the black evidence bag and produced a remote encased in a plastic bag.

"Thank you, officer. Mr. Jackley, your fingerprints were not on the murder weapon. We know that from the prints you submitted ten years ago for a liquor license for a restaurant – a restaurant, by the way, that was destroyed by a gas explosion. You collected the insurance from that, I believe. The insurance company suspected it was deliberate, but they couldn't prove anything."

Gordon Jackley said nothing.

"But we did find your prints on this remote. What we don't have is your DNA, and I'm betting we'll find your residual DNA on the murder weapon. DNA usually sticks around. I believe you wiped your prints off the top, where you'd picked it up and used it to kill Hector Moreno."

"But you said Roberta's prints were on it."

"Yes, but only on the base. They're old prints. Maybe she nudged it at some point to tidy up. But to leave that pattern wound, you'd have to grab the top with both hands and bring it down directly on the victim's head."

Jackley's mouth fell open.

"Here's what I think happened that afternoon. Moreno was outraged that you had cheated his niece out of nearly ten thousand dollars, so he put together a file of other people you'd cheated over the years. Maybe he used that as a threat to make you return the money. Roberta Moreno knew about the other people you'd cheated, so I'm guessing your old college buddy looked the other way as long as he could. But when he finally confronted you, you turned psycho and killed him."

Simms shook his head. "Your old roommate."

"Then you destroyed the file he'd collected by burning it in the fireplace. But you remembered the security system had a motion detector, and had recorded your arrival. With only one other person in the house, you had to cover up the crime, and you came up with the brilliant idea of staging a gas explosion."

"Yeah, brilliant," said Simms.

A sheen of sweat glistened on Gordon Jackley's cheeks.

"Step one was to make sure the fire was out in the fireplace, so you doused the ashes with water. We know that because the videos from one of the EMT bodycams show the fireplace floor was wet, even though the fire department had not hosed down the living room. Then you sneaked to the furnace and sabotaged the gas line regulator – something I believe you've done before. You knew it would take at least an hour for enough gas to fill the house, so you waited. You waited those long, agonizing minutes. I can just imagine you sweating, wondering if Roberta Moreno would notice."

Simms leaned close. "Like he's sweating right now."

"Maybe more." I tapped the evidence bag. "You were headed toward the tornado room with this. It's the remote for the gas fireplace. You planned to wait until enough gas had built up for an explosion that would level the house, then lock yourself in Moreno's tornado room and turn on the pilot. But you made a sloppy mistake."

Simms whistled. "I'll say."

"On your way to the tornado room, you accidentally hit the igniter on the fireplace remote, and the blast blew you into the wall at the end of the hallway. It also hit Hector Moreno's body from behind and into his desk. That's what broke his ribs. When you hit the wall, you broke your ribs, as well as your forearm, and injured your right rotator cuff. All frontal injuries. The fireplace remote was at your feet when the EMT found you."

Gordon Jackley opened his mouth, stared at the remote, at the armadillo. "But Roberta..."

"No way," I said. "You told me you and Hector were working at his desk when you left to go to the bathroom. So by your own statement, he was alive when you last saw him. The explosion occurred while you were headed *away* from the office, not *toward* it. You were only about thirty feet from him when the blast occurred. That means Roberta Moreno did not have time to kill her husband and take cover in the garage."

Simms leaned back, his arms folded across his chest. "Yeah, someone with greater foresight would've proceeded more wisely, and made sure he didn't hit the fireplace remote."

Jackley said nothing. He worked his jaws, and his eyes flashed with a fierce light.

I tilted toward him. "Is there something you want to say?"

He took a deep breath, and in a quivering voice, replied, "I did – *not* – push that button."

"I believe you." I offered a deep sigh. "I think I know what happened. When you burned the file, some smoldering ashes drifted up into the flue, and later, before you made it to the tornado room, some of them floated back down. It happens every Christmas when people burn wrapping paper in the fireplace. It only takes one spark."

Gordon Jackley's head sank into his shoulders.

"You know what's ironic, Mr. Jackley? The file Hector Moreno put together *did* stop you after all."

Simms stood and pulled out a pair of handcuffs. "Yeah, that's the word. Ironic."

Death on a Pedestal

Edward Lodi

When I arrived at my office I found two men standing in the hallway. The sight of them made me want to turn around and go home. It must be a nightmare, I figured. Or the DTs. Then I thought, maybe if I blink they'll go away.

They didn't.

The first guy was the skinniest human being I've ever seen: a veritable bundle of bones. Those Stick Insects whose defense against predators is to resemble a twig – blow up a photograph of one, and that's what this guy looked like. The second guy is easier to describe. He was of average height, of average build, with a head shaped like a chicken's.

I'm sensitive to people's feelings, so I did my best to conceal my shock. When I was able to speak I said: "You gentlemen here to see me?"

The skinny guy pointed at the gold lettering on the office door. "You him? Tony Atti, Private Investigator?"

"One and the same," I replied as I unlocked the door.

They followed me in.

"What can I do for you?" I asked once we were all comfortably seated, me at my desk, the two of them on chairs

I'd salvaged from the salt marsh below my office window. The locals use the salt marsh as an unofficial dump. You never know what treasures you might find there.

The men seemed nervous. I indicated the pink Depression-glass dish in the center of the desk. "I'd offer you some peanuts but I see the mice have been at them." A few rodent droppings don't put me off my feed, but some folks are fastidious. Out of politeness I removed the dish from my desk and shoved it into a drawer.

"Someone we know has been murdered. The cops won't do nothing," the skinny guy said.

"And you'd like me to…?"

"Find out who did it."

"I don't know," I said. "I don't like going up against the police, especially when they're investigating a homicide."

"There ain't no investigation," the skinny guy said with a note of bitterness. "Cops say it's an accident. Me and Geek know better, don't we, Geek?"

The guy with a head like a chicken's nodded. "Mickey was murdered. Nobody can't convince me different."

"Before we go any further, fellows, suppose we introduce ourselves. You know my name: Tony Atti. You're…?"

"Jake Jones," the skinny guy said. "This here is Geek."

I extended my hand to Jake. We shook. I turned to Geek. "What's your real handle?"

"Geek'll do."

"You don't mind being called Geek?"

He shrugged but said nothing.

"This Mickey who you say was murdered. He have a last name?"

"Gavoni," Jake said. "But he never used it. He went by Mickey the Mighty."

That clinched it. What I'd suspected. These guys were circus folks. Sideshow freaks. It's a cruel term and I don't like it but that's what they were labeled. Maybe they didn't like it, either, but they accepted it. They had no choice.

"Okay, tell me what happened."

"We're with Casper Brothers Circus," Jake said.

I remembered now. I'd seen ads in the New Bedford *Standard-Times*. "Came to town when? Last week?"

"Five nights ago. Yesterday morning Irma found Mickey with his neck broke."

"Irma?"

"The Fat Lady."

This case was beginning to intrigue me. Like any red-blooded American I'd loved the circus when I was a kid. Elephants. Giraffes. Big cats. Jugglers and sword-swallowers and knife-throwers. Acrobats without nets performing death-defying acts. Girls in skimpy outfits balanced precariously on the backs of fast-moving horses. Trained seals. And of course the clowns.

But there was a darker side, designed to appeal more to adults I suppose, anyone with prurient tastes. The Freak Show. Unfortunates compelled by necessity to display themselves for yokels to gawk at. Not as bad in the circus as in some of the seedier carnivals, but bad enough. I'm no crusader, but I don't like to see people exploited. I decided then and there that I might just take the case. If, that is, it included free entry to the Big Top.

Which raised the question of my fee. I generally charge a hundred bucks a day plus expenses. Judging by the threadbare clothes these guys had on they'd be hard pressed to scrape up half that. "Gumshoes don't come cheap," I said. "I charge twenty-five dollars a day. I'll waive my usual retainer, provided I get a free pass."

Jake gulped. His Adam's apple bulged in his throat like a pig stuck in a python. The two men exchanged glances. "We could pass the hat," Geek suggested. "The others'll kick in."

Jake shook his head. "We can't pass it twice. We still need dough to bury Mickey."

"Look, gentlemen," I said. "If I take this case I'll get to see the inner workings of a circus, something I've always wanted to do. Tell you what. You can pay me on the installment plan. Just fork over a dollar now to make it legal."

Geek fished in his wallet and came up with a dollar bill so frayed it might have been printed when George Washington was still president. The formalities over with, I said: "Mickey the Mighty. Was he the Strong Man?"

Geek looked at me and guffawed. He sounded like a rooster crowing. I found the sound unnerving.

Jake chuckled. "Mickey's a midget," he explained. "Twenty-nine inches tall. Only he didn't like 'midget.' 'Little person' was how he called hisself."

Geek grew serious. "Them cops. A big joke with them, a midget dead. One of 'em says, so's everybody could hear, 'Maybe the Fat Lady sat on him.'"

"This Fat Lady. Where'd she find the body?"

"On the pedestal drum in the center ring."

"Pedestal drum? The thing elephants balance on when they're doing tricks?"

"Yeah," Jake said. "Irma found him sprawled on his back, like he was put on display. It wasn't no accident."

"Did the police determine a cause of death?"

"His neck was broke."

"So you're telling me the cops just walked away from this?"

"Yeah," Geek said. "To them we're just freaks. Less than human. So what if one of us dies under mysterious circumstances. Somethin' to joke about when they're having their coffee and donuts."

"'Must of fell off the trapeze,' they're saying," Jake added. "But we know that ain't possible, don't we Geek? Mickey was scared shitless of heights. He'd no sooner climb up on that trapeze than he'd walk a tightrope across Niagara Falls blindfolded."

"Gentlemen, this case is beginning to pique my interest," I said. "I've got nothing else pending this afternoon," (or any other afternoon, for that matter), "so why don't we get started right away."

My clients had cadged a ride that morning from a delivery truck driver, so I chauffeured them back in my car. They rode along in the front, with Jake squeezed between me and Geek. Whenever we took a curve Jake's elbow dug into my ribs like the point of a bayonet.

On the way I gleaned a few more details, like the fact that

Mickey the Mighty had not been, to put it mildly, a popular fellow. Jake and Geek were willing to impart that piece of information, but hesitant to explain why the murder victim had been disliked.

I didn't press them. I figured I'd soon enough find out why. I did ask them to explain why, if Mickey was *persona non grata*, the two of them were willing to cough up hard-earned dough to find his killer.

"Matter of principle," Jake said. "Mickey was one of us."

Geek explained further: "Lotta people think our lives ain't worth shit. We disagree."

"I think I understand," I said. "But what if it was…"

Jake finished the sentence for me. "One of us? In that case we'll just have to sort it out."

It was mid-morning when we arrived at the grounds. The visitors' lot was empty. I parked near the gate and we walked in with only a cursory glance from the security guard. The first thing that struck me, other than the hustle and bustle even at that hour, was the smell: familiar, yet somehow different from the way I remembered it as a kid: a mélange of roasted peanuts, cotton candy, elephant dung, caged cats, roustabouts dripping sweat. And something else. It took me a few moments to recognize it. Fear. I could smell fear.

"Where you wanna start?" Jake asked as we approached the Big Top.

"Inside. I'd like to see where The Fat Lady found the body."

The huge tent was deserted. The pedestal drum sat in the middle of the center ring like a sacrificial altar awaiting its next victim. "You said Mickey was on his back, like he'd been placed on display?"

"Yeah," Jake said. "Soon as Irma found him she come directly to our unit. We was having breakfast, wasn't we, Geek?"

Geek bobbed his head, like a chicken pecking for insects. I couldn't help wondering if the movement was natural, or had become ingrained from being part of his act for so long. "She was all flustered and couldn't hardly talk. We come here right away."

"Irma wasn't so flustered as to lose her appetite," Jake said wryly. "She et our breakfast whilst we was gone."

"That was just nerves, Jake. Irma can't help herself."

Jake shrugged. "Anyways, Mickey was on the drum on his back, with his arms and legs spread out even, not crooked like he'd of been if he'd of fell like the cops claim."

"Who do you think would've done that, and why?"

"Who, I don't know," Jake said. "We're hoping you'll find out for us. Why, I can guess. To send a message."

"What kind of message?"

Jake glanced at Geek. At first neither spoke. Then Geek said: "Mickey was a sneak."

Jake elaborated: "He spied on people. Twenty-nine inches – he could hide places, know what I mean? Hear and see things he shouldn't of."

I glanced at the drum and pictured the diminutive corpse lying there. "What you're telling me, gentlemen, is that Mickey the Mighty was a blackmailer." Jake and Geek remained silent. "Well," I continued, "everyone's got secrets. Obviously you two didn't kill Mickey to keep him quiet, else you wouldn't hire me to stir things up. So tell me, who in this outfit has most to hide?"

Geek shuffled his feet like a chicken scratching for feed. "It ain't up to us to say."

"I don't know, Geek," Jake said, staring at the drum. "Maybe we oughta loosen up. It don't make no sense, us hiring a private detective, then not sharing what we know."

Geek shrugged. "I guess there can't be no harm."

"Everybody knows Ella is carrying on with Andy," Jake said. After my blank stare he explained that Ella, the circus's star equestrienne, though married to Otis, the lion tamer, was having an affair with Andy, the knife thrower.

"Everybody knows, 'cept Otis," Geek said with a semi guffaw. "Just like it ain't no secret that Sam and Sondra are playing hide-the-salami."

"Sondra's one of the acrobats," Jake said for my edification. "She's hitched to Al. Al's just a roustabout. Sam's the circus strong man. 'Samson, the Muscle Man,' he calls hisself."

"Andy and Sam. Either one of 'em married?"

Jake shook his head. "Nope. Both is single."

Once I'd got the two adulterous triangles straightened out in my head, I said, "It doesn't seem likely that either Sam or Andy would have much to lose if Mickey informed either of the respective husbands they were being cuckolded. Sam the Muscle Man sounds like he can take care of himself. Likewise Andy, with his knife-throwing skills. Which leaves the women. Can you picture one or the other of them breaking Mickey's neck?"

Geek and Jake both indicated the negative. "Still, you never know," I reminded them. "Best to keep an open mind."

"*Cherchez la femme*," Geek remarked unexpectedly.

A cluster of clowns strolled into the Big Top and, milling around, eyed us with suspicion. "Let's move on," I suggested. "It's time I met Irma."

The performers were housed at the rear of the circus, away from the Big Top and sideshow tents, in units hauled from city to city on railroad cars or flatbed trucks. Each was the width of a railroad car, and half the length. Irma's was easily identifiable. The caricature of a Fat Lady rollicking with laughter was painted on the side.

"Irma's just like in the picture," Jake informed me as he rapped his knuckles against her door.

As we stood on the low wooden steps outside Irma's unit I caught a glimpse, from the rear, of a distinctly Junoesque figure entering a unit three doors down. Geek saw me gawking and reading my mind said, "Nice figure, huh?"

"Not bad," I agreed. "She one of the acrobats?"

Geek smirked, as if at some inside joke. "Jake and me'll introduce you later."

When Irma answered Jake's knock he explained my presence. "A detective!" Irma exclaimed. "And good-looking!" (Full disclosure: not all dames would agree with that.)

"Geek and me'll wait outside," Jake said.

It's just as well they did. The Fat Lady lived up to her billing, and then some. Most performers were housed two to a unit. In Irma's case there simply wasn't room for anyone else. Even the rail-thin Jake would've found sharing her quarters a challenge.

And it wasn't just her size, or the bulky furniture her weight required, that made moving around difficult. There was also the clutter. "I just finished washing my unmentionables," Irma apologized, as, attempting to reach the chair she proffered, I squeezed past a clothes rack draped with bras, underdrawers, and stockings the size of wind socks. "But you're a man of the world," she tittered. "You've seen such things before."

Not on that scale, I hadn't.

She offered me coffee but I declined. "What time was it when you found the body?" I asked.

"Five or ten past eight. Sure you don't want something to drink? A beer maybe."

"Only if you're having one."

"Of course." She got up and navigated her way to the refrigerator. "We have electricity but no running water," Irma informed me. "The showers and toilets are outside. A real hassle, when you gotta go at night." She handed me a Dawson, then lowered herself onto a settee that groaned like a human when she sagged into it.

I took a healthy swig. "What were you doing in the Big Top so early?"

"On my way to see Emily." Irma tilted her bottle to her lips and drained it in one gulp. "I use the tent as a shortcut. The inside of my thighs chafe when I walk any distance," she added.

To be polite I downed the rest of my beer. "And Emily is…?"

"My best friend," she said, eyes twinkling. "She's the only friend I've got who's bigger than me."

I raised my eyebrows.

"Emily's an elephant," Irma explained. She laughed, the way you'd expect a circus Fat Lady to laugh, uproariously. I wondered how much of it was genuine, how much an act. "I visit her every morning," Irma continued, when the laughter subsided. "She likes peanuts. I always bring her a handful. Another beer?"

It was obvious that Irma was lonely, so I accepted the offer and stayed longer than I normally would've, nursing my beer. But in the end I learned little of value. On the subject of who might have wanted Mickey the Mighty dead, Irma The Fat Lady was noncommittal. Finally, I thanked her and left.

When I stepped outside Geek and Jake were nowhere in sight. As I stood pondering my next move something whooshed past my ear. My first thought was: a bird. Then I saw the knife sticking in the side of Irma's unit. Instinctively I spun around. A tall lanky man stood grinning at me.

"You must be Andy," I said. The knife thrower Ella the equestrienne was having an affair with.

"That's right," he said.

"I don't like people tossing knives at me."

He shrugged. "Just a friendly warning, pal. Some folks around here don't care much for nosy parkers."

"I'll keep that in mind. Pal," I added, with as much disdain as I could muster.

Jake and Geek came around a corner. Geek spotted the knife and immediately took in the situation. "Knock it off, Andy." He pulled the knife free and tossed it onto the ground at the knife thrower's feet. Andy scowled. Bending, he picked the knife up. I braced myself for trouble but needn't have. The knife thrower muttered something under his breath and walked away.

"Don't pay him no heed," Geek said. "He's just a jerk."

I agreed. If Andy was the killer it was unlikely he'd call attention to himself by threatening me. Even so, I'd be wise to stay on guard.

"Now where to, gentlemen?"

Geek looked at Jake. "If anyone was close to Mickey, it was Bea, ain't that right, Jake?" Was it my imagination, or did I see him wink?

The man billed as The Human Toothpick nodded. "Bea and Mickey go a long way back."

Bea's unit was a few doors from Irma's: the one the statuesque dame had entered. This was one interview I looked forward to. That is, until the door opened and the reason Geek had winked became clear. Though Bea had the figure of a goddess, her face was somewhat off-putting. Not that her features were unattractive, or anything like that. She might even be considered beautiful, if not for her dark, bushy beard.

Jake introduced me.

The Bearded Lady looked me over, like a cut of meat she might buy for supper. "I don't know as I can be of any help, Mr. Atti, but come in. You two boys stay outside. I want this hunk to myself."

In striking contrast to Irma's cluttered unit, The Bearded Lady's was the picture of neatness. A place for everything and everything in its place. She had on an ankle-length dress which showed her full figure to advantage. Before meeting Bea I would've expected a bearded woman to have mannish features. More disconcerting than the beard, was I think, Bea's indisputable femininity.

She invited me to sit. "In case you're wondering, 'Bea's short for Beatrice, not 'Beard.'"

I smiled at the witticism.

"We have the place to ourselves, Mr. Atti. Or may I call you Tony? We can speak frankly. Last week my roommate left unexpectedly." She paused a beat. "Trudy worked the gate. I guess the temptation was too much. She ran off with the night's receipts – along with Cory, the sword-swallower." She laughed throatily. "Can I offer you a drink? Scotch okay?"

"You having one? Okay then. Neat, no ice." What the hell. "Geek and Jake tell me you've known Mickey quite some time."

"Poor fellow." She handed me my Scotch. "Tony, I'll be square with you. Mickey was a stinker. Nobody liked the little bastard. I was no exception." She stared into her drink. "Still – to have his neck broken."

The Scotch was the way I like it, pungent, reeking of smoldering peat fires. I had to go easy or I might end up staying the afternoon. "So when did you first meet him? Here at the circus?"

She shook her head. "About ten years ago, at a two-bit carnival I hooked up with when…" She trailed off and gazed at the floor, as if lost in the mists of time. I could picture her: a young woman. With hair on her chin. As if reading my thoughts she tugged at the beard. "Who'd hire me? Can you see me waiting on tables? My family…" She took a sip. "The carnival came to town. I hadn't had a square meal in days. So

I joined up and became a freak. Officially."

"And Mickey?"

"Mickey the Mighty. The sideshow Strong Man. That was the draw, you see: a midget who lifted weights, who performed amazing feats of strength." She gritted her teeth, swished Scotch around in her mouth. "That's how we met. After a few weeks I left the carnival and joined the circus. Mickey stayed on. I didn't see him again until a couple months ago, when suddenly he shows up here. It was an acquaintance I wasn't eager to renew."

"Why is that? You said Mickey was a stinker. In what way?"

"You know he was only twenty-nine inches high?"

I nodded.

"He used that to his advantage. Hiding in places you wouldn't expect. Spying. Seeing things he shouldn't. He said it was all in fun." She paused. "Nobody else thought so."

"Did anyone threaten him?"

Bea laughed and polished off her drink. "Can you see Otis the Lion Tamer or Samson, the real Strong Man, threatening to punch him out?" She shrugged. "What could people do?"

"Especially if he had a hold on them," I said. "Things he knew which they wouldn't want made public."

Bea let that ride. Seeing my empty glass she got up and refilled it, along with her own. We sat for a while drinking in silence. Eventually I asked one or two more questions, to no avail. The Bearded Lady had said all she had to say regarding the dead midget.

Finally I took my leave. Bea said she was sorry to see me go and I believed her. One more Scotch and I might have stayed. Even to this day I wonder…

As before, when I got outside my clients were nowhere to be seen. This time, however, no knives came whizzing past my ear. The closest I came to danger was hearing a lion roar. Or maybe it was a tiger. Or a sideshow barker practicing his spiel.

I was hungry. It was past my lunch time and the Scotch I'd drunk, floating on top of the Dawsons, was making my mind cloudy. I strolled around. Maybe I could find a hot dog stand.

I was in luck. With a matinee scheduled for later, the gates stood open to let the suckers wander in and squander their money on sideshows. In anticipation of the crowds the food concessions stood ready. I bought a couple of frankfurters. The dogs, though greasy, tasted okay. What might have been ground up to produce them was anyone's guess. Jimmy Hoffa, for all I knew.

When Geek showed up at my elbow I wasn't surprised. I figured one or the other of my clients would be in contact. He handed me an envelope. "I got you a free pass, good for the Big Top and all the sideshows."

I thanked him and tucked the envelope into my pocket. "Can I see Mickey's quarters? I assume he shared a unit." Geek pecked at the air with his head. It took me a while to realize he was nodding.

"He bunked with Phil."

"Think Phil will mind if I poke around?"

"Naw. Phil's a good sport. We better hurry, though. The shows will be starting soon and we gotta be in place."

When we arrived Geek stood on the steps and hollered,

"Phil! It's Geek. You got a visitor." A male voice shouted for us to enter.

Phil was seated barefoot on a comfortable armchair. The reason for the absence of shoes and socks was self-evident. Phil had no arms. In lieu of fingers he depended on toes to perform everyday functions.

"This here is Mr. Atti, a private detective me and Jake has hired to find out who killed Mickey. Okay if he looks around?"

"Be my guest, Mr. Atti. Nobody's bothered to clear out his stuff so it's just like he left it. Can I offer you a cigarette?" I told him I'd quit a few years back. "I wish I could," Phil said. He shook one from a pack, brought it to his mouth, struck a match and applied its flame to the tip, all by using his toes.

Phil the Armless Wonder had blond hair and was strikingly handsome. I put his age at around thirty. "How well did you and Mickey get along?" I asked.

"Not too bad, considering he was a little prick. Once he learned he couldn't push me around we actually got along fine. He kept to his end of the unit, I kept to mine."

"Can you think of anyone who might've wanted him dead?"

Phil took a deep drag of his cigarette before answering. "Draw up a list of everyone in the circus. That would about cover it."

"Phil, we oughta get going," Geek interjected.

"Feel free to rifle through Mickey's junk," Phil said as he slid off the chair. "If you find anything that might incriminate his killer, destroy it. Whoever did the runt in did the rest of us a favor."

After he and Geek left I made a thorough search of Mickey

the Mighty's earthly belongings, beginning with his clothing, crammed into drawers set against the wall. Handling the doll-size articles was like pawing through a dead child's wardrobe. But I soon dismissed that notion. If his many detractors deserved credence, in the afterworld Mickey wouldn't be wearing a halo. He'd be carrying a pitchfork.

After twenty minutes I was ready to call it quits. What had I hoped to find, anyhow? Mickey trafficked in information. Secrets he could peddle, or threaten to peddle. Information he stored in his head.

The only item of interest I came across was a photo album: publicity shots of Mickey the Mighty, in tights, performing amazing "feats of strength" in various phases of his career. Other than his diminutive size, the photos showed a perfectly proportioned male adult, albeit more muscular than the norm. The extra meat presumably came from working out.

There was something else extra, though. Something I almost missed. Several of the photos seemed thicker than the others. That was strange. I slid one of the fatter photos from its protective plastic sleeve.

There was a second photograph concealed beneath.

I stared at it, then removed it from the sleeve and placed it on the floor face-down. I went through the album and came up with four additional photographs in the same vein. I set the album aside, scooped up the five photographs I'd confiscated, and slid them under my shirt.

I looked at my watch. It was too late to catch any of the sideshows. That was too bad. I'd like to have seen some of my new-found friends in action, Geek in particular. But maybe it was just as well that I didn't. I'd rather remember them as people I'd met and interacted with, than as sideshow freaks.

I had a good idea now as to who was responsible for Mickey's death. The existence of the photographs provided motive. There was also one piece of additional evidence, purely circumstantial, nothing that would hold up in a court of law, but which I found compelling.

I still had time to catch the performance under the Big Top. Confronting the killer, and revealing that person's identity, would have to wait.

As I stepped down from the unit a man wearing tails and a top hat approached me. The long whip he wielded in his right hand indicated he was probably not the ringmaster, but rather Otis, the Lion Tamer. The scowl on his face suggested this was not a chance meeting.

"You," he said. "You're the private dick that's been snooping around."

"And you must be Otis."

"Circus people don't take to outsiders interfering in our affairs." For emphasis he gave the whip a snap.

"My clients seem to disagree. Now if you'll excuse me."

"Them two freaks? They don't count. Me, I'm telling you to clear out."

"Go play with your pussycats." I began to walk away.

I felt the whip caress the nape of my neck before I heard the crack.

"That's just a warning," Otis said.

Now my dander was up. "If you're afraid I'll discover your

wife's infidelity and make it known, thereby making you the laughing stock of the circus, you're too late. It's already common knowledge."

Otis's eyes bulged and he let out a roar.

"That's a nice impersonation of a lion," I said.

Furious, he raised the whip. I'd anticipated that. The animal tamer was skilled at bullying beasts of prey, not wily private eyes, or so I reasoned.

The whip stung me across the shoulders. Suddenly I didn't feel quite so wily. The pain felt worse than a sock to the jaw. That made me really angry.

On instinct I dropped to my knees then rolled onto my back, with my hands and feet raised, like an animal playing dead. The maneuver took Otis off guard. Whatever he'd expected me to do, it wasn't that. I took advantage of his confusion and leapt to my feet. While his brain was still processing what had happened, I rushed forward, wrenched the whip from his hand, and using the butt end whacked him across the face. Twice. Dropping the whip I hauled back with my fist and hit him hard in the solar plexus.

Gasping for air he dropped to the ground like a deflated balloon, with his top hat still perfectly positioned. It looked ludicrous on him, so I snatched it from his head and placed it on my own. I left him there, winded and dazed, and strolled along, feeling like Dapper Dan. People began staring at the hat so I ditched it behind a sideshow tent, took out my pass, and headed on into the Big Top.

The pass Geek gave me allowed me a seat near the center ring.

I enjoyed the show. The trapeze artists performed their death-defying act with the greatest of ease, as did the acrobats, including Sondra, who, although married to a roustabout named Al was carrying on an affair with Samson the Strong Man. The scantily-clad equestrienne, Ella, put her horse through the paces then ended the act by standing on its bare back and riding around the ring. Hopefully she'd be equally adept at handling her hubby Otis after the show.

I enjoyed the clowns. And the elephants, my favorite being Irma's friend Emily. The biggest surprise was Otis. After our altercation I thought he might call in sick. However, bloody but unbowed he showed up on time. The bandages on his face created a certain mystique, as if he'd been mauled by an unruly lion. The only thing missing was his hat.

When the show ended I made my way to the housing units. Bea promptly answered my knock. "Tony!" She invited me in. "What a pleasant surprise. Did you catch my act? I didn't notice."

"Sorry, no. I didn't have time." I could tell she was puzzled by my presence. It could be she thought I had romance in mind. And maybe I would have, beard notwithstanding, under different circumstances.

She poured two Scotches and handed me one.

"Bea, these belong to you." I handed over the photos I'd found in Mickey's album.

She took one glance, then placed them face-down on the floor. Crimson splotches blossomed beneath her beard.

I contemplated the amber liquid in my glass, then took a sip.

She smoothed a fold in her dress before breaking the silence. "It was when I joined the carnival. Mickey offered me money. At the time it seemed like a lot. He said that for some men hair on my face would be a turn-on. All I had to do was pose. He didn't bother to describe what kind of poses he had in mind."

"He slipped you a date drug…"

She nodded. "I was naive. I hated myself afterwards. But by then it was too late."

"Is that when the blackmail started?"

"No. Soon after he took the pictures I left the carnival and joined the circus. More Scotch?"

"Thanks, but I'd better not. I've got a long drive home."

She hesitated, then poured herself another. "You know I killed Mickey, don't you?"

I met her gaze. Her eyes were soft, gentle. Not the eyes of a calculating killer. "I wasn't sure. The photos suggested blackmail. But others besides you could've had the same motive."

"What else, then? Do I look like the criminal type?"

I stared longingly at the half-empty bottle. Heaven help me if she insisted on pouring me another.

"Look around you, Bea. You're a stickler for neatness. A place for everything, and everything in its place. The way Mickey was laid out, on the pedestal drum… Jake and Geek thought it was done as a warning. But that didn't make sense to me."

"Obsessive-compulsive is what the shrinks call it. The need

to make everything just-so. Sure you won't have a drop more?"

I shook my head. "I'd like to hear the whole story, though."

"There isn't much to tell." She reached for the Scotch. "Mind if I pour myself a little more Dutch courage?" She refilled her glass, then sat quietly before continuing. "The blackmail started three months ago, when Mickey suddenly appeared, as if from nowhere." She took several pensive sips.

"Look Bea," I assured her. "I'm not going with this to the police. They think, or pretend to think, that Mickey's death was accidental. I'm content to leave it at that."

"It's funny, Tony, but it really was an accident. I mean, I didn't plan to kill him."

"How did it happen?"

"It was at night. I was on my way here after cleaning up the kiosk. As I passed one of the sideshow tents I saw Mickey laying on the ground. He had a camera and was taking pictures through an opening under the flap. The son of a bitch was bleeding me dry, and now he was going to do it to someone else. Tony, I just lost it. I grabbed him by the ankles and tossed him away from me, like I was ridding myself of trash. He landed hard on the ground. That's how his neck broke."

"No one saw any of this?"

She sighed. "Not as far as I know."

"Then what?"

"I couldn't just leave him on the ground. So I carried him into the Big Top, to the pedestal drum, where I knew he'd be found eventually."

Most people wouldn't have bothered, I thought. They

would've just walked away.

"What about the camera?"

"I brought it here, smashed it, and tossed it into a dumpster."

I got up from the chair. "I'd better be going, Bea." I wanted to say more but felt at a loss for words. "One more thing. Do you trust Jake and Geek?"

She fumbled for the Scotch bottle, picked it up, then put it down again. "I'll have a big enough head tomorrow as it is," she said, with a half-hearted laugh. "Yes, I do trust Jake and Geek. They're true friends."

"I think I should tell them. But I won't if you object."

"No, Tony, I don't object. They'll understand."

With reluctance I took my leave.

"Mickey got what he deserved," Jake and Geek affirmed after I'd given them a summary.

"Maybe I should go talk to Bea," Jake said. "You know, to console her."

Geek gave off a characteristic guffaw. "You'd like to console her, all right."

"And what do you mean by that crack?"

"You always did have a crush on her."

"That ain't so."

"No? Remember that time we got drunk on muscatel? You said you'd like to shave off her beard, to see what she looks like without it."

"What about you? You always had the hots for Irma."

"So what if I do? It ain't no business of yours."

I figured this was a good time to make my exit. As I slipped away toward the parking lot I could still hear them wrangling. Goodbye fee, I told myself. But I was wrong. For months afterwards, every once in a while an envelope would arrive in the mail, postmarked from some place far away, with two or three dollars tucked inside.

Bitter Love
Lynn Hesse

My day, muggy and hot, started with a call out of a triple homicide in a parking lot of a ritzy multiplex in Dunwoody, Georgia.

Bowlegged Detective Ralph Jackson waddled over to me while I squatted over the young female's body with a lotus tattoo on her right thigh. Her skirt was hiked up around her waist, showing her chartreuse bikini underwear. I dropped the sheet over the body and stood to talk to Ralph, who was sensitive about being deaf in one ear, an injury from Desert Storm. "What the heck happened here?" he asked.

"Looks like the wife shot her no-good cheating husband, the girlfriend, and herself, but it's too soon to tell. No I.D. on this one. The .45 semi-auto is lying next to the Mrs. over there near the silver Lexus."

Ralph grunted. "Who's processing the scene?

"Norma."

I yelled at the uniform near the crime scene tape. "Tell those bystanders to turn their cellphones off or point them toward the building unless they want them confiscated. Not one video better surface on the web."

"Norma Rae Rae." He smiled. "Norma's a little spitfire, doesn't take any guff from anybody. At least we caught a break there."

"Yeah, Norma's the best. She'll be finished with the photos in a few."

"What's this marker for? I don't see anything."

"Somebody picked up the shoes. I caught the numbnuts trying to slink away with the stilettoes. He petted them before he returned them to me."

"I bet, the perv. Or just wanted a souvenir from a triple homicide scene?"

"Probably both. Sexual fetishes run the gamut." I shrugged.

I've been doing a lot of shrugging in the last year. When my husband asked me if his mother could stay with us to recoup from her fall, I shrugged and walked away. I knew he meant live with us until the end of time. Later in bed, I blurted out, "I'm not changing her diapers."

The old bitty wasn't that bad off. She could still get around with a walker and disappear fast enough if you needed her to stay put in a dollar store. She didn't want Samuel to marry me because I was a divorcee with a seven-year-old son. It made little difference that my fiancé was divorced with an eighteen-month-old daughter to raise. The way I looked at it, his party-animal ex and my can't-keep-a-job ex evened things out.

Ralph interrupted my reverie. "Direct me toward the witnesses, and I'll take the statements."

I pointed to a group of unhappy techies under a mezzanine drinking their lattes and typing on their cell phones. They probably could care less about going to work, but the muggy August heat in the South wasn't pleasant at any time. I couldn't blame them for wanting to return to their air-conditioned office cubicles. I imagined them shooting paper clips at each other during breaks, their excitement for the day. Although I'd heard on the news, gaming for this generation was replacing office romances and sexual encounters—a weirder world than even I lived in.

Radio announced a bank robbery in-progress on Mount Vernon Road less than a mile away. No backup was available.

I cleared on the call. "Ralph, you need to handle the on-scene. I'll be down the road apiece, be back to help with the death notification."

I'm good at death notification.

I had to tell my husband his father had passed. Doris had called my work phone from Florida to spare herself from telling her youngest son the bad news. Before my father-in-law died, I nursed him back to health from a stroke while his wife sat on my living room couch, never peeled as much as one potato. She watched me raise her grandchild and drag in at midnight after working uniform in the highest crime area in the county without a word of praise.

Of course, dear Harry checked out five years later in Clearwater, Florida. He left my mother-in-law alone, barking out her ludicrous opinions as people walked past her third-floor condo balcony. Once I heard her yell, "Take that ring out of your nose for Godsake snowbird," to a pre-teen walking a pug.

"You're killin' me," Ralph said. "I've been workin' three straight days without any sleep."

"Must be a full moon. Sorry, Ralphie, we're all in the same boat." Hate boats. Once Doris pushed my son out of a fishing dinghy. The water wasn't over his head, but it scared him. She claimed it was an accident. Other people's children were all the same to her. Hoodlums.

"Probably," Ralph said. "You go get'em, Rodeo Queen." His dimples flickered. In my younger days, before I was a mother, I rode the rodeo circuit on weekends barrel racing. I won some prize money along the way and—the last time I fell off my horse—a bum left knee.

Ralph interjected, "I'm so tired if the bank perps walked up and confessed, right here, they would have to handcuff themselves. I couldn't chase them. So, go on."

I laughed, but my partner's belly hung over his belt about six inches, and he hadn't run after a perp in twenty years. I handed him my crime scene sketch.

"You owe me one," he said. "Your pretty face and a bottle of whiskey at Copper's bar after work are my preferences."

I gave him a sideways glance as I opened the door to my unmarked city vehicle and rolled down my window. "For doing your duty?"

"You don't expect me to handle this cluster with county pay as my incentive?" Ralph pointed at each mound covered with a sheet like they were carcasses, not human remains.

"Naw—but sometimes I forget you lack human kindness and a work ethic."

He huffed.

A female sergeant walked over to us and offered to help make the death notification to the family. She had to be newly promoted. Nobody volunteered. I raised my eyebrows at Ralph, who had found himself a rookie sergeant to do his bidding. I drove away.

When I arrived at the bank, the first uniform patrol car screeched into the parking lot. The officer parked on the far side of the lot from me, all hyped from running the blue lights and siren to get there. He motioned for me to stand down, pulled his duty weapon, and approached from the side of the building. Unimpressed with his shaved head and bulging muscles, I took out my binoculars and scanned the front glass doors for movement inside. Nada. The front parking lot contained eight cars; I estimated half of them belonged to employees, leaving two or three owned by customers. I hoped the surveillance cameras were working and the perps wouldn't take hostages. The top of the building looked clear. No snipers.

Uniform was on his talkie with the volume blasting while he waited for what he considered appropriate backup.

I walked around to the rear parking lot and saw a white-panel van idling near the rear entrance. I called in the tag number and tried to raise Muscle Man on the radio. No response. I considered approaching the van, but I couldn't see the front of the van or tell how many occupants were inside. The driver might be armed with an AK-47 emulating the bank robbers from Center Precinct last week.

Radio advised the van was reported stolen a couple of days ago from the Ace Hardware Store about a mile away on Hammond Drive.

An older woman in a broad-brim sunhat got out of a Beemer.

The van driver gunned the engine.

I raced toward Sunhat as I fetched my 9mm out of my

shoulder holster. Wouldn't you know it? She pepper sprayed me.

My eyes lit up to a million degrees, and tears and snot flew from my eyes and nose. I lifted the tail of my T-shirt and wiped my eyes with the underneath side. "I'm Detective Robinson. Don't go near the van. There's a robbery in progress inside the bank."

I saw the blurry woman's figure stop halfway between me and the van. "Oh, God. They're coming out of the bank. What should I do?" Sunhat said.

"Go back to your car and leave," I demand. I informed radio I needed backup and repeated the white-paneled van description.

I laid flat on the pavement with tears streaming down my face and tried to focus. The skin on my abdomen burned from my sweat mixing with the residual pepper on the T-shirt. With my arms extended straight out in front of me, my 9mm double gripped, I rolled toward a parked red SUV. My ID badge lanyard flopped from side to side. I scrambled into a squatting position near the front passenger door and located the van swinging around and closing in fast on what distance was left between them and me. They fired before I braced myself against the hood of the car. I fired back and missed. They braked and stopped twenty feet past the SUV. I scrambled under the car.

Red clown shoes hit the pavement attached to yellow polka dot pants, shiny ones. *What the...*

Then I heard the devil incarnate speak. "I should kill her."

A horn blasted somewhere close by. Maybe God himself

said, "Dummy, get back inside. Now. We're leaving."

The van burned rubber as it raced out of the parking lot into the alley.

I crawled out from underneath the SUV and bent over, placing my road-rash hands on my scraped knees. I willed myself to breathe to control the adrenaline.

A uniform car screeched to a halt. "You injured?" a baby-face officer asked.

"No. They're dressed like clowns. Go." I pointed in the direction the van had gone. He took off.

"Radio, I'm okay," I said as I limped back to my car.

It was only ten o'clock in the morning.

*****

Back at the station, I was writing reports when my husband called. Samuel had heard about the robbery and shots fired. He didn't know it was me. I stalled and didn't tell him the details. He pressed the issue. I thundered into the phone. "It was me. I'm fine. Just some self-inflicted road rash when I hit the pavement."

"You need to quit and get a real job." His tone came across as cold and critical.

The argument was old, and I was in no mood to deal with it. The implication his free-lance graphic designer job made *real* money struck home. "Right, geek commando, I'll phone you when I can. I.A. and uniform want their reports yesterday."

"Gloria, wait. While you were out playing Wonder Woman, I took mom to emergency again. Her blood sugar spiked. I need you at home. And maybe some time to take a leak in peace."

"She's your mother, and I didn't sign up to be her nurse."

"That's frickin' clear. You're not interested unless you're at the center of the universe."

I didn't know which one of us cut the connection first. I allowed the silence to sink in before I put the phone in my pocket. Maybe he was right to some extent. My days of catering to others whims and needs were long gone. I couldn't do it anymore. I'd lost mom from Parkinson's disease and dad from a heart attack without a word of sympathy from my husband's side of the family. My photo-journalist son, living in Texas, rarely called home because he knew his stepfather disliked him. When I watched the stepchild I'd raised from diapers get married in her birth mother's church in Portland, Maine, I cried. Kate left the sanctuary holding the hand of Dwight Farmington, a man who expected my bubbly daughter to kiss his ring every day. Something broke inside of me as I watched Dwight destroy Kate's spirit.

Since the birth of her children, Kate had relied on anti-depressants. She was on every committee in her gated community and at her children's private schools. Her three-year-old diagnosed with social anxiety went to a special school with an annual tuition close to my yearly salary. Lately, I noticed on social media Kate wears pink to every event and perky smiles.

My lieutenant was hovering near my desk. I needed another cup of coffee, but I didn't want her to see my left knee was swollen and worthy of another injury report. "The incident report is almost ready, minus the lady's name," I said.

I could tell the lieutenant thought I should've obtained Sunhat's name on scene as I blew streams of mucus in the air and saved the woman's life and my own. I added with my standard charm. "Unless you want to write this report for me LT, back off. Let me type."

She gave me her drop-dead look and walked out of my space, yelling over her shoulder. "Hunting and pecking isn't typing. When I come back, it better be done."

I mumbled to myself, "You wish you were me, hard ass." I grinned, satisfied because everyone knew thirty-something was sleeping her way to the top. My stomach growled like an angry cat. I pulled at a baggy T-shirt and hoodie somebody had thrown at me when I entered the precinct.

I had to look like a drowned rat from the EMS decontamination washing procedure. At least my eyes had quit stinging.

The desk phone rang. It was Ralph. He wanted me to meet him at the morgue. "Bad news?" I asked.

"Come see for yourself."

Accustomed to Ralph's tendency to relish withholding info, I changed the subject. "Did you make the death notifications?"

"The girl's mother went berserk, and I left her with sarge." He paused. "Hum, the sergeant, she's kinda cute."

"Really. You could be her grandpa."

"I can dream, can't I?"

"No. It's icky."

"Jeez, if I can't have you, I gotta do something?" Ralph said.

"*What* do you want me to look at?"

"Signs of some poison inside the middle-aged woman's nose and mouth."

"Dang, so much for my theory," I said.

"M.E. says she was probably dead before being displayed at the homicide scene."

"I'm en route." It was noon when I left the use of force report half done in my computer, dodged the lieutenant's office by using the backstairs and headed for the morgue. My left knee was throbbing like a toothache.

*****

Standing in the morgue hallway, Ralph told me a story about the mixed-used development owner showing up at the crime scene. He held his pinkie out and used a nasal tone. "Gordy and I paid a small fortune to live where our children wouldn't be exposed to robbery and such."

I laughed. I needed to laugh. By "such" the civilian meant death. "Yeah, the folks in the finest parts of Dunwoody prefer to die behind closed doors with their dignity preserved by hired help, a nurse or companion, watching over them in their last days. The hired help cleaning up the mess before the family arrives to cry over the dead body."

I didn't like the privileged, but then I had a rep of not playing well with others. Being a county detective for ten years had one advantage. The smarter brass left me alone. I cleared their cases, and they put up with my bad attitude. Going on three to four hours of sleep a night since my children were small might've contributed to my disposition.

I yawned. "I need coffee."

"Let's get something to eat," Ralph said as we left the

morgue and the rancid air from the dumpster in the parking lot hit my nostrils.

"No thanks. I need to finish my reports and go home to fight with my husband about my mother-in-law. Although he might've to argue with himself while I fall asleep."

"Better you than me. I would eliminate that problem. That's why I live alone."

I felt Jackson watch me hobble away. It was one o'clock in the afternoon.

*****

A little less than three hours later, I'm wedged in the pharmacy line at a supermarket between first-of-the-month pensioners and their carts. My husband's back pain had kicked in, and he had told me he couldn't face getting in the car again. He texted, "It's your responsibility to help out," as I left the precinct. I was obliged to clean the house, do the laundry, buy the groceries, and refill Doris's pill organizer each week too. She needed a new prescription filled. This bottle of god-knows-what made her twenty-seventh medication.

Although I disliked my mother-in-law, I had mentioned several times I thought some of Doris's meds were interfering with others, but my husband dismissed my worries. "The doctors know what they're doing," he said.

I hobbled forward in line as I grabbed a power bar off the shelf. I took a bite. It tasted like fake chocolate coating over a chalky flour paste, but I gobbled it down. I took another step forward. Pain shot up my left leg. My left knee was the size of a grapefruit. I crumbled up the wrapper before I realized what I was doing. I reached the checkout counter and smoothed the wrapper out as best I could.

The young pharmacy employee with heavy eyeliner shook her head when I handed her the wrapper with the bar code torn in half. "It's borderline stealing when you eat it before you pay."

"I haven't eaten all day." I shrugged.

"Are you a cop?" She focused on the bulge made by my duty weapon under my sweatshirt.

"A detective," I said.

"Figures." She punched in the numbers at the bottom of the bar code.

She took her time finding the prescription in the "D" basket for Doris, not under our family name Robinson, and made me pay full price because I didn't have my mother-in-law's insurance cards on me.

I didn't thank her when she handed me the package.

It was five o'clock, and Doris liked to eat promptly at six o'clock in the evening. Damn, I should've bought a roasted chicken while I was inside the store," I said out loud as I drove my battle-scarred Volvo down the lot aisle. A car shot out of a parking spot at warp speed, and I swerved, missing a bag lady pushing a buggy full of her possessions by inches. She yelled obscenities at me and beat on the hood of my car. Her last descriptive sentence ended with "dickhead." I shrugged and spelled the word SORRY in sign language through the closed window. My mom taught the deaf.

The bag lady cocked her head and stared.

I drove home in a daze. At a four-way stop, the driver behind me honked and honked. I was less than a mile away from my house, and I wasn't looking forward to my next angry encounter. *No respite.*

*****

My husband and his mother were seated at the dining room table playing cards with seagulls printed on the sides. They ignored me until I dropped the pharmacy bag on the table.

They looked up.

"I'm going to take a shower. Please take out a package of chicken from the freezer, put it in warm water to thaw, and preheat the oven to three seventy-five degrees."

I looked like I'd had been through hell, but my husband's face registered nothing. Doris wrinkled her nose.

Grateful for the temporary ceasefire, I took a fifteen-minute shower and put antibiotic cream on my scratches. The small bandages decorated with quirky superheroes—endorphin boosting in the store—made me wince when I covered the sores. My hipbones were bruised, and my left knee needed ice and elevation. Dressed in a faded maxi dress, I found the duo at the kitchen table eating bowls of salad from a prepackaged salad mixture. "Mom was starving so we're eating salad until the chicken is done," Samuel said.

"Have you put the chicken in the oven?"

"No." His attention never wavered from his mother's lettuce-chewing mouth.

I slapped the frozen chicken breasts in a roasting pan, slung mushroom soup over it, and slammed the oven door shut.

They zeroed in on me and stopped talking as I upped the heat to four hundred and fifty degrees.

I glared at them. "If you can manage to fit it in your busy schedules, nuke three potatoes in forty-five minutes. I'll be in the bedroom putting ice on my knee."

They resumed eating as if I wasn't there. I filled a plastic baggy with ice, poured myself a Seven and Seven, and tromped toward the bedroom.

*****

We sat at the dining room table eating chicken, white bread, and barbeque potato chips on the china plates my mother-in-law had bought for Samuel and me as a wedding gift. I drank another whiskey.

Doris devoured part of her chicken breast in silence.

My husband ruined it. "This chicken is still pink in the center."

Doris pushed her chicken toward me. "You can't expect me to eat this raw meat."

I stacked their plates and silverware and threw everything in the trash. "Then I guess you're done," I said, propping my hands on my hips. I threw heat rays of animosity at them until they left the room.

*****

I must've dozed off on the couch. About nine o'clock in the evening, I woke up from a dream about refilling Doris's pill organizer. I realized Doris was overdue on taking her meds. I grabbed the organizer from a top shelf in the kitchen. My mother-in-law tended to take more of the "feel good" pills, the ones that calmed her down, than were prescribed, if I left them within her reach. I found her evening meds and dumped the pills in her favorite candy dish, a blue-glass chicken toothpick

170

holder, and fetched her a glass of room-temperature filtered water. No ice.

When she finished taking the pills, I checked her blood sugar. It was normal. I picked up the candy wrappers on the floor. My husband insisted on letting her buy candy bars on their weekly outings to a local dollar store.

"If you care, my son went out to buy me some food I can digest without getting salmonella."

She meant fast food. "I see," I said. "We all make choices."

My phone rang. I hopped down the hallway to the kitchen on my good leg holding on to the walls. I picked up my cell.

It was Ralph. "Do you need anything, Rodeo Queen? I'd share a bottle with you."

"No, thanks, I'm good, and you better not be outside my door like last time," I said as I reached into the back of the medicine shelf and took out my husband's back pain medication. I palmed a pill and washed it down with some water. Half a dozen pills beckoned inside the bottle, but I left them alone. Samuel wouldn't notice one missing.

"Naw, I'm at a bar. Worried about you taking shit from your family. They don't appreciate you." Ralph said, slurring the last few words.

I didn't hear any background pub noise, but he wasn't knocking on my door. "I'm being good to myself," I said. "I plan on sleeping like a baby in my bedroom with or without Samuel on the couch. Talk to you later."

"One more thing, give me Officer Stevenson's cell number. You took his card. Right?"

"From the murder scene, yeah." I hobbled to my bedroom

and shuffled through my dirty clothes, and found the card. I didn't ask why he needed the number.

I ended the conversation with Ralph and heard my husband's squeaky car door slam shut in the garage, but I didn't have the energy to engage with Samuel again tonight. I left a living room lamp on, peeped in on my sleepy mother-in-law, and turned down her television white noise, then I went to bed across the hall.

The next morning Doris was stone-cold dead, and my husband was MIA.

*****

While the detectives working for the Medical Examiner's Office crept about in Doris's room, I went to the kitchen for a cup of coffee. My hands shook so badly I couldn't hold the spoon to stir in the sugar. *Where was my husband?* I searched for a breakfast granola bar in the pantry, and not finding one; I searched another shelf where I kept packages of dried fruit. I bumped a bottle on the counter.

My husband's bottle of pain meds was open and empty. A wave of nausea hit my stomach. I called my husband. It went to voice mail. *Damn it.*

I walked to Doris's room. I knew the older detective. I liked him. "Jim, I need to show you something." He followed me into the kitchen. "I took one of these pills before I went to sleep. There were maybe five or six left. I don't know if I put the bottle away, and I don't know if Doris took the rest of them."

He gave me a sympathetic look. "Have you heard from your husband?"

"No. This isn't like him. He wouldn't leave without letting me know." I sat down. The chair made a creaking sound.

Jim photographed the pill bottle. "This is your husband's prescription?"

"Yes."

The second detective, a younger version of Jim, clean-cut, medium height, and stocky, came into the room carrying a handful of candy wrapper he put into a plastic baggie and labeled. "Didn't you say your mother-in-law was diabetic?"

"My husband lets her sneak sugary snacks into her bedroom. It's a game with them. But I checked her blood sugar before I went to bed. She was fine."

"Pretty strong stuff," the young detective said, lifting the bottle of pain meds with a gloved hand and putting it in a separate baggie.

"I tore up a knee yesterday working a bank robbery and didn't go to the emergency, so I took one of my husband's pain pills."

Disapproval flooded his face. "It was an on-duty injury. Why not go?"

"Look. I volunteered the information about the pills. I don't have anything to hide. I wish my husband would show up. I'm worried."

Jim took my cell lying next to me on the table and passed it to the young detective to bag. "Check the security cams," he said. He turned back to me. "Probably a natural death, but because your husband's missing, we're going to treat it as a suspicious death and rule out any foul play."

"Excuse me?"

"The glass in Doris's bedroom still contains some water."

"So?"

"It smells bitter." He touched his nose. "Potassium cyanide, but I could be wrong."

The young detective whispered to the older one.

A chill ran through me. "You suspect poison?" I ran to the filtered water pitcher near the sink and held it up. "I used this same water to make coffee this morning. That doesn't make any sense."

The detectives exchanged wary glances.

"Not my husband. My husband loves her. He would've checked on his mother when he came home, gave her more water, but—"

"Gloria, please sit down. We need to talk," Jim said.

"I heard him in the garage late last night. Was the garage door open?"

Jim shook his head. "According to your security cams, your husband never left home last night. Are you sure you don't know where he is?"

*****

It was nine o'clock in the morning, less than twenty-four hours since I worked the domestic homicides in the Dunwoody parking lot. Now I sat in jail awaiting my arraignment for murdering my mother-in-law. "I'm living in a nightmare that won't end," I said to my lawyer, an up-and-coming defense attorney who'd eviscerated me in the courtroom last year.

I explained how I might've contributed to my mother-in-law's death by leaving the pills out.

She shook his head. "M.E. ruled water laced with cyanide killed her."

"That eases my conscience some."

She shook her long braids. "Honestly, it doesn't look good for you. No trace of your husband. Your brothers in blue think you killed him too."

"They'll need a body and forensic evidence."

"Maybe. They found blood on a T-shirt in the garage."

"News to me." I rubbed my temples.

"Do you think your husband set you up?" she asked.

"For sure, Samuel has the computer skills to sabotage the security cameras. Nobody else has a motive, except him or me. Unless my partner Detective Jackson did me a favor." I winked.

"Would Jackson know how to gain entry into your house?"

"Yes, but that's nonsense. Samuel must've hidden his true feelings about his mother. He couldn't take any more of the old bag or me or both." I shrugged. "He chose cyanide to kill his own mother and essentially get rid of me—that's some bitter love.

Conestoga Number Four
Kelly Zimmer

"Stella!"

Imogene's scream pierced the Sunday morning silence. Abandoning the cart of beer and booze I'd lugged to the bar, I raced across the lot toward the covered wagon and dashed up its weathered stairs. I reached the head housekeeper a second before she stepped backward off the wagon's rustic porch.

"What is it?" I blurted before sucking in oxygen.

Imogene pressed one hand to her chest and pointed with the forefinger of her free hand. "Inside. There's a man."

Though still catching my breath, I forced a chuckle. "What? Is he naked?"

Imogene's pale lips worked silently, and my smile faded.

"Stay here," I said, and stepped through the cabin's improbable French doors to the deluxe accommodations beyond.

The Florida sun reached only narrow fingers through the towering oaks, and the draperies behind the queen-sized bed were pulled, deepening the gloom. Squinting, I made out a thin man lying face down on the faux-Native American blanket beside the bed. A butcher knife protruded from his back, and the blood staining his grey t-shirt had dried to a brown crust.

I backed from the scene as Imogene had, but without the screaming. After another deep breath, I pulled out my cell phone to call my old nemesis, Sheriff Dante Bullock.

My history with Sheriff Dante went back to my high school days when I hung out with the wrong crowd, drank on public beaches, and raised hell. Between fourteen and seventeen, I was snagged by the Angel Grove Police regularly but never charged. After the last incident, the local cops grew tired of dealing with me and called in Dante Bullock to scare me straight.

Built for the job at six-five and nearly as wide, the African-American sheriff policing an agricultural, read "cracker" county took no shit. The trailer-trash brat of a meth addict proved no problem for him. After my last bust at an illegal beach bonfire, he explained he could either send me off to juvie or I could figure it out. Not being stupid, I figured it out.

During my senior year, I rarely went home, leaving Mom to deal with her issues alone. Though both anger and guilt gnawed at me, with Sheriff Dante's help, I stayed focused. When not passing greasy bags out the drive-up window at the local fast food, I studied. If Mom's trailer got too chaotic, I escaped to the Angel Grove police station with a handful of local hard cases. In an under-used interview room, we did homework, napped, or hid from domestic drama. Sheriff Dante checked in with us occasionally but rarely spoke, which was fine. A silent sheriff was an appeased sheriff not threatening us with prison.

Though it had been five years since graduation, I'd never deleted Sheriff Dante's number, and it was natural to call him instead of nine-one-one. The local cops arrived first to secure the deluxe camping cabin until the county's crime scene van arrived. Imogene and I huddled at the edge of the gathering crowd, watching the techs haul their equipment up the rustic steps to Conestoga Number Four.

Sheriff Dante and his deputies arrived next. He unfolded himself from the car, caught my eyes, and inclined his head. Imogene and I sidled over. "Can you tell me what's happening here?" he asked.

Imogene's words flooded out. "I knocked, but there was no answer, so I went in, and there was a man with a knife in his back."

"Who is this unit rented to?" Dante asked.

"It isn't the guest," Imogene said. "The Ackleys took the Saturday night river cruise and won't dock until eleven this morning."

The sheriff pulled a notebook from his back pocket. "Who is he, then?"

Imogene buried her face in her hands. "I don't know."

"What time did you find the body?" Dante asked.

"I heard Imogene's scream at about nine-thirty," I said.

The housekeeper raised her head to me. She was pale and shaky. "That's about right. I started at eight with the early check-outs and got here around nine-thirty."

"Did you go inside, Stella?" Dante asked.

"Just for a moment," I said. "Long enough to see he was dead."

"Do you recognize him?"

"No, he's face down, and I sure didn't turn him over."

"What about the knife? Have either of you seen the knife before?"

Imogene and I exchanged a glance. "We didn't look at it that closely," I said.

He flipped his notebook closed and wrinkled his nose. "Where are the owners?"

"The Glovers are coming," I said. "I called them right after I called you."

Dante pulled off his mirrored sunglasses and frowned at me. "You told them you found a body, and they didn't rush right over?"

I waggled my head, sending my pigtails bobbing. "I suspect I woke them. Alex and Betty were still partying with the guests when I closed down the bar last night."

Dante grunted. "You closed last night and opened this morning?"

"Do it every weekend. I get off after the lunch rush on Sundays, then don't work again until Thursday afternoon. It's a pretty sweet deal, actually."

He returned his sunglasses to his broad face. "We need to interview the staff and the guests. Where can I set up?"

"There's the community center," I said and nodded toward the pool.

"I'll need a list of guests and employees who were here either last night or this morning," Dante said.

"Got it," I said. "I'll unlock for you."

"Thanks, Stella. You'll be at the bar if I need you?"

I winked at him. "Always."

Thanks to the dead guy, I didn't get the bar open until almost eleven. Everybody wanted to know what was happening at Conestoga Number Four, but I was too busy to chat. They'd find out when Dante interviewed them, anyway.

Most Sundays, I handled the sparse crowd alone, but that morning the curious filled every barstool. I hustled my butt off until Greg bounced over to lend a hand after the overnight river cruise docked.

I huffed a relieved sigh as he logged into the register. "Thanks, Greg. I'm dying here, but doesn't Harry need you at the marina?"

"Boats can't launch until the sheriff gives the okay." Greg leaned in close and whispered, "I saw Imogene leaving. She was crying and in a big hurry to get to her car. What's that all about?"

"Later," I said and hustled down the bar.

With the crowd thickening to Saturday levels, Greg, Shelly, and I worked at the bar until four when the evening shift arrived. Greg jogged off toward the dock to help Harry, but I clocked out, dragging toward my eight-year-old Toyota, dreaming of a shower and a nap. I'd closed the bar at 2:00 a.m., returned at nine to open, found a body, and was dead on my feet when Iris came flapping after me.

"Stella, you've got to hear this." Iris stopped her fluttering and beckoned me closer.

"If you're going to tell me about the dead guy, I already know," I said.

"Yeah, Dante told me you and Imogene found him." Iris

flipped her waist-length black hair over a shoulder. "Did they show you his picture?"

"Not yet. Did you recognize him?" I asked.

Though I'm only five-five, I towered over the diminutive spa hostess and had to bend from the waist to catch her whisper. "Not at first; at least I told the cops I didn't." Her forehead creased with worry. "I feel like I've seen him before, but I can't remember where and I don't want Dante to think I lied if it comes to me later."

I cupped a hand over her shoulder. "Dante comes off all gruff, but he's a good guy. As long as you didn't murder anyone, you've got nothing to worry about."

Unconvinced, Iris glared over my shoulder. "Here he comes," she hissed. "I'm so out of here. Call me if you recognize the guy in the picture, okay?"

I promised I would and turned to meet the sheriff.

"You on your way home, Stella?" Dante asked in a comforting baritone rumble.

"I was."

"Can you spare a moment?"

"Sure. Iris tells me you're showing around the dead guy's photo. Does that mean you haven't identified him?"

"No ID on him. We'll run his fingerprints, but knowing who he is will help us catch his killer, so the sooner we ID him, the better."

"What time did he die?" I asked.

"Too soon to say, but the tech says he'd been dead at least five or six hours. Can you handle a look at his photo?"

I pressed my shoulders back and straightened my spine. "Let's see him," I said.

Dante passed me his phone. The corpse's eyes were wide open and frozen in shock, and his whiskered jaw tense. I covered my mouth with one hand.

"Take your time," the sheriff said.

Fifty, maybe. Greasy, gray-brown curls surrounded a pale, bald crown. Stubbly, sunken cheeks and nasty teeth told me he'd lived a hard life. "Looks like a down-and-outer," I said.

"You don't recognize him?" Dante asked. "Maybe a customer at the bar?"

"A glamper? Are you kidding? Guys who drop three hundred bucks a night for a yurt or fake Conestoga wagon can afford a decent haircut and some dental work."

Dante grunted and pocketed his phone. "So this luxury glamor camping is a real thing?"

"I'd hate to think about the unemployment rate in Angel Grove without it. The Glovers turned a dull-as-dirt RV campground into a destination."

"You trust the Glovers?" he asked.

"Hell, yeah." I scrunched my face at him. "Why do you ask? Did they know the dead guy?"

"They say they don't recognize him, but I have a feeling something's off."

Dante's feelings about people were legendary. They're what kept me out of juvie. But the Glovers? "I don't know, Dante. Even with my reputation, they let me clean cabins with Imogene when I was in high school, and the day I turned twenty-one, they put me behind the bar. My income doubled overnight, got me out of my Mom's trailer."

"That has more to do with how you fill out your Glover's Getaways t-shirt than a generous spirit."

"Bull. Alex Glover even gave my mom a shot at a housekeeping job over Betty's objections. Everyone knew she wouldn't work out, but he did it for me."

Dante heaved a sigh from deep inside his chest. "Go home and get some rest. If you have any ideas about the deceased, call me."

"I will," I promised and headed toward my car.

"And, Stella," he called.

"What?"

"I'm proud of you, kid."

*****

I stepped out of a hot shower and into yoga pants and a sweatshirt at six that evening. When I'm working, I don't drink, so Sunday is my wild night with a light beer on my front porch. Staying sober gives me a sense of control, something I need as I'd basically had to raise myself.

As I rocked on the porch swing of my tiny rental enjoying the early October evening, my landlord rumbled up in his primer-gray pickup. Ed Dobbs was coming up on ninety and had grown up in the one-bedroom house I rented. Back in the day, he, his brother, and sister shared one of the two bedrooms. In the nineteen-forties, the family built a roomier place closer to town. They kept the old homestead, renting it out after remodeling the kids' room into a bathroom with indoor plumbing and everything.

"Heard you had excitement at work today." Ed lowered himself into the rocking chair. He was all elbows and knees and wiry hair and would likely see his hundredth birthday.

"Dead guy in a Conestoga wagon," I reported and raised my beer. "Want a drink?"

"Got any bourbon?"

I stepped inside, retrieved the bottle from beneath the kitchen sink, and poured him two fingers' worth into a juice glass.

"Nobody knows the dead guy," I said, "but Iris says he looks familiar. And Dante thinks the Glovers are hiding something."

Ed sipped his bourbon and squinted into the setting sun. "That man's instincts are usually spot on, but Alex Glover seems like a straight shooter. As for Betty, she's the best of a bad lot, but I've never known her to be anything but fair."

"They're probably just concerned about how a murder will affect business," I said.

"They'll manage. Turning the orange grove into an RV park saved the economy around here, and when this whole fancy-schmancy camping craze took off, they jumped on it. They're sharp, that pair."

"And generous," I said. "I'd be flipping burgers if they hadn't gambled on a messed-up kid."

"Not much of a risk. They saw a bright girl who wanted to work and needed a break."

"They sure didn't hesitate to gamble on the luxury cabins and the riverboat. That stuff must have cost a fortune."

"It's paying off," Ed said. "Imogene says they're booked out months in advance. I understand she found the body."

"Imogene's pretty shaken up. She rushed home as soon as Dante finished questioning her."

Ed nodded sagely. "Spooked."

We rocked in silence, watching the orange and yellow sunset fade to indigo.

"I hope this murder doesn't close the campground," I said. "Angel Grove needs the jobs. Hell, I need the job."

Ed drained the last of his bourbon, stood and asked, "How old are you now, Stella?"

"Twenty-two."

"You saving for college?"

"You know I am."

"Well then, go. It's time you got out of Angel Grove and started living your life."

"Are you evicting me?" I asked with a sassy grin.

"You're too smart to spend your nights serving drinks to self-important assholes. Put Angel Grove in your rearview. Go to college, get away from your mother, make a life."

"I can't leave now. It's snowbird season. We'll be packed with Midwesterners and Canadians dodging winter."

Ed huffed, climbed into his ancient pickup, and trundled down the road. I stumbled off to bed without giving the dead man another thought.

*****

Angel Grove doesn't have a chain grocery store, just a family-owned convenience store with pretensions. Imogene said it was going bankrupt until Alex Glover's grandfather opened the campground. Grove Groceries began stocking firewood and camping supplies, expanded the fresh food section, and added all the little sundries you need on the road. When Glovers Getaways became a glamping destination, the store added IPA beers, decent wine, and organic produce.

On Mondays, I did my shopping and caught up on the Angel Grove gossip I'd missed while working my butt off over the weekend. This week's talk was all about the murder. As I pushed my mini-cart up and down the aisles, I picked up bits of drivel, such as Imogene killed the guy, then just pretended to find the body. Also, Dante arrested the Glovers, and the campground was a front for drug dealers. It wasn't until I loaded my bags into the car that I got legitimate news.

Iris approached me in the parking lot, a bag of lemons for the spa clutched in a white-knuckled hand. Her black eyes darted around, and she spoke in a tense whisper. "I think I remember where I saw him before, the dead guy. What do I do, Stella?"

"You tell the cops," I said.

"I know I should, but I'm afraid. Come with me."

"Fine. When?"

The tension left her jaw. "Pick me up at twelve. I'll take an early lunch."

"Sure, but tell me about the guy. How do you know him?"

"Later. It's complicated, and I'm already late." Iris scooted off.

As I slid into the Toyota, my cell buzzed with a call from Betty Glover.

"Stella, I'm so sorry to bother you on your day off," she

began, "but we're in a terrible mess here. Imogene quit."

"What! Why?"

"Because of the murder. I told her to take all the time she needs, but Imogene insists she's leaving town."

Dante won't like that, I thought. "I'll call her."

"Later. What we really need is your help. Shelly's coming in early to fill Imogene's housekeeping shift, but we'll need you on the bar. Greg's opening, so you won't be alone."

"Of course," I said, then remembered my promise to Iris. "I can be in at one."

"Perfect, thank you."

My day off blown to bits, I unloaded my groceries at home, then changed into my bar outfit: a sky-blue Glover's Glamping Getaways t-shirt over cut-off denim shorts. After pulling my blonde hair into high pigtails, I did my makeup and shot out to collect Iris at the spa.

She'd already flipped the sign to "*Closed, be back soon!*" and locked up. I pounded on the door. "Iris, it's me. Let's go."

Nothing. I tried again. "Iris, come on. I have to work at one!"

Again, nothing. I pulled my phone from my back pocket and tried her number. A calypso beat rang behind the door. Iris, or at least her phone, was inside. The hairs on the back of my arms quivered as I rang Betty Glover. "Betty, I need you to open the spa. Iris is inside and not answering her phone."

Betty ended the call without a goodbye, and her golf cart pulled into view within two minutes. Her face set in a forbidding grimace, she shoved past me with the key. Inside, we called out, but all was quiet except for bubbling from one of the pedicure chairs beyond the beaded curtain separating the reception desk from the spa. The beads clicked as Betty stepped past them, then clattered again as she stepped back into the reception area, her eyes wide and wild. "Call nine-one-one."

I punched in the numbers and pushed through the curtain. Iris was on her knees in front of a pedicure chair, her head pushed beneath the fragrant bubbling water. When the emergency dispatcher answered my call, all I could say was, "help."

*****

This time, Dante ordered the campground, marina, bar, and restaurant closed. The employees were sequestered in the resort's community room, and guests were told to remain in their cabins or RVs until police took their statements.

Dante held his interviews in the kitchen off the community room, and I was his first customer. "When someone finds two bodies in two days, we consider them a person of interest," he explained. The concerned, fatherly eyes were now brown lasers shredding my self-confidence.

Unexpected teenage petulance rose in my voice. "I'm not even supposed to be here. Iris wanted me to take her to the Angel Grove PD. She thought she recognized the dead guy from yesterday." The challenge in my tone turned into a whine. "I wouldn't hurt Iris. She was my friend."

"Who else knew Iris recognized the victim?" Dante asked.

"I don't know."

"Wouldn't she have told the Glovers?"

I raised and lowered a shoulder. "Probably. Imogene's

worked for them for over twenty years."

"And you're sure you don't recognize the man from yesterday?"

I shook my head. "You haven't identified him yet?"

"We're going public today, putting his photo out there. What exactly did Iris tell you about the guy?"

"Yesterday, she said he seemed familiar, but she wasn't sure why. This morning she remembered where she'd seen him, but she was running late and said she'd tell me later."

"What time this morning?"

"Right after I finished my grocery shopping, a few minutes before ten."

"And the spa opened at ten?"

I shrugged again. "As far as I know. On a Monday, she'd be alone unless there were appointments."

"There were two appointments in her book. Both were for mid-afternoon," Dante said. "Do employees use the spa?"

"Yeah, we get a discount."

"So an employee could have stopped in, requested a pedicure, and killed Iris?"

Tears pooled, but I forced them back. "I suppose."

Dante nodded and rubbed his face with a meaty hand. "Here's the thing. The page for Saturday is missing, ripped from the spa's appointment book. Who had appointments on Saturday?"

"Dante, I worked practically non-stop from Thursday afternoon through Sunday. Other than the bar, I don't know what went on at the spa or anywhere else."

He heaved an exasperated sigh. "You go on now and send the Glovers in, please."

Betty and Alex remained in the kitchen with Dante for almost an hour. Afterward, I joined them in the office to help check out the campers who'd given statements. Most guests were quiet, withdrawn, even apologetic. All were eager to leave. A few raised hell and one couple was so full of entitled outraged, we thanked them when they swore they'd never return.

Other employees joined us in the office as Dante finished their interviews. By five-thirty, abandoned by our guests, the staff slumped around the table in the conference room, convinced we were destined for the unemployment line.

"Can we go home?" Shelly asked.

"Not until Sheriff Bullock releases us," Alex Glover said as the man himself stepped through the door.

"Sorry for the delay, folks," Dante said. "I have one more question for you. Where is Imogene Carter?"

Alex cleared his throat. "Imogene didn't come to work. She quit today; we told you that."

"My deputies can't locate her. When did you last speak with her?"

"Nine-thirty, maybe later," Betty said. "She said she was leaving town."

"Any idea where she might have gone?" Dante asked Betty. When she didn't respond, he cast his gaze around the room but was met with blank stares. "Okay, everyone's free to leave except the Glovers and Stella Riley."

The blank stares turned to me.

"Go on," Dante said, "before I change my mind."

Chairs scraped across the wood floor as my coworkers bolted. When the dust settled, it was just the Glovers, me, and Greg at the conference table.

"Greg," Dante said. "You can go now."

Greg crossed his arms over his chest. "Not if you're keeping Stella. I want to know what's happening."

"I can handle Sheriff Dante," I said. "We go back a long way."

"Whatever," Greg said, but remained seated.

Warmth bloomed in my cheeks. So focused on making a buck, I hadn't noticed Greg's interest in me. He had the non-threatening preppie look Alex liked in his male employees but was a decent-looking guy and fun to work with. Maybe, I thought, after this is over.

One corner of Dante's lips twitched. "Fine, now Mr. and Mrs. Glover—"

"Betty and Alex," Alex said irritably. "You've known us for years, Dante. Knock off the official stuff."

"This is a murder investigation," Dante said, "and I want to know why you didn't identify the dead man yesterday."

"Because we don't know him," Betty snapped.

"You should," Dante said. "He's your brother."

Betty's mouth dropped open. She shook her head, sending graying chestnut curls swaying.

Alex reached toward Dante's phone. "Let me see that photo again."

Dante pulled up the picture and passed his phone to the

Glovers. "That photo went out with a press release at noon today," he said. "Ed Dobbs called within an hour, identifying the man as your brother, Michael James McKenzie. Why didn't you identify him, Betty?"

Recalling the photo Dante had shown me the day before, I said, "I can answer that. Mike McKenzie was a drunk—a fat, red-faced bully. He wore his hair long and was pushing three-hundred pounds the last time I saw him."

"And when was that?" Dante asked.

"Five years ago. Betty and Alex sent him packing not long after I started working here."

Fingers pressed to her temples, Betty gawked at the phone Alex held and said, "It can't be him. The eyes are so empty."

Alex thrust the phone back to Dante. "If Betty didn't recognize her brother, how can Ed Dobbs be so sure? The man's what? A hundred?"

"Eighty-nine," Dante said, "and he recognized the mangled ear."

Betty pressed the fingers of one hand to her lips. "The puppy! When he was ten, our new puppy nipped his ear. I suppose it could be Mike, but what was he doing here? And why does he look like that? What happened to him?"

"I was hoping you could tell us," Dante said.

"How? I haven't heard from my brother in five years." Betty collapsed into herself. "Could I have some water, please?"

I popped to the mini-fridge in the corner and pulled out an armload of water bottles. As I passed them around, Alex Glover explained about Mike.

"Betty and her brother didn't part on good terms. Like Stella said, Mike was a bully and a loudmouth. He helped around the property, but we had endless complaints from employees about abusive language, and..." Alex faltered to a halt.

I helped him out. "He harassed the female employees, myself included," I said.

Betty pulled herself together. "It was a Sunday morning, and we had a lot of cash on hand. Alex caught Mike at the safe, helping himself. I was already pissed about Mike's roving hands, and his petty thievery pushed me over the limit. I told my brother to leave the property and never return."

Dante expelled a cubic ton of air and moved his gaze from Betty Glover to me. "You witnessed his dismissal?"

"Mike and Betty were in the office next door, arguing. Imogene and I were in this room reviewing the day's checkouts and heard the whole thing," I confirmed.

"Do you think Imogene recognized Mike McKenzie? Is that why she's run away?" Alex asked.

"Maybe," I said, "Mike grabbed her ass, too, and she was afraid of him."

Dante's eyes bored into me. "Were you afraid of him?"

I raised my chin and grinned. "No, but I didn't recognize him, and I didn't kill him."

A deputy leaned into the conference room and motioned for Dante to step outside. While we waited, Betty slumped sideways into her husband's arms. I turned from the distraught couple to Greg. "Thanks for sticking by me," I said. "This is all so weird."

"To think I moved out here for the peace and quiet," Greg said.

I stifled a laugh.

"Seriously," he said, "when I graduated from college, I wanted to live in the real world, actually support myself for a while."

"You can't make a career out of fueling boats and tending bar," I said, channeling Ed Dobbs.

Greg slid his eyes toward the Glovers. "I know, but I'd hoped the party would last a little longer."

Dante strode back into the conference room but didn't sit. "You said the guests had left," he said.

Betty pulled herself erect. "I thought we'd checked everyone out, but it's been hectic."

"What about the people from Conestoga Number Four?" Dante asked.

"They left yesterday afternoon," Betty said. "They couldn't return to their unit, and I didn't have another space to offer them."

Aggrieved voices carried into the conference room. Mr. and Mrs. Ackley entered, trailed by a Sheriff's Deputy.

Betty gaped at them. "Ben, Joan, I didn't know you were still here."

"We weren't," Ben Ackley said. "We moved to the hotel that you recommended."

Mr. Ackley was a big man, barrel-chested and with lots of wavy black hair. His wife was slender and fair. Both appeared offended, with mouths set in dissatisfied frowns.

"Why did you come back?" Dante asked. "And what were you doing in the Conestoga wagon?"

"Your deputies wouldn't let us pack our things ourselves. Stuff is missing," Ben said.

"So you walked past crime scene tape to find it?" Dante asked.

"That tape doesn't apply to us," Joan Ackley said. "It was our room."

With a friend dead, another missing, and my employer's brother murdered, I wasn't in the mood for her elitist sense of entitlement. "I see you got a pedicure on Saturday," I blurted.

Dante's head spun to Mrs. Ackley. "You had a spa appointment on Saturday?"

"I certainly did not," she said.

"Sure you did," I said and bobbed my head toward her feet. "The little orchids on the big toes are Iris' work."

The Sheriff's eyes dropped to Joan Ackley's shell-pink pedicure. A white orchid decorated the nail of each big toe. "Were you at the spa on Saturday, Mrs. Ackley?" he asked.

She patted at her bangs. "Yes, but I didn't have an appointment. We decided to take the river cruise that afternoon, and I wanted to spruce myself up."

"Did you tear out the appointment page for Saturday?" I asked.

The blonde's face crumpled in confusion. "Why would I do that?"

I craned my head around to Dante. "I'll bet that's what Iris remembered."

"What do you mean, Stella?" Dante asked.

"Iris didn't recognize the dead guy, but she told me she remembered where she saw him. What if it was Saturday at the spa? What if he was meeting Joan Ackley?"

Ben Ackley huffed. "I don't think so, kid."

"Hold on," I said. "He might have approached your wife for spare change or something."

"If he did, I'd call security," Joan said. "And why does it matter? I didn't kill that guy. Ben and I were away on the overnight cruise."

"That's true," Greg said. "I worked Saturday's cruise. I helped Mrs. Ackley onto the dock at Rascals on Saturday night, then back on the boat at midnight. You know how it works. Once everyone's accounted for, we moor in the river for the night. No one leaves unless they swim to shore."

I deflated. "If Mike McKenzie died six hours before Imogene and I found him, the Ackleys are in the clear," I said reluctantly. I really wanted it to be them.

"Mike McKenzie," Joan said. "Did you say the victim's name was Mike McKenzie?"

Dante screwed up his face at her. "You knew him?"

"Possibly," Ben said, "but not under that name." He turned to Dante. "Could we speak with you privately?"

Dante narrowed his eyes. "Betty, Alex you can leave. I'd like Stella to stay."

The Glovers exchanged a glance but left without protest. Under the table, Greg's hand slid to my knee. I didn't object, and Dante didn't throw him out.

Ben and Joan Ackley told us they collected vintage firearms and were big into Civil War-era stuff. They answered an ad from a guy offering a Model 1862 Sharps and Hankins Army carbine for five hundred bucks. I didn't believe a word of it and, judging from the creases in Dante's forehead, either did the sheriff.

"Why did you meet him here at Glover's?" I asked Joan. "And why didn't you admit to recognizing him?"

Joan exhaled and raised her face to the ceiling. She nodded at Ben, who explained. "Ms. Becker and I aren't collectors; we're insurance investigators. After a claim has been filed and paid, the insurance company is curious when lost items turn up for sale online. We posed as buyers. We'd never met the seller face-to-face. He said his name was Mack Jorgenson and the item he offered was from the McKenzie fire. It's got to be him."

Dante's thick black brows raised, and he looked as puzzled as I'd ever seen him.

"We communicated via email," Joan said. "He said he'd look for us at the bar on Saturday morning, but he never showed. By two, we figured he got cold feet. I went for a pedicure, then we got on the river cruise." Joan threw a wink Greg's way. "Just like the handsome young man said. We popped back to the cabin to see if maybe the police missed something meant for us. We didn't know about the second murder and got nabbed."

I twirled the end of a pigtail as I thought. "Mike knew you had the cash for the buy. I bet he was watching you," I said and raised my gaze to Joan, "to make sure you and Ben got on the boat because he planned to rob you while you were out. Did you leave the five-hundred in the unit's safe?"

Ben Ackley snorted. "No way." He patted his hip pocket. "I carried it on me. Anyway, we never intended to pay him."

"But Mike McKenzie didn't know that," I said. "And if he was still pissed at his sister, he probably thought it would be a hoot if her fancy resort got blamed for the loss."

"But how did he get in the wagon?" Ben asked. "There was no forced entry."

"Housekeeping key," Dante said. "Practically everyone on staff has one, and every key is accounted for."

"Which means," I muttered, "one of our staff let Mike McKenzie into Conestoga Number Four."

*****

Dante insisted the campground remain closed for forty-eight hours. Ben and Joan were released after promising to share their email conversations between them and "Mack," the antique firearms dealer. Betty and I called and canceled the few Tuesday and Wednesday reservations. Check-ins were heaviest on Thursdays and Fridays. With luck and brilliant detective work, the week wouldn't be a total loss. Still, Betty and Alex appeared pale and worn when Greg and I left them in the resort's office that evening.

Thick clouds obscured the sunset when we reached my car, and the breeze whipped Greg's tawny hair around his face. "What do you think?" he asked. "Will this place make it?"

"It has to," I said. "Glover's Glamping Getaways is the town's biggest employer. Without it, Angel Grove is just another orange grove ghost town."

"It really is an oasis out here, isn't it?"

"Yep, a ritzy watering hole in the middle of derelict groves and cattle ranches. The Glovers saved this town," I said. "We can't let them go under."

"How did they pay for all this?" Greg asked.

"Alex said his family owned the land going back to the eighteen-hundreds. When the family got out of cattle and citrus, Alex's grandfather sold acreage to fund the campground."

"But what about the riverboat, spa, and luxury yurts? Where did that money come from?" Greg asked.

"I assume they got a loan. Mortgaged the land."

"Hell of a mortgage," Greg said and wandered off to his car.

On my way home, I stopped at Ed Dobb's place to share a glass of bourbon and asked him to fill me in on the local history. After all, he'd been around for most of it.

The Glovers and the McKenzies founded the town in the eighteen-seventies. The families flourished for a hundred years, then the cattle industry turned sour. Betty's family sold their land and, Ed said, did little after that. When the family home burned down, Betty's dad went into a decline. He passed away a couple of years later.

The Glovers experienced similar business setbacks, but Alex Glover's grandfather sold only a portion of his land and started the campground as an ordinary RV park on the rest. The park was nothing special but provided jobs for the dying town, making the Glovers hometown heroes. Alex and Betty's marriage was like a royal wedding in Angel Grove, and the new couple devoted themselves to reviving the local economy. Betty was Angel Grove's Queen Bee, chairing committees and arranging fundraisers. Betty McKenzie Glover valued her reputation as the First Lady of Angel Grove, so people weren't surprised when she sent her trouble-making brother packing.

"I was sure glad he was gone," I said. "Do you think Imogene killed Mike and ran off?"

"It sure looks that way," Ed said. "She might have called to you to witness her finding the body."

"Imogene had no more motive than me or a dozen others," I countered. "The knife came from the restaurant, and most of us have keys to the cabins."

After tossing around suspects and their motives, Ed and I agreed there were plenty of reasons to kill Mike McKenzie but couldn't fathom why Iris had to die. The answer didn't come to me until the next day when I filled Imogene's housekeeping shift.

*****

Dante's deputies said if I stayed away from the murder scenes, I could go about my business. After I finished with the cabins, I automatically headed toward the spa with a basket of towels and robes but stopped myself halfway.

A glance at my phone told me it was two o'clock. Imogene always finished her rounds with clean towels and robes for the spa at around two. At two on Saturday, Joan Becker was inside the spa while Mike McKenzie lurked outside. If Imogene spotted Mike, she might have confronted him, and Iris would have seen them from the reception desk. Busy with clients, the incident didn't make an impression until the following day when Iris recognized the man talking to Imogene as the dead guy.

When we talked in the grocery store parking lot, Iris didn't know Imogene had quit. If Imogene showed up for a quick pedicure, Iris would think nothing of it. If Iris mentioned seeing her arguing with the dead guy, would that be enough for Imogene to kill Iris? Seemed unlikely.

Who else might Iris have told, and did that person kill her? When the answer came to me, I dropped the linen basket and called Dante Bullock. He'd reached out when I needed a helping hand. It was time to repay the favor.

*****

By four, we were back in the conference room. Alex Glover greeted Dante and his deputies eagerly, hoping to learn when he could reopen the resort. Ben Ackley and Joan Becker appeared curious. Greg was worried, and so was I. If nothing else, I was about to lose my job.

The Sheriff addressed Alex Glover. "We have some answers."

Alex practically melted, relief oozing from every pore. "Thank you, Dante. Who killed them?"

"Not about the murders. I have answers to some questions Stella put to me earlier."

"Stella?" Alex said with a chuckle. "What did she want to know?"

"For starters," I said, "where did you get the money to expand this place? The spa, the boat, all the fancy cabins must have cost upwards of a million."

"I don't see how that's your business," Alex said as the smile slipped from his face.

"Also, Mike looked like a homeless guy, a drunk who'd

been living rough for years."

Betty shook her head. "Drink does that to people. It ruins lives."

"Yeah, but how is he selling stuff online?" I asked. "Where did he get it, and why was he using a fake name?"

"Selling what?" Betty shook her head again. "I don't know what you're talking about."

"Ed Dobbs," I continued, "told me Mike started working at the resort right after your father died."

"That's true," Betty said, "and before you ask, there was life insurance. Every penny of my share went into the resort."

"I figured as much," I said, "but life insurance wasn't enough to fund everything. The insurance money from the fire was, though."

"Investigators found enough in the wreckage," Ben said, "to convince the insurance company the claim was genuine, so they paid."

"That check beefed up your father's estate," I continued. "But you had to split it with your brother. You kept the cash to fund this place while Mike kept the pile of goodies you two stole from the family home before setting the fire."

"That's a lie!" Betty rose from her chair, but Alex pressed her back.

"What's prompting these accusations, Stella?" Alex asked. "We've always gone the extra mile for you."

That was true, and it pained me to blow his world apart, but I continued. "I suspect when Betty sent her brother packing, Mike was happy not to be fixing toilets and repairing A/C units all day. He disappeared, living off the family heirlooms for years until fake collectors agreed to meet him here."

"Joan and I agreed proximity to the McKenzie fire scene would convince the seller we knew more than we did," Ben said, "so we met him here. We had no idea we'd hooked an actual McKenzie. When he didn't show at the meet, we assumed he chickened out, so we pulled the plug on the plan and joined the river cruise to dig for local gossip about the fire."

"What does the fire have to do with Mike's death?" Betty asked, her words sputtering out.

I ignored her and continued along Ben's train of thought. "Mike didn't get cold feet. He stalked Joan to ensure you two would be out of the way. Imogene arrived at the spa with fresh towels at two on Saturday and recognized Mike."

Alex ran a hand through his sandy hair. "So Mike killed Iris?"

"Of course not," I said. "Mike was already dead when Iris was murdered. But, after seeing Mike on Saturday afternoon, Imogene went straight to Betty."

Betty drew back from the table. "She did not!"

"Imogene brought you a message from your brother demanding you meet him at Conestoga Number Four after the bar closed down. When Imogene stumbled on his body the next morning, she knew you'd kept that appointment and killed him."

Alex lept to his feet. "You're saying Betty stabbed her brother in the back?"

"Mike didn't want to work," I said. "He wanted to drink.

He sold the family treasures for pennies on the dollar until the goodies ran out, then came here to hit up his big sister for more cash."

"If he'd come to me, I'd have given him money," Betty said, her voice a dangerous hiss.

"But he didn't go to you," I said, "at least not right away. He wanted one more score and targeted the Ackleys. Unfortunately, Imogene recognized him and tried to chase him off. That's what Iris saw. I'll bet Iris saw them arguing, and the page torn from the appointment book was a note Iris made to herself."

"We found it in her kitchen," Dante confirmed, "on the fridge door."

"I'm guessing Mike threatened to go to the cops about the fire unless you gave him cash. When Mike turned up dead the next day, Imogene lied to Dante, said she didn't recognize the corpse then ran to you. You told her to forget she saw your brother and leave town. How much did you pay her to leave?"

Betty slapped the table with both palms. "I gave her nothing."

My heart slipped to my stomach. "Then Imogene's dead. Once Mike's identity was uncovered, you'd be the prime suspect, so you made Imogene disappear, hoping the police would assume she killed your brother and ran."

"You're insane," Betty said, "and you're fired. Get out."

Dante cleared his throat, a deep rumbling in his chest. "Not yet, Betty. Stella has one more question."

Alex blinked at Dante. "Is that why we're here? To answer our bartender's questions?"

"Stella and I go way back. We help each other when we can." Dante turned his massive head to me. "Ask your question, Stella."

I aimed a smug smile at Betty. "Did you make Iris paint your toenails before you drowned her?"

Betty shoved herself across the table, her fingers bent into claws. Blood oozed at the scratches stinging my throat before Dante pulled her off me.

*****

It took weeks to sort it all out. Emails between Betty and her brother going back five years supported the arson and insurance fraud. Dante found evidence in Mike's Ft. Myers condo that proved he sold off the remaining family heirlooms online while trying to drink himself to death.

Imogene's body turned up after a month-long search. She had no family, and Ed Dobbs was the only one with the stomach to identify her.

"If I live another ninety years, I'll never forget the sight," he said as I handed him the keys to my rental.

"You'd better live another ninety years," I said, "or at least long enough to visit me in Gainesville."

"Oh, I'll be around," Ed assured me.

"How's Alex?" I asked.

"Miserable. Alex Glover put his heart into that fancy-ass campground. He has to sell, and the money will go to the insurance company and Betty's lawyers."

"He's losing land that's been in his family for generations," I said. "I'm so sorry."

"Don't be. Alex should have been more curious about how Betty funded the expansion. It's the town I'm worried about. If Glover doesn't find a buyer, Angel Grove will fade away into nothing." Ed kicked at the gravel. "The old fool."

"The town will carry on, just like you," I said and kissed his stubbly cheek. "Greg, bring me that bottle of bourbon from under the kitchen sink."

A moment later, Greg popped out the front door with the bourbon bottle in one hand and my backpack in the other. "Here you go, babe," he said.

I passed the bottle to Ed. "Think of me while you're sipping bourbon on the porch." Ed accepted the bottle with a nod and drove off.

Greg added my backpack to the bags and boxes in my backseat. "Ready?" he asked.

"Wagons Ho," I said as I climbed into the driver's seat.

Triangles
John M. Floyd

At eleven a.m. Michael Boone looked up from his crossword puzzle and rubbed his eyes. TGIAL, he thought: thank God it's almost lunchtime. Yawning, he rose from his chair, refilled his coffee cup, and looked through the third-floor window at the sunlit park across the street. Unlike his office, the park was busy this time of day: two old men studied a chessboard on a picnic table, a woman with a ponytail jogged along behind a baby stroller, a thin guy in a scruffy gray beard leaned against a lamppost, and two teenagers took turns tossing a frisbee to a bouncy white dog. *You should be down there*, Boone told himself. *Sitting on a bench in the shade eating a hot dog, watching the ladies stroll by in their summer dresses.*

Then his eyes narrowed. One of those ladies was looking up at him. She had stopped on the sidewalk between the park and the street and was standing there alone, staring straight at him. A brunette, probably late thirties, white blouse and flowered skirt. As he watched, she lowered her head, glanced both ways, and crossed the street toward his building. So did Gray Beard and Jogging Mama, taking advantage of the break in traffic, and within seconds all of them moved out of his line of sight. He stood there a moment more, then went back to his desk.

Boone focused again on his puzzle. Fifteen across: a seven-letter word for *irresponsible*. Reckless? Careless? No, those were too long. He was mentally counting the letters in "negligent" when he heard footsteps in the hall, and a knock on the frame of his open doorway. It was the woman from the park.

"Mr. Boone?" she said. "My name's Willie Decker."

He leaned back in his chair. "Willie?"

Her face softened a bit, but didn't quite smile. "Wilhelmina."

"Come in, Ms. Decker. Have a seat."

She stepped inside, closed the door, and settled into the chair facing his desk.

"I saw you outside," Boone said.

She nodded. "I was wondering whether to come up to your office."

"I wonder that every morning," he said.

This time she did smile.

"Can I get you some coffee?"

"No, thanks." She cleared her throat. "I… well, I saw your ad in the *Chronicle*."

"Ah, yes." Boone put away his half-completed puzzle and said, "My cousin works for the paper. She talked me into the ad."

"It said you're a private investigator."

"At least that much was true," he agreed, thinking it probably should've also said he needed the work. "How can I help you, Ms. Decker?"

She hesitated. Looked down at the tiny purse in her lap and up again.

"I think somebody's trying to kill me," she said.

A long silence passed.

"You're in the wrong place," Boone said. "You need to be talking to the police."

She shook her head. "I can't."

"Why not?"

"Because I stole something from him. I don't want the police to know about that."

"Him? So you know who this is, who wants to kill you?"

"Yes. It's my husband, Gus Decker. Gustav, actually. He's from Austria."

Boone took a moment to process that. *Gustav and Wilhelmina.* Sounded like a foreign movie. "What happened, exactly?"

"Two things. About a week ago the brakes failed in my car, and I had to drive into a ditch to avoid a busy stoplight. Scared me silly, but I was okay."

"You think someone tampered with it?"

"The repair shop found a brake-fluid leak. But the car's only a year old."

"What else?" Boone asked.

"A van almost ran me over the other day, in a parking lot at the Galleria. I recognized the driver—I think he works for my husband."

"Did you get a plate number?"

"No. But it was Texas."

"Local? Harris County?"

"I couldn't tell."

"And you're sure this wasn't an accident?"

"I'm not positive," she said. "But the van barely missed me. There were no witnesses."

"You know the driver's name?"

"No. I don't know much of anything about Gus's business."

"What does he do, your husband?"

"He owns a trucking company. Decker-Fuhrman Transport."

Boone paused, thinking. "And what exactly did you 'steal' from him, Ms. Decker?"

"A piece of artwork," she said. "A painting he acquired before we met. We're separated now, but I still have a house key, and I snuck in and took it, a few days ago."

"Trucker and art collector. Interesting combination."

"He's neither one, really. He just runs the company. And that painting probably came to him in ways I don't want to know about."

"Well, as far as theft goes," Boone said, "a concept called spousal immunity would probably keep you from being either sued or prosecuted. At least in this state."

She looked up at the ceiling a moment, as if trying to come to a decision. "Let's put it this way, then. Illegal or not, I took something of my husband's, that he wants back."

"And you think that's the reason you're in danger? Because you took the painting?"

"And lost it," she said.

"How did you lose it?"

She shifted a little in her seat. "I sold it."

"For how much?"

"Thirty thousand dollars."

Boone raised his eyebrows.

"It was a Meissonier," she said.

He tried to look as if he knew who that was. "So, let him have the money. Maybe he can buy it back."

"I'm going to give the money away."

Boone could feel the beginnings of a headache. He took a sip of his now-cold coffee, which didn't help, and said, "I can see why he might be upset. But you said he wants to *kill* you. What am I missing?"

"I'm going to give it to the man I've been having an affair with."

The office went quiet.

"And your husband knows this? Knows you plan to give it away, and who to?"

"Yes. I told him." She added, "He wants to kill us both."

The silence stretched out. They sat and studied each other.

"Ms. Decker," Boone said, "I need the rest of the story."

"What do you mean?"

"You still haven't told me the real reason you can't go to the police, about… well, your suspicions."

She heaved a sigh. Half a minute passed.

Finally she said, "It's complicated. For one thing, I have no proof."

"What else?"

"This man in my life—his name's Everett—has debts. Gambling debts."

"And?"

"And he's an elected official. If such a damaging secret were revealed…."

"Are you talking about Everett Nelson?" Boone asked. "The city councilman?"

"Yes."

"So this thirty thousand—it'll get him out of trouble? Out of debt?"

"Not quite, no. But it'll help."

Boone shook his head and said, "This doesn't sound all that complicated, to me. It sounds simple. The question is, would you rather protect Everett Nelson—or stay alive?"

"That's why I'm here, Mr. Boone. I'm trying to do both."

Boone did a palms-up. "Then I don't know what you expect from me, Ms. Decker. Even if your brake malfunction was no accident, and if this man you saw in the van does work for your husband, there's no proof, as you said, of any of this. And do you think I can guard you? Or bail out your boyfriend? I can't."

"I'm not asking you to. But you could talk to him."

"Talk to your husband, you mean?"

"Yes. There's a place he goes every night, alone, on his property. You could meet him there. You could reason with him."

"I don't even know him."

She leaned forward, balanced her elbows on her knees. "I've checked you out, Mr. Boone. I'm aware of your background. Your reputation."

"What exactly is my reputation?"

"You were in the papers awhile back."

"You mean, besides my ad?"

"Besides your ad. I'm referring to that business about the kidnapping."

Boone shrugged. "I was just on the sidelines, Ms. Decker. I happened to be there when the cops caught the guy."

"I heard *you* caught him."

"The police caught him. I slowed him down."

"You shot him, you mean."

"He was trying to shoot me."

"And that other thing, those two arms dealers—"

Boone shook his head. "I'm told that's an ongoing investigation."

"But you found them, when nobody else could. Prevented a terrorist attack, I heard. A bombing they'd planned. My point is, Mr. Boone, my husband watches the news, like I do, and he probably knows who you are and what you're capable of—"

"What I'm capable of?"

"And if you meet with him," she said, "I think he might listen to you."

"In other words, I might threaten him."

"Your involvement might threaten him." Willie Decker swallowed, and wiped a tear from her eye with the back of a hand before fixing him with a stare. "I have no place else to go, okay? I'm honestly afraid for my life."

Boone sighed. "You should be careful how you use the word 'honestly.'"

"But you'll do it. You'll help me. Right?"

He looked back at her for a moment. He could hear the traffic in the street below, the wail of a distant siren, the yapping of a dog. He wondered if it was the one chasing the frisbee.

"Yes," he said. "I'll talk to your husband."

She took a long breath, nodded, and swiped at her eyes again. "Thank you."

"I'll need an address."

"You'll need more than that," she said. "Are you available tonight? Around seven?"

"Why?"

"I'd like you to come to my apartment. We'll leave your car there and I'll drive you to Gus's place. Mine and Gus's, actually, but you know what I mean."

"You'll be with me when I talk to him?"

"No—I won't even tell him you're coming. But I need to be with you when you enter the area. It's gated and manned, and Gus doesn't like visitors. I'm your only way in."

"If he doesn't like visitors, I'm sure he'll be pleased when I stroll onto the grounds unannounced. That sounds like trespassing."

"It's not. The place is half mine, and I'm saying it's okay."

Boone could see all kinds of problems with that, but it was a little late to back out. They went over the payment terms, and she wrote a check, gave him her address, thanked him twice more, and left. After she'd gone, Boone sat there in the silent office and studied the open doorway. He was still looking at it when he had an unbidden thought. It was the seven-word answer for fifteen across:

Foolish.

"Damn right it is," he said aloud.

*****

At seven o'clock that evening, with Wilhelmina Decker's down payment in his checking account and serious doubts in his heart, Boone parked in front of her apartment building, met her at the door, and rode with her in her black BMW to her previous (and her husband's current) address. As it turned out, Gustav Decker lived on the bottom edge of a exclusive three-sided subdivision called the Triangle, west of the city. They drove through the guarded entrance—*Good to see you again, Ms. Decker*—without incident and parked two minutes later on a heavily wooded street just past a red-brick mailbox with DECKER printed on the side. Boone climbed out of the passenger seat and walked, as instructed, to a three-story home with a curved driveway in front and then trudged around the side of the house to the edge of the forest that supposedly covered half the ten-acre property. Willie had told him Gus always strolled through those woods between seven and eight or so, and it would be best to catch him out there rather than ring the doorbell. He usually refused to answer the door anyway, she said. This only added to Boone's negative opinion of the man, and they'd not even met yet.

It was a dark, warm night, with a quarter moon low in the sky and winking in and out of the clouds, and when Boone rounded the back corner of the residence he glimpsed a shadowy movement in the trees beyond. Instinctively his hand started toward the pistol in his shoulder holster, but he stopped himself. He was glad he did. A calm voice said, "Do not move."

Boone watched the shadow emerge from the woods at about the same moment the moon emerged from the clouds. The owner of the heavily accented voice, Boone saw, was short and blond, and holding a handgun. The wife had said he was usually armed.

"Gustav Decker?" Boone asked.

"That is correct."

"Don't shoot," Boone said. "I was asked to come talk with you. That's all."

The man with the gun moved forward in the gloom, and stopped beside another shadow—the stairpost of a set of steps leading up to what appeared to be a huge wooden deck along the back of the residence. Then the moon vanished again. "I take it you are Michael Boone," Decker said.

Boone blinked in surprise. "She told you?"

"Let us just say that I know you. I will need your weapon, please." Decker held out a hand, and when Boone had surrendered his pistol without argument Decker stooped in the darkness and pressed what must have been a switch recessed into the stairpost. Floodlights lined up along the back eaves suddenly came on, momentarily blinding Boone and bathing the whole scene in a stark yellow light. The deck was indeed immense, with long redwood benches just inside the railings and brick-lined flowerbeds along the perimeter below.

"Come," Decker said. "Let us go inside."

*****

Up close, the house looked even bigger. Decker steered Boone at gunpoint through the back door and into a huge den with a conference table in the center. Decker motioned for him to sit, then pocketed Boone's revolver and took a seat on the opposite side of the table. Decker placed his own gun—a black automatic—on the walnut tabletop in front of him. In the light of the lamps scattered about the area, he turned out to be white-haired rather than blond, but was still fairly young, by Boone's standards. Early forties, maybe.

"Do you want to give me your version of what you are doing here?" he asked.

Boone stared at him. "My version?"

Decker tilted his head. "I was told that you have come here to do me harm, Mr. Boone. I find that disturbing."

"What do you mean, you were told?"

"I received a call only moments before you arrived—I was walking as I usually do, in the woods out back. It was a call from a number I did not recognize. The voice was low and garbled, but it informed me that a prowler had just been spotted, inching around the east side of my home. You can imagine my concern."

"A prowler?"

"I was told that he—you—had a firearm."

"How would someone know that? It wasn't out and visible."

"Your face was. I might have shot you, otherwise. I almost did."

Boone frowned. "But you called me by name. How'd you recognize me?"

"Night-vision goggles," Decker said, taking them from his pocket and holding them up.

"That's not what I meant. How'd you know my face? We haven't met before."

"I knew you from your photograph. It appears you have gained weight."

"What photograph?"

"The newspaper. The relevant articles are online." Decker raised his chin and seemed to examine Boone more closely. "A kidnapping case, was it not? Also, you located those two gunrunners some time ago. The averted terrorist plot."

"What I'm asking is, why'd you look me up at all?"

"Because I found out my wife Willie met with you this morning," Decker said.

"How'd you know that?"

"I have been watching her, ever since she—well, since she took something from me."

"She told me about that." Then: "So you followed her, today?"

"No—I had her followed."

Remembering the park, Boone said, "Let me guess. Skinny guy, ratty gray beard?"

"That is correct. How did you know?"

"I'm a detective," Boone said. "Tell him I said he's too ugly for undercover work."

"I will. What else did my Willie reveal to you, in this morning's meeting?"

"She told me her life was in danger. She's had some close calls recently."

"And she thinks…?"

"That you're behind it. That's why I'm here—she asked me to come talk with you."

Decker smiled, as if at some private joke. "Then I believe we can safely assume she was the one who called me."

"Who warned you, you mean? Just now?"

"Yes. She can be quite deceptive, my Willie. And to think I am the one who taught her how to disguise her voice. And the benefits of a throwaway cell phone."

Boone shook his head. "None of that makes sense. If your wife asked me to come here, on her behalf—why would she then call and tell you I was sneaking around, with a gun?" He pointed to Decker's pistol, on the table between them. "And if you knew someone was coming, why were you waiting for him with that? Why didn't you just call the police?"

"I told you, I only found out just before you arrived. And in my business, I have been forced to deal personally with violence from time to time. As I said, I almost shot you."

"That's my point," Boone said. "Why would Ms. Decker want you to shoot me?"

Decker seemed to realize that was a fair question. He glanced around the room as if searching for answers, then let his gaze settle on his automatic, there on the table. And frowned.

After a long pause he turned, looked thoughtfully at the row of windows, and took a remote from another pocket and pressed a button. The shades in the room lowered, slowly, until all the windows were covered. Then he reached for the pistol in front of him. Boone tensed, but Decker said, "Let us declare a truce, Mr. Boone. I only want to check something."

He picked up his gun with one hand and used the other to rack the slide and eject the chambered cartridge. He picked the cartridge up off the tabletop and looked at it. "As I feared," he said, and rolled it across the table to Boone.

Boone looked at the cartridge, felt its crimped nose, and understood. It was a blank round.

Decker, who had taken out the clip and was inspecting the other shells, nodded as if agreeing with himself. "They are all blanks." He looked up at Boone. "If we had had a shootout, you and I, blanks in my firearm would effectively guarantee the outcome, would you not say?"

Boone tried to think of a reply, and couldn't. During the silence, Decker rose from his chair. "Please excuse me for a minute," he said, and left the room.

It took three minutes. Then he returned, and sat again at the table.

"What's going on here, Decker?" Boone asked.

Gustav Decker ran a hand through his hair, stayed quiet a moment, then said, "Consider this. My Willie knows I would not call the police, she knows I carry this pistol on my walks, and she knows I would try to defend myself if I felt I was in danger."

"So?"

"So, she also knows I am not very proficient with a gun. And she knows that you *are*."

Boone frowned. "Let me get this straight. You're saying she set it up for *me* to kill *you*?"

"I am saying I think she wants me dead and cannot or will not do it herself. So she gives you some sad story about being in peril, hires you, convinces you to contact me, and then calls to alert me that someone is skulking around my home with a weapon. In my opinion, that is setting things up rather well."

"But why would she want you dead? To protect herself?"

"To help herself. We are still married, Mr. Boone, and I am heavily insured. Willie is the beneficiary of a policy on my life for more than two million dollars. Besides, I suppose she told you about this love triangle with Councilman Nelson. With me out of the photograph—"

"The picture."

"Yes. With me out of the picture, she would marry him in an instant."

"I doubt she'd do that," Boone said.

"Why?"

"Because that would make her Willie Nelson."

Decker gave him a bored, wooden-faced stare. "You are a strange man, Michael Boone. To find humor in a situation such as this."

"*I'm* strange? You walk around in your yard wearing infrared glasses."

"It is fortunate for you that I do. I just find it interesting that you think all this is funny."

"I don't," Boone said. "I think it's crazy." Which was an understatement. "Tell me this: Even if your wife did plan your death, and planned for me to carry it out—how did she do it?"

"You mean, how did she manage to load my pistol with blanks?" Decker said. "That is simple. Remember, she still has a key. I doubt she has had this planned for long, but she could certainly have come here earlier today—I always go to my club from two until four. The house is empty then, and she knows where I keep this weapon. She must have exchanged the live cartridges for blanks, and left."

"But it was my understanding that you take your gun with you, when you're out."

"Only when I am here, outside on the property. I keep a second pistol in my car."

Boone shook his head. "It still doesn't add up. If she wanted you dead, why wouldn't she just do it herself?"

"Because she would be a prime suspect, that is why."

"She'd be just as much a suspect if I killed you and then it came out that she'd met with me this morning. She'd be implicated up to her diamond earrings."

"Not if you were dead too."

Boone blinked. "What?"

"Think about it," Decker said. "How could she have called to tell me what she told me, if she were not here already, watching? How would she have known exactly where *you* were, at that moment?"

Boone paused, thinking. "You're right about that much. She *is* here. She's waiting for me in her car, out there on the street."

"No. You might have left her in her car, but I suspect that she got out and followed you, unseen, and phoned me then. That is why I lowered the blinds just now. And when I left the room a moment ago I locked the other windows and dead-bolted the doors." He nodded toward the back and said, "Willie was probably hiding out there when we first met, waiting for you to shoot me—in self-defense, I admit—and if you had, she would have then sneaked up and shot *you*, and placed her smoking gun in my lifeless hand."

Boone thought about that for a moment. "It wouldn't have worked," he said. "There'd be no gunshot residue on your hand. The police would know you weren't the shooter."

"She probably never considered that," Decker said. "I did not say it would work—I just said she *thought* it would work."

Again Boone shook his head. "All this assumes she's capable of doing such a thing."

"I believe she is."

"It also assumes that she owns a gun."

"She does."

"Then that, too, wouldn't make much sense."

"Why not?" Decker asked.

"Because it'd be her gun that was used to kill me, and not yours."

"No, it would be mine. I gave her the pistol she has—it is registered to me." He paused, apparently satisfied with his logic. "Except for the absence of gunpowder traces on my hand, as you said, the scenario would be perfect, for her. I would have been killed by you, she would be rich and free, and you, who are dangerous because of the knowledge you have since she met with you this morning, would be dead as well. Her reasoning was off, but her intentions seem clear."

Silence. Then, in a lower voice, Boone said, "So, if what you're saying's true, she's still out there right now. Watching us and waiting."

"I would suspect so. What do *you* think?"

"I think I wish I hadn't come in to the office this morning." Boone studied the shaded windows. "Seriously, I'm thinking you're both overreacting to just about everything. Either that, or there's some truth to all this, and if so, I'm not sure I'd trust you *or* her."

Surprisingly, Decker smiled. "Well, meanwhile, I suggest we confront her on our terms, and find out what is really happening. I further suggest that you go out the back, and I will go out the front and work my way around. Nobody ever uses the front door."

"So I've been told."

"I will also cut the lights. This is no need for either of us to wind up silhouetted against a window." He rose to his feet and crossed the room to a desk, where he opened a drawer and reloaded his automatic with what Boone assumed were live rounds. Then he took Boone's revolver from his pocket, handed it back to him, and smiled again. "I doubt this is how you thought you would be spending your evening."

Boone stood also. "Believe it or not, this morning I was bored."

Decker walked to a bank of wall switches, turned off the room and deck lights, and left. Boone took a moment to let his eyes adjust to the darkness, then drew a deep breath and exited through the back door as planned.

*****

The moon was higher now, but still ducking in and out of the drifting clouds. His mind whirling with a dozen questions, Michael Boone quietly crossed the darkened deck. He paused near the spot where he remembered the short staircase should be, the one with the light switch in the stairpost. When he raised his eyes again, he saw her—or what was probably her. A flicker of moonlight through the trees, reflected on something shiny. He dropped to one knee and rested his gun arm on the bannister.

"Don't move, Ms. Decker," he said. "I know where you are."

A small voice replied, "All right."

She walked out of the trees at almost the same place her husband had done, twenty minutes earlier, and slowly approached the steps. Boone kept his pistol aimed and steady.

"Hold both hands out to your sides," he said. "I really don't want to shoot you. Okay?"

"Okay."

With his left hand Boone dug his cell phone out of his pocket and touched the "flashlight" key. He pointed it and saw her face, yellow-white in the surrounding darkness. He moved the beam downward. In one of her hands was a snubnosed revolver, and in the other was something flimsy and black, hanging by a strap.

"What are you doing here?" he asked her. "You said you'd wait in the car."

"I know I did. The situation changed."

"I agree." Boone carefully descended the steps. "Come here, and hand me the gun," he said. She held it out, and he took it with his phone/flashlight hand.

"I couldn't do it," she murmured. "Not until I was sure."

"Sure of what?" he asked. He put his own gun away in its shoulder holster and studied her face in the beam of light. She didn't look scared, or angry, or anything he'd expected. Mostly, she looked confused. No more than he was, he thought. "What's going on, here, Willie?"

"You tell *me*," she said. "I got a call from Gustav ten minutes ago, while I sat in the car. He was whispering and sounded terrified, said he was your prisoner, said he'd locked himself in the bathroom. He said you'd told him you were going to kill him and then come to my place and kill me." She swallowed and asked, "Did you kill him?"

"*What?* Of course I didn't kill him."

"Where is he, then?"

"He's around front, somewhere," Boone said. "And why would I kill him? Why would I do any of those things?"

"For the money he keeps here at the house, he said—plus the thirty thousand I told you about, at my apartment. He said you'd tricked me from the very start."

Boone tried to make sense of what he was hearing. Decker must've called her when he'd left the den for several minutes, earlier. Why had he lied? What the hell *was* going on, here?

"He told me he'd had me followed," she continued, "so he knew I came to your office today. That's how he knew who you were. He told me I've been wrong about him, and that he forgives me for the things I've said and done."

"And you believe that?"

"I don't know what to believe, right now."

Join the club, Boone said to himself. Then he had another thought. "Your gun," he said, tapping the revolver he held in his hand. "Is this the one he gave you?"

"He never gave me a gun. That's the one he told me to take, when he called me just now. It was in the glove compartment of his car, parked in the driveway out front. He asked me to come help him, quick, and he said the only way was for me to get his pistol and shoot you with it. He said to come watch the back door, and kill you when you stepped outside." She paused and gulped a breath. "Are you saying he was lying to me, about all that?"

"He's been lying to both of us, about everything. He told me *you* called *him*," Boone said. "But let's take one thing at a time. How were you supposed to see me, out here?"

She raised the object she was holding in her other hand. It was a pair of infrared goggles. Good grief, Boone thought. All God's chillun got night vision.

"This was in the glovebox, along with his gun—he told me to duck into his car and get both of them on my way back here." She sighed. "I could see you… but I couldn't shoot you, Mr. Boone. I couldn't make myself do it."

"Good thing you didn't," he said. "For me and you both. If what I'm thinking is true, he would've killed you too."

"He what?"

Boone switched off his light and pulled her down into a crouch, there on the bottom steps of the deck. The moon was hidden again, and even though everything was now pitch black, he thought he finally saw—in his mind, at least—what was happening here.

Quickly, he filled her in, telling her about Decker's suggestion that she wanted not only to kill him for the insurance money but to also kill Boone because of how much he now knew. Which made Boone think of something else.

He looked down at her gun in his hand—a shortbarrelled .38, like his—and, working blind, popped the cylinder and ejected one of the shells. Then he took out his cell again, turned on its flashlight, focused on the cartridge, and nodded.

"What?" she asked.

"It's a blank. Gunpowder, but no bullet. If you'd shot at me, you'd have been shooting blanks." Apparently, when Gustav got an idea, he stuck with it. Boone replaced the cartridge and snapped the cylinder shut.

She sighed. "That bastard. So he wanted *you* to kill *me*."

"There's a lot of that going around." Boone switched off the light, pocketed his phone, and looked up at her, thinking. "In a way, you gotta admire the guy. This was all planned out, Willie. Planned fast and careful, after he heard what you told me in my office this morning. His spy relayed to him the time

I'd be here and the fact that you'd be bringing me. Decker put blanks in his own gun so he could later show it to me and convince me you were out to get him killed and me too, and he also put blanks in the one he left for you to get, in his glove compartment."

"But—how would he know what I told you in your office?"

"Because he did have a man following you, a man who'd been told to hear as well as see. He must've crept up the stairs behind you, in my building, and listened to us outside my door."

Boone could hear her breathing as she mulled that over. "So Gus knew that I thought he wanted me dead," she said.

"And everything else too—including the fact that you still have the money from the painting. He'll probably send his eavesdropper to your apartment at some point, to steal it back."

"That's the least of my worries. If you have all this figured right, he plans to kill us both."

"Not if we can get out of here." Boone stood, and pulled her up with him. "Put your night goggles back on. We'll head for the woods, then loop around to your car before he—"

"Too late," Gus Decker said.

*****

Both of them swiveled toward the sound of his voice, which had come from the yard beyond the deck. Boone could see nothing in the blackness.

"My, my," Decker said. "Another triangle. The husband, the wife, and her hired help." His voice hardened. "Do not move a muscle. Either of you."

231

Boone's mind was spinning. He realized they were right where Decker wanted them: with his night glasses he could see them but they couldn't see him. Even worse, the gun Boone was holding was Willie's, and useless. His own was tucked away in its holster.

When Decker spoke again, he seemed to have moved closer.

"As I am sure you have guessed, I have my weapon aimed at your heart, Mr. Boone. Place your gun on the ground at your feet."

Boone did, very slowly. "You don't want to do this, Decker. It won't work."

"I will be the judge of that. Before we proceed, however, I need an answer to one question. How much did my wife tell you this morning about my operation?"

"Have you been operated on?"

Decker chuckled in the darkness. "Funny until the end, are you not? I mean my business, Mr. Boone. How much did she tell you?"

"She said she didn't know much about it."

"Ah. She did not mention the smuggling of ammunition across the Mexican border?"

"Guns, you mean?"

"No. The cartels down there already have guns. The beauty of it is, the guns are of no use without bullets. My trucks move the ammo. It is smaller, easier to hide, less risk."

Boone suddenly understood. "Unless someone's late with a shipment, or shows up with less than he's supposed to. Plenty of risk then, right? Is that what happened to the guy who was murdered last year? Did the two goons who killed him—the ones who were planning the railroad bombing—did they work for you?"

Decker hesitated, then said, "You are sometimes too perceptive for your own good, my friend. Yes, they were part of my extended organization, although it is structured such that they did not know of my involvement, and I knew nothing of their terrorism plans. And yes, that is a grudge I have held against you for some time. But my question is—"

"So you steered your wife to me, didn't you. Probably after your attempts on her life failed, and you saw she was getting suspicious."

"Now that you bring it up, I might have left a newspaper so she could see it, folded to your ad. I knew she was going to seek help, and I certainly did not want her going to the police." He chuckled again, a wicked sound in the ink-black darkness. "Willie is fairly quick about most things, are you not, Darling? And so gullible about others."

"Screw you, Gus," she said.

"Mr. Boone, my question is," Decker continued, "were any of my business dealings discussed, in your office this morning?" In a sharper tone he asked, "Willie, did you speak of such things, to this man?"

"Why?" she said, glaring at him.

"What do you mean, why?"

"I mean why does it matter, if you're going to kill us both?"

Boone spoke up before Decker could reply, as the thought occurred to him: "The guy with the gray beard, who followed her today," Boone said, "the guy listening outside my office.

You need to know if he heard any of that, and failed to mention it to you. Right? So you'll know whether to murder him too."

A long silence passed. "Earl Pinkston," Decker said, "was useful, yes, but he is a complication as well. A loose end. Perhaps it *is* best that he die also—just in case he did hear too much." Decker paused. "Not that that should matter, as my dear wife has said, to either of *you*."

Something in Decker's voice told Boone time had run out. "Wait," he blurted. "Wait a second. I meant what I said—this won't work. You can't just kill us. If you're going to get away with this, it has to be done the way you must've planned it, earlier. Either Ms. Decker or I will have to shoot the other. If neither of us has gunshot residue on our hands afterward...."

"I remember our conversation, Mr. Boone. I have already considered that."

"And?"

"And I have decided you are correct. You will have to shoot my wife."

A deep silence fell, there on the steps of the deck. Boone heard Willie Decker gulp.

"Pick up your gun," Decker said, "and shoot her. Now."

Boone hesitated only a moment, then stooped to pick up her revolver. As Boone's fingers closed around it, Decker said, "I warn you, Mr. Boone, do not point it in my direction."

Silently, in his mind, Boone said, *Trust me, Willie. Remember, this is your gun, not mine.* Without another word he turned his back to Decker, grabbed her behind her neck, and pulled her to him. Then he pressed the barrel of her gun into her stomach and pulled the trigger.

There was a muffled blast, and—God bless her, he thought—she spun away and collapsed face-down into the grass beside the flowerbed at the bottom of the steps.

"Now drop it," Decker said. His voice was shaky; it was obvious he hadn't expected Boone to actually go through with it.

For the second time Boone let her gun slip from his fingers. Then he took a slow step to the left, away from Willie. And closer to the stairpost.

The moon came out again then. Only for an instant, then everything went dark again—but long enough for Boone to know exactly where Decker was standing. He might need to know that, if he had trouble finding the light switch on the stairpost beside his left arm. If he could somehow press that switch, and if the floodlights blinded Decker for even a second or two, Boone's right hand might be able to get to his gun, the one with the real bullets, inside his coat.

He tensed his body, got ready to move—

And felt the cold muzzle of Decker's gunbarrel against his throat. Boone hadn't even heard him approach. "Allow me," Decker said. Forcing Boone backward a step and holding the automatic tightly against the soft skin just under Boone's chin, Decker leaned forward and pressed the switch. The four floodlights along the roofline blazed to life. In an instant Decker's night goggles were off and cast aside.

And he was smiling.

"A good try," he said. "Goodbye, Mr. Boone."

It was the last thing he ever said. At that moment his head jerked to one side, his gun fired into the air an inch from

Boone's right ear, and Decker staggered backward into the yard. His wife, growling like an enraged beast, took a step in his direction, the bloodstained brick in her hand raised for another strike—but at that moment her husband turned, blinking away the blood from his scalp, raised his pistol, and aimed it at her. Boone's gun was out of its holster now and ready, but she was standing between them, and suddenly he knew he was too late.

Then a shot rang out. Willie stopped in her tracks and Boone froze also, and they watched together as Decker's eyes rolled up into his head and his mouth fell open and he toppled forward into the grass. In the middle of his back was a dark red splotch the size of a softball.

Behind him, holding a smoking shotgun, stood the thin, gray-bearded man—Pinkston?—that Boone had last seen this morning. He looked up at Boone and Willie, his eyes wide, and lowered the shotgun.

Boone—his right ear still ringing—tried to speak and found that he couldn't. He cleared his throat, tried again, and said to Pinkston, "You heard what he said?"

"I heard enough." The gun slipped from Earl Pinkston's fingers as if suddenly too heavy to hold, and then his knees seemed to give way. With trembling hands he eased himself to the ground and sat there beside the shotgun. "Thanks for turning on the lights," he murmured.

*****

Boone holstered his pistol, took Willie by the shoulders, and turned her so he could look at the front of her dress. It was blackened a little, but most of the impact of the blank charge had been absorbed by Boone's left palm, which he'd shoved between the gun and her stomach just before he'd fired. It hurt like hell.

"Are you okay?" he asked her. She swallowed hard and nodded. Numbly she dropped the brick she'd been holding. Boone looked down and saw the empty slot where it had been, at the edge of the flowerbed.

When he was sure she wouldn't pass out Boone walked to Decker's body and pried the automatic from the dead man's fingers. Then he continued across the yard, his shadow stretching out in front of him, to stand beside Earl Pinkston. Gently Boone helped him to his feet.

"I didn't know none of that he was talkin' about," Pinkston said. "He just hired me to follow his wife today, and listen if she spoke to anybody. Paid me five hundred bucks."

"I believe you," Boone said. "He fooled all of us. But why are you here now, tonight?"

"Mr. Decker called me, maybe twenty minutes ago. Said the guard at the gate would let me pass. Told me to come quick, and wait out there in the woods for him."

He had probably made the call just after he phoned Willie, Boone thought. "He wanted you here so he could kill you, I imagine."

Pinkston nodded. "I expect so."

"Why'd you bring the shotgun?"

"Don't know. Somethin' told me it'd be a good idea."

"It was," Boone said. He looked up and saw Willie on her cell phone, probably calling nine-one-one. He sighed and added, "It's about to get busy around here."

Pinkston didn't reply. He had sagged again onto the ground, sitting there with a blank look on his face and his hands in his lap. Boone patted his shoulder once and walked over to stand beside Willie at the edge of the flowerbeds. She stood facing the house, as if trying to literally put her dead husband behind her.

She disconnected from her call and said, "The cops are on their way."

Boone nodded, cradling his damaged left hand. All of a sudden he felt exhausted.

"This is like a bad dream," she murmured. She was hugging her elbows, and trembling despite the heat. "What's hardest is that I actually believed him, for awhile there."

"So did I," he said.

She studied his face a moment. "You saved my life, Mr. Boone."

"Michael. My name's Michael." He looked again at Decker's body, lying face-down in the grass. "You saved mine too."

"And the guy over there—Pinkston? He saved us both."

Boone nodded again. "Now I'm sorry I said bad things about him."

A warm wind blew in from the west, riffling her hair and smelling like pine trees. Crickets chirped in the woods, still and dark beyond the reach of the floodlights.

Willie drew a shaky breath and let it out. "Not your usual day, huh?"

"No. Most of my cases last at least twelve hours."

He saw a tiny, tired smile on her face. "So what's next?" she asked.

"About a thousand questions, from the Men in Blue."

"I mean, after that."

Boone shrugged. "In stories like this, the knight and the princess are supposed to run away together."

She turned to face him. He could see that the thought had at least crossed her mind. "Can't," she said.

"Edward?"

"Afraid so."

Boone let out a sigh. "Yet another triangle."

"Actually," she said, smiling again, "I think you'd like him."

"I'll like him when the city fixes the potholes on my street and the water problems in my building." He paused and added, "I bet your councilman never came to your rescue, in your hour of need."

"He never shot me in the stomach, either."

Boone nodded. "Good point."

Several minutes passed, both of them staring into the night and listening for the approaching cruisers and adrift in their own thoughts. Boone's were mostly positive. Long-range, he now knew enough to have the Feds launch an investigation into Decker-Fuhrman Transport, and to expose and stop what would probably be one of the biggest arms-smuggling operations in recent years. The police would love him, and owe him as well. Short-range, Edward Nelson or not, Boone planned to spend some time with Wilhelmina Decker. If a private eye couldn't outcharm a gambling-addicted city employee, what was the world coming to?

"What are you grinning about?" she asked him.

"Just thinking."

"Tell me," she said.

"Two things. First, I was thinking about tomorrow. Second, about a shady bench in the park across the street from my office."

"What about it?"

"I bet it's a good place to watch the ladies stroll by, in their summer dresses."

"And what's special about tomorrow?"

He turned to look at her. "You like hot dogs?" he said.

Alligator in a Sweatsuit
Shannon Lawrence

On a day as swampy as the Okefenokee, I tangled with a python, a prostitute, a crazy person, and a dead guy, in no particular order.

It started that morning with a body lying on a hotel room floor, his flesh covered in a sheen of moisture from the humid air. The dead man wore only a tie, a single black sock, and a condom. His eyes had been frozen wide open as if his last sight had been a big surprise—which I was sure it had been—and his mouth gaped, black fillings visible on his bottom rear molars.

Not only could I not find the other sock anywhere, but there was no sign of the rest of his clothing either. Surely, he'd worn pants to this crappy motel room. Shorts, at least. Shirts seemed to be optional in the Florida heat these days—at least for men; we women still had to cover up—but I assumed underwear hadn't gone out of style. And what about shoes? Car keys? A wallet? Not a trace.

I'd have to wait on the coroner to know cause of death, but my semi-practiced eye didn't catch any obvious signs, such as holes of various shapes and sizes, blood, a dented head, or ligature marks. His eyes showed no signs of petechial hemorrhage, his face bore no discoloration, and I couldn't see any bruising. Could be natural causes or poison, of course. Or a billion other things.

As for why the crime scene techs and I had been called here when there was no obvious sign of murder, well, his belongings being absent was one reason. The other reason being the coiled, also deceased, baby python left on his chest like an unholy gift. No sign of its cause of death either. At least not that I could tell from the wide berth I gave it to keep the fear shudders away.

I left the crime scene folks behind to photograph the scene, dust for prints, and look for the hidden clues only they could find. Likely, there wouldn't be any more, but we cops must go through the motions, whether we're flailing at shadows or not. My first stop was the front desk of the motel, where I hoped to at least get a name, possibly even a description of the person who'd entered that room with the guy. Unfortunately, the room hadn't been rented out, and the only other tenants at the hotel were two couples, an obese salesman, and an elderly woman and her poodle. My flash of a cell phone photo of his face proved to be unrecognizable to the dipwad behind the counter whose nametag read "Randy." His eyes strayed to a barking television mounted on the lobby wall as he talked to me.

"I haven't seen that guy before. He's not someone I checked in."

"Odd. So you think he broke in?" I turned to look out the windows on the front and side of the building. From here, I could clearly see the room in question, uniforms standing right outside the door. This guy was either lying or incompetent. Probably both, judging by our interaction, so far. "Wouldn't you have seen someone sneaking in?"

"Not necessarily. I have to leave the desk sometimes."

"Do you still keep copies of licenses when people check in?" The larger hotels had moved away from doing this, but hole-in-the-wall joints like this still made it a point, what with so much of their business being cash-based. Their typical clientele were illicit in some manner, drifters, or those too poor to stay at a real hotel with a continental breakfast and mini-fridge.

"Yeah."

We stared at each other a moment, and then his eyes drifted back to that damn TV set.

"Can I see them?" I'd thought this was implied, but apparently not.

His gaze drifted back my way. "Oh, yeah, sure." He pulled a short stack of paper from under the counter and placed it in front of me, one sheet drifting down to the floor.

I bent over to pick it up, and when I came up, paper in hand, he'd looked away again. This guy had the focus of a butterfly and the looks of a pelican, skin sagging below his chin almost all the way to his chest, despite the scrawniness of the rest of his body.

The license photos aligned with what he'd claimed. None of the images matched John Doe. I set the pages back on the counter and slapped my business card down in front of him. "If you remember anything other than the local TV listings, give me a call." I cut my losses and headed out, directing a rookie onsite to question the other tenants.

Often, the solution to a crime comes from the oddest places. In this case, the oddest clue I had was the python, followed closely by the man's missing property. Due to the insane number of pythons in the Florida wild, there were strict laws governing who could own pythons, and I was fairly certain no one was supposed to be breeding them except perhaps for scientific reasons. This snake had come from the wild or someone permitted to handle them. Luckily, I knew a herpetologist, and she didn't live far from the motel.

Myra's neighborhood was one step up from seedy, so a mild improvement over the area around the motel, which I'm sure was full of disease and random body parts if I felt like looking a little closer. These houses looked like their owners mostly tried to maintain them, but rot from the morbid humidity had seeped into many of them, and I winced at the level of mold this neighborhood must have been producing and projecting into the atmosphere.

Myra's house, on the other hand, was clean and tidy, her lawn well cared for. Oddly, though not for those who knew her, the house was a reptilian green with blue trim and merry white lace curtains in the windows. Despite its pleasant appearance, I had to brace myself before going in.

She responded to my knock promptly and cheerily. "Mads! How are you? Come in and see my newest acquisition."

I wondered if she'd been standing at the doorway, waiting to ask some unsuspecting fool into the house to see her snake. If I'd been delivering the mail, would she have greeted me the same way? Probably.

"What is it?" Hopefully she couldn't sense the wariness behind my question.

"A coral, and she's a beauty." She turned, blonde hair whirling at a rate a millisecond slower than the rest of her, and traipsed to a wall of glass terrariums with various types of lamps beaming warm light into the room.

I followed her to a terrarium on the lowest shelf, where she kept her nocturnal snakes. The day she'd informed me of this, my heart had frozen in mid-beat at the mere thought that there were night snakes. I'd previously felt safe trekking through tall grass at night, but not after that terrifying lunch. Instead, I now face random heebie-jeebies in the most central part of a grassy field, right when I have the greatest distance in any direction to get to safety. Like when I'm in a hotel, sitting on a toilet in the dark of night, and I suddenly think of one of those news stories of snakes coming up through the toilet plumbing and biting people on the ass.

The snake was definitely pretty, which made it easier to give out the appropriate level of oohs and aahs. The alternating bands of black-yellow-red-yellow shone under the lamp, reminding me of the old warning poem:

Red touch yellow, kill a fellow;

Red touch black, friend to Jack.

Something like that, anyway. I didn't figure I'd remember that when faced with a banded snake in the wild, but it was nice to pretend I might be able to stay safe in a possible snake-attack situation. After all, I was a badass cop. I'd saved lives, taken down bad guys. A tiny snake was no big deal.

Unless it could kill you with a bite.

"Did you really need another poisonous snake?"

"Sure, why not?"

"I don't know. Because if it gets out, it might kill you?"

"Corey wouldn't kill me, would you, baby?" Her voice got high and squeaky, like she was talking to a baby. Perhaps she was.

In a nearby terrarium, a large rattlesnake shifted drowsily. "What about that one? Would Rattley kill you?"

"That's Rick, and you've met him before. Don't act like you

don't remember his name."

I didn't, but that didn't seem important right now.

"Myra, I need to ask you some questions about pythons. Do you have a few minutes?"

"Oh, I've always got time to talk snakes. Burmese? Reticulated?" She turned to face me, and I noticed pink stains on the skin around her neck and one arm.

"Why's your skin all irritated?"

Her brows furrowed. "What?"

"Your skin, it's all pink." I pointed at my neck.

"Oh, that. I had a run-in with an anti-snake psycho at a rally. He dowsed me with his red Slurpee. It mostly washed off, but as you can see, it stained. Anyway, what kind of python?"

I showed her a photo of it on my phone.

"A Burmese! Beautiful, isn't it? It's hard to tell by the photo, but it doesn't look very old. What's that it's on?"

I could see why she'd wonder. He'd been a hairy man. The snake was curled up on what looked like a matted rug. "That's a man's chest. A dead snake was found on a probable murder victim today, and I'm trying to trace who might have had access to pythons since I know individuals aren't allowed to own them."

"Poor baby." Her lips drooped for a moment, but then her forehead crinkled and a thoughtful expression took over. "Everyone has to have a Reptile of Concern license to own a python, though there are tons of private collectors who get them illegally. For the legit ones, Florida Fish and Wildlife has a record of license holders. There are, of course, probably thousands in the wild around here, too. I get why you're asking, but I'm not sure it would be worth your time to track down the folks with licenses. There are hundreds."

"Are they allowed to breed them?"

"No, though there may be some research labs who are allowed to do that. That's one thing we regular license holders certainly can't do." She thought for a moment, a thin snake in the terrarium behind her rising along the glass, tongue flicking. I knew what that meant. That bastard was tasting me, sensing my presence on the other side of the glass.

A shiver ran up my spine, followed on fleet feet by a full body shudder. Luckily, Myra was deep in thought and didn't see it.

"You know what?" she asked, eyes widening. "Let me see that photo again. Any legal ROC has to be microchipped if it's over one inch. Let the coroner or whoever will be handling the autopsy know for when they do the necropsy. If it's legal, there's a chip."

Eager to get out of the Den of Snakedom, I thanked her and backed toward the door. "We need to meet up for lunch soon. Have you tried that new place down on Meyers?"

"I haven't. Let's do it this weekend! If you're not working."

"I have Saturday off. Noon?"

"Yep. See you then!" She turned her back on me before I even reached the door, cooing at Tasty McSnifferson.

My phone rang as I approached my car. I answered in my customarily polite way: "What do you want?"

The caller hesitated before speaking. "We've got a witness at the hotel who saw a woman go into the hotel with our John Doe. She's meeting us downtown." Ah, the rookie.

"I'll be there." I hung up and climbed into the car, rolling down the windows as soon as I had the engine on. I felt like a baked ham, and not the honey kind. More the rancid, moldy kind. My phone tolled that a text message had come in. I scanned the information in order to mentally prepare on the way.

The drive downtown was quick. I'd managed to miss morning rush hour, skating in at the tail end with the other stragglers. I parked in the Police Plaza garage and took the elevator to the third floor, and the interview rooms. The scents of coffee and fear circulated through the hallways. In another two hours, the smells of lunch would override the fear for a short time, before being wrestled back under again.

Yapping greeted me as I neared Interview Two.

Inside the room, a small gray poodle sat atop the interview table. A fake plant stood in the corner, four seats were arranged around the table, and a neutral, hotel-room-style painting graced the wall. We kept this room for witnesses, rather than criminals, so it had amenities the others lacked, such as cushioned chairs.

In the end, it was still an interview room in a police station.

The plump woman sitting at the table sported well-coiffed, bright red hair, and appeared to be around eighty, though she'd aged nicely, her skin soft, albeit wrinkled. Her makeup was pristine, and large, jeweled rings graced her fingers. As I stepped inside, the dog licked her nose, eliciting a raucous laugh that lapped at the walls, nearly causing me to laugh with her.

Good thing I'm a hardened police woman, with magical abilities to hold back a laugh.

"Hello, Ms. White," I said. "I'm Detective Barnes."

She nodded. "You can call me Doris."

"Doris, then."

I got the preliminaries over with then said, "How long have you been staying at the hotel?"

"I've been there about two weeks. I'm between houses."

They tell me you saw the victim with someone?"

"Yes, a young lady. She giggled a lot, stumbled around on giant heels. I'd say she was a pro."

"A pro?"

"You know, a *prostitute*." She whispered this last word.

"What makes you think that?"

"The way she dressed, for one. I get that girls dress all kinds of slutty these days, but the dress hem came to just below her butt cheeks, and it was only by the grace of God that her nipples didn't pop out of the top of her dress. There were cutouts along the sides, too." She absently petted the poodle as she talked. "All in all, I'd say she had on about three square inches of fabric, spread out across her top half."

I liked this lady.

"Have you seen her before?"

"Yes, with other men."

"Is it always in that room?"

"Yep."

"What did you see, exactly? Walk me through from the beginning."

She took a moment to collect her thoughts. The dog settled onto its belly in front of her, tongue hanging out one side of its mouth. "They drove up in his car when I was out walking Pansy."

"What time?"

"Last night around ten p.m. Pansy and I like to stay up and watch movies, so I usually take an intermission and walk him around that time before finishing the movie and going to bed."

Pansy. Him. Huh.

"They pulled up and he got out of the car. He walked

around to her side and opened the door for her. She cupped his privates as she got out and giggled at him. It pretty much lasted all the way to the room." She paused. "The giggling, not the cupping."

"Go on."

"They walked to the room. She kissed him as he was unlocking the door, so it ended up taking a few tries. Those card keys are a pain in the ass. Then they went inside and shut the door."

"Other than her clothing, what did she look like?"

"Long black hair and dark skin. Skinny. Her knees were bruised." Another pause. "You think that's a hazard of the job?"

"Possibly. Did you see anything odd during your walk? Or the next morning?"

"There was a man hanging around across the street this morning. A homeless guy. I didn't really see his face, though. He was wearing a gray sweatshirt with the hood pulled up, and it hid his face."

"You said he was homeless. How could you tell?"

"I guess I just assumed. He was filthy, his clothes didn't fit quite right and were mismatched."

"Did you see when this woman left the room?"

"Nope. They were locked up tight when I went back to my room. I wanted to see how the movie ended."

"Did you hear any names exchanged?"

"He called her Candy; she called him Sexy. Over and over. I think she thought it sounded sexier than it did. Then again, he certainly seemed to like it."

"Did you notice what kind of car he drove?"

"It was an expensive one. Dark blue. Maybe a Jaguar."

"What was he wearing?"

"He had on jeans and a polo shirt, tucked in. Dark blue. And cowboy-type boots, though they looked a bit odd. I wasn't paying so much attention to them since her heels were about six inches high and sparkly. I think they distracted me from his boots."

"You've actually been more helpful than most. Quite a memory."

"It's nice of you to say, but it's really because I'm nosy. I take in everything."

"We always appreciate that sort of attention to detail from our witnesses." I stood up, extending my hand with a business card in it. "Thank you for your help. If you think of anything else, give me a call. Would you like an officer to walk you to the front?"

"Nah. Good memory, remember? I can find my way out." She picked the dog up from the table and waved his paw at me. "Say bye to the nice police woman, Pansy."

I inadvertently waved at the idiot dog, who most certainly did not care if I felt like saying bye. Still, it made Ms. White smile, and I figured she'd earned that. In other circumstances, she would have made me laugh.

I checked in with the rookie who had been canvassing the hotel guests. "Anybody else see or hear anything?"

The rookie was a short, stocky man, his shoulders twice the width of his hips. He looked perpetually puzzled, but not in a daft way. More a curious way. "One of the couples thought they heard screams early this morning, but they didn't look out the window or anything. Nor did they look at a clock. When I asked them to guesstimate the time, he said eight a.m., and she said nine." He shrugged. "They argued about everything the whole time. I'm not sure why they're on vacation together. Pretty sure they don't like each other at all."

"Did you happen to talk to a homeless man hanging out in the area?"

"Never saw him. You want us to look for him?"

"No, I'll head out and see if there's anyone around. I need you to see if there are any cameras in the area and get footage. The victim's car was dark, pricy, possibly a Jag. I need an image of his passenger. Also, did you check the cars in the lot against the sign-in information yet?"

"Yeah. All vehicles were accounted for."

"Okay. Find me that footage."

He nodded and took off, torso hardly moving as his bottom half practically marched out the door.

So far, I had a dead John Doe with a pet snake, a probable hooker, and a homeless guy with a hoodie. Time to go back to the hotel and check a few things. I doubted the homeless guy had gone far, so he'd probably be hanging around. Maybe he'd seen something.

*****

Back at the hotel, I set off on foot, looking for shady areas where someone might hide away from the sun that now beat down on the pavement, sending up waves of heat that rippled through the air.

About twenty minutes in, I walked over a culvert with a small stream running below a wood and concrete footbridge. Something rustled underneath the bridge, and a muffled voice sounded. I leaned over the railing, aiming for a better look, but couldn't see anything. Maybe it was the homeless guy.

Trees stood along the edges of the culvert, the grass knee-high at least. Perfect snake depth, which put me on edge. The stream babbled in its merry forward march. My feet sunk into the damp soil and I slid downward, barely keeping my balance. My right foot slipped into the tepid water, the mud sucking at my shoe. I reached down to grab the shoe to ensure it wouldn't slip off then I lifted my foot. It came out with a mild sucking noise.

Something hissed.

Slowly, I lifted my head. There, in the tall grasses beside the water, the massive blunt head of a full-sized python stared at me. I must have startled it when I fell into the stream. Having seen video of these suckers attacking, how suddenly they struck, I fell into an immediate internal panic. It was about three feet from me, which helped some, as I recalled how close pythons got to the prey in those videos. If they were anything to go by, pythons couldn't strike from a distance.

Of course, maybe they could, and just preferred being closer.

With smooth, slow movements, I reached for the service weapon at my hip. The snake hadn't moved, its vacant eyes aimed in my general direction. The sheer size of this thing up close was terrifying, yet amazing. The head was about the size of a dinner plate. I brought the gun in front of me, aimed, and began to squeeze.

"Wait, don't!" A man popped out from the grass, his head and shoulders the only parts of him I could see. "She won't hurt you!"

"She?"

"You startled her, is all. If you back away nice and slow, she won't follow you."

I decided to do as he said before launching my argument. I retreated several steps before the python's head disappeared back into the grass, at which point I realized I preferred having a visual on the bastard. Blood pumping through my veins, breaths pumping in and out, I scurried up the embankment without looking back, afraid that at any moment that jaw would unhinge and wrap around my leg, pulling me into its cavernous guts.

At the top, I stopped, bending over to pant for a second. I could now see parts of the massive body visible in the grass, and I choked back the scream that wanted to bubble out of me.

Only now did I allow my attention to stray to the man standing fearlessly beside the snake. He wore several layers of clothes, the outermost a light jacket. Under that jacket were jeans and a blue polo shirt that looked cleaner than the other layers, though I made out a small, red stain on the pants. He shifted, the tops of a pair of cowboy boots showing above the grass. "Hey, you weren't at the Starburst Hotel up the road this morning, were you?"

He shifted his eyes, likely looking for an escape route. I figured the snake was a damn good promise of escape all on its own.

"You're not in trouble," I said, "but I'm really hoping you saw a woman leaving the hotel. We need to ask her some questions. She might be in danger." People were often more willing to help if they thought they were saving someone versus pointing a finger.

His long, greasy hair stuck to his head, not moving much in the wind. He had thick stubble and one eye squinted more than the other, which leant him an expression of doubt by default. "Why do you think she's in danger?"

"She might have witnessed a crime."

"That guy on the floor in the hotel room?"

Taken aback, I asked, "Did you see him?"

He scratched his head with fingernails so black I could see the dirt from where I stood. "I saw someone." One of his hands slid into his jacket pocket.

I still had my gun out, and I pointed it at him. "Stop. Do not reach into your pocket."

He froze, looked confused.

"What were you reaching for?"

Before he could answer, his pocket moved. At first, I thought I'd imagined it, but then it moved it again, and a small, dark head poked out of the pocket.

"What is that?" My voice came out much closer to a screech than I'd intended.

"Just a baby."

"A baby what?"

He gestured at the giant python. "Snake, of course."

Right. Of course. What was I thinking?

"Why do you have a snake in your pocket?"

"I'm keeping it warm so Marsha can have a break."

He'd named the python Marsha?

"Well, leave it where it is." Trying to wrest control of the situation back, I continued, "Tell me what you saw this morning."

He shuffled from one foot to the other. "I saw a lady running out of the room. She hardly had any clothes on at all. She drove away in a super nice car. I don't think it was hers."

Sexist. "When did you see the dead man?"

"She left the door open when she left, and I wondered why she looked so scared. So I went to the room and peeked inside. The man was on the floor, not moving. He looked so alone."

"Did you…did you give him the baby snake?" The head

poking out of that pocket looked pretty similar to the dead snake's.

"I thought they could keep each other company. She had just died, poor little thing. She just wasn't strong enough to make it."

That explained the dead snake, and it was obvious where the man's discarded clothing had gone, but I was still no closer to identifying John Doe or the prostitute. "Would you be able to identify the woman if I showed you a picture of her?"

"Sure. She's at the hotel all the time. I've seen her before. Sometimes she slips me some money or food. She's nice."

Creepies crawled up my spine as it struck me to wonder where the other baby snakes were. Pythons didn't just hatch two babies at a time. I needed to leave. "Do you know the nice lady's name?"

"No, but the guy at the front desk talks to her all the time. He's pretty skeezy. Sometimes they close the door."

"Okay, one more question. Can I get your name for my notes? In case I have more questions?"

"Sure can. It's Stanley Kalowitz."

Throwing my thanks his way, I darted back toward the hotel. Once on safe ground, I called the rookie, gave him Stanley's location and information, and asked him to get a couple uniforms out to pick him up. He was a suspect, and someone who could easily disappear. I did my good deed for the day and warned the rookie about the snakes, asking him to get someone out to pick them up, as well.

"Any info for me?" I asked.

"No video footage around there. There's a camera near the hotel, but it's been out of service a long time."

"Thanks." I hung up. No sense drawing out a conversation

where no real information was being passed along.

My phone rang again as I approached the front office. "What is it?"

"Hello to you, too, Madison." Ben, our coroner, didn't sound too happy.

Shit. "You got any information for me yet?"

"Cause of death is a myocardial infarction, but I found a needle mark in his back. I'm still looking to see what substance might have been injected to cause the MI."

"So a heart attack caused by some kind of poison?"

"Yep."

"Okay, thanks, Ben. Let me know when you find out something more."

I strolled into the office, enjoying the look of misery that overtook the clerk's face. This time, I walked up to the counter, reached for the remote, and turned the television off, keeping the remote so he couldn't turn it back on. "Can you tell me about a blonde prostitute, possibly named Candy, who frequents your hotel?"

"We don't allow prostitution here."

"Good. Now that we got that out of the way, I've got a witness who's seen you with Candy multiple times. Want to try again?"

'He sighed, eyes briefly drifting to the TV, despite its current dead state. "Candy rents rooms off the books sometimes. It's none of my business what she uses them for. She just needs a place to sleep, and she pays full price, plus a bonus."

"Right. I can guess what that bonus is. You're about one step off from pimpdom. Did she rent a room last night?"

"Yeah."

"Did she give you any information on the john?"

"No. I told you, it's none of my business."

"You should make it your business. Do you have contact information for Candy? Know where I can find her?"

"She calls me. I don't call her. But I know she calls me from Sandy's Pub, down off Clinton and Esposito sometimes. Maybe she lives around there."

"Describe her for me."

"She's real pretty. Dark hair down to her waist, tan skin, dark brown eyes."

"Anything that stands out? Tattoos? Scars?"

"She's got a butterfly tattoo on her left shoulder and a rose on her lower back."

I didn't want to think about how he knew about the rose. "It would have been nice to have this information earlier, Randy. I'll be in touch about possible charges."

He blustered at my back as I walked out, the remote still in my hand. Let him walk to the TV if he wanted to watch it. He'd wasted half my day with his lies.

I called a friend in Vice on the way to my car. "Hey, Herbert." Yes, that was his real name. "I need to know if you're aware of a prostitute named Candy who frequents the Starburst Hotel and Sandy's Pub. She's a possible murder suspect."

His gruff voice itched my ear through the phone. "You know how many of those girls go by Candy?"

"A lot?"

"Maybe not so many as you'd think, but definitely more than one. Any other information?"

"Yeah, two tattoos—one on her shoulder, one on her lower back."

"I do know a Candy that sounds about right. Try the Elsinore Apartments right there by Sandy's Pub. Unit 314, I think."

"Thanks, Herbert. I owe you." He hung up before I did. What was this, a fast hang-up competition? I made note to hang up faster next time.

The Elsinore was in a seedy area near the waterfront. Palm trees lined the street on the water side, waving in the breeze, which did little to lessen the effects of the high temperature. It had grown increasingly hotter as the day progressed, and I was sweating at a volume nearing Niagara Falls. I looked around for the Jag, but cars were parked everywhere, stretching down side streets, and I didn't see anything nice within view.

I approached the front of the building and walked through the unlocked door, the scent of dead fish following me in, amplified by the narrow, thinly carpeted hallway and cracked, peeling walls. A creaky set of steps took me up to the third floor, the scent of urine overpowering. I avoided a dark puddle, wondering if that was the source of the odor, or something entirely new.

Room 314 stood near a turn in the hallway. No one answered the door the first two times I knocked, but the third time brought the sound of shuffling steps and a shadow in the peephole.

"I'm not buying anything," a quiet voice said.

"I'm not selling anything."

"What do you want?"

I held my badge up to the peephole. "I need to ask you some questions. Please open the door."

Silence greeted my request. I could practically hear the profanity running through her head. I bet she wished she lived on the first floor, but she wouldn't be the first to try leaping from a third floor.

"Open the door now."

Technically, she didn't have to, but what citizens didn't know couldn't hurt me.

Another thirty seconds passed before I heard the *skink* of a chain being drawn across the door, and the click of the lock. A small, dark haired woman opened the door, her boobular circumference probably about equal to her height. She wore a thin cotton nightgown that fell at mid-thigh, and her hair stuck up in a clump at the side. Her makeup had smeared across the left side of her face.

"I didn't kill him."

"If that's true, you also didn't call the police or an ambulance when he dropped dead."

"Is that a crime?"

"Yes."

"Oh." She thought a moment then, with a slumping of her shoulders, invited me in. "You want some coffee?"

The thought of poison crossed my mind, and I declined, motioning for her to take a seat across from me. "So tell me what happened if you didn't kill him."

She clutched her hands in her lap, squeezing them enough to whiten the knuckles. "He started acting funny last night, slurring his speech, acting confused sometimes. But he performed just fine." Here, she stopped and shot me a look. "I mean, he got it up okay."

I nodded, not wanting to have this conversation.

"But when we woke up this morning and tried to have one last bang for his buck, he was still slurring, and he fell out of the bed. He tried to walk across the room, but he kept stumbling. I asked if he was diabetic or something. Did he need some juice? He said he wasn't, but then he fell over and didn't move. I panicked and took off. I swear I wasn't trying to steal his car, but I didn't know what to do or where the buses were. My johns usually pick me up."

"Do you know his full name?"

"Yeah, actually I have his wallet." She went back to the purse and pulled it out, handing it to me. "It's all there. His money, I mean. I wasn't robbing him. I just panicked." She pulled a black fabric bundle out of the purse, untying a knot in it as I watched. Finally, she turned the bundle upside down and dumped out some cheap jewelry. Thrusting the fabric toward me, she continued, "This is his, too. I…I wasn't sure what to do with my jewelry, and I didn't want to lose it. I always take it out before, you know."

I took the sock, grimacing as I stuck it in my pocket before going through his wallet. His driver's license told me his name was Kurt Lancaster. Did his parents do that on purpose? "Take me back to the beginning. Retrace the date from start to finish."

"All right. I met him at Sandy's yesterday, about eight o'clock. From there, we drove in his car to some ritzy place for dinner. There were all these people out front with signs about saving the pythons or something. Some lady got in Kurt's face, screaming about his boots. I guess they were snakeskin or something."

My mind was starting to go somewhere I preferred it not, but I allowed her to keep talking, as much as I didn't want to.

"She hit him with her sign and called him a murderer. She kept hitting him. There were other people coming over now, and they were all yelling, too. Some guy tried to get past us, and he was holding this big cup. Kurt grabbed the cup from him and sloshed it on her. Scared the crap out of me, at first, because it was red, and my brain screamed, 'Blood!' But it was just a Slushee or something."

"Candy, do you remember anything strange before the hotel?"

"Yeah, actually. He yelped and said something had poked him. He kept rubbing at his back while we were at the dance club."

Shit. It couldn't be.

"When did the poke happen?"

"Right after he threw the Slushee at that lady. As we were walking away."

I asked her a few more questions, but didn't get anything more helpful than I'd already gotten. "Thank you for your time, Candy. I'll be in contact later. Don't leave town."

All I could think about was getting across town. There had to be a different explanation than the one shrieking through my head right now.

I called Ben, but had to leave a message. He never answered the phone while busy with a body. "Call me when you get a chance. I need to know if snake venom could be the cause of death of our John Doe. By the way, his name is Kurt Lancaster. Not a joke."

In the car, I called the rookie, whose name turned out to be Steinem. His last name, anyway. Eventually, I might even learn his first name. I gave him Doe's name and asked him to run it. He could take care of the easy part. I also passed along Candy's name and location so she could be picked up, along with a request for them to look for the car. Candy and Stanley might not be killers—only one person fit that bill—but they'd each committed crimes, for which they'd have to answer.

The acid green of the house now struck me as poisonous instead of amusing. I felt sick to my stomach, sitting in the car for several minutes to gather my thoughts. The phone rang. Ben. I picked up, staring at my friend's house. "Hey, Ben."

"It could have been coral snake venom. They're native to the area, and the effects of their venom can take hours to kill the victim. He had an elevated white count, which can be an indication. You onto something?"

"Yeah. I'm definitely onto something. Call you back later."

I climbed out of the car and scuffed my way up the sidewalk, hoping the ground would open up and swallow me. The muggy air crept up on me like an alligator in a sweatsuit, adding to the weight on my shoulders.

Myra's front door popped open. "Twice in two days! How'd I get so lucky?" She looked so chipper, happy to see me. I wished I felt the same.

At least our visits would be sans snakes now. No snakes allowed in prison.

The Usual Unusual Suspects

Mike Job was born in 1943, and following high school, attested in the British South Africa Police (Rhodesia). There he served 15yrs in a variety of functions – dog-handler, general policework, including investigation, sub-aqua, medico-legal work, anti-terrorism and court prosecution, before returning to his home-town, Durban. After moving to Cape Town, he served 32 years in the City's Safety and Security branch before retirement. Married with one daughter, currently teaching English in South Korea.

Jill Hand is a member of International Thriller Writers. She is the author of Southern Gothic thrillers White Oaks and Black Willows, from Black Rose Writing. Her work has appeared in many anthologies, including Windward: Best New England Crime Stories, The Corona Book of Ghost Stories, and the Pulp Horror Book of Phobias, Volumes I and II, among others.

Joe Giordano was born in Brooklyn. He and his wife Jane now live in Texas.

Joe's stories have appeared in more than one hundred magazines including *The Saturday Evening Post, and Shenandoah*. His novels, *Birds of Passage, An Italian Immigrant Coming of Age Story* (2015), and *Appointment with ISIL, an Anthony Provati Thriller* (2017) were published by Harvard Square Editions. Rogue Phoenix Press published *Drone Strike* (2019) and his short story collection, *Stories and Places I Remember* (2020).

Joe was among one hundred Italian American authors honored by Barnes & Noble to march in Manhattan's 2017 Columbus Day Parade. Read the first chapter of Joe's novels and sign up for his blog at http://joe-giordano.com/

Michael Thomét is a writer and game designer from the dry desert of Arizona. He believes that every story should have at least a bit of mystery to carry one from line to line. Although this is his first time publishing prose, he has released several digital narrative works such as games, interactive fiction, and what he calls "a text play delivered over Twitter." His other narrative works can be found at http://incobalt.me.

Michele Bazan Reed's short stories have appeared in *Woman's World* magazine and several anthologies, most recently *Detective Mysteries Short Stories, Mid-Century Murder, Malice Domestic 15: Mystery Most Theatrical, Masthead: Best New England Mysteries 2020, The Fish that Got Away* and the forthcoming *The Big Fang* (autumn 2021).

A member of Sisters in Crime and its Guppy Chapter, Private Eye Writers of America, and the Short Mystery Fiction Society, she won a 2017 Daphne Award in the unpublished mainstream mystery category.

Paul R. Paradise is the author of the *Theo Jones* detective series, and the first in the series is *The Counterfeit Detective* (Koehler Books); the next is tentatively titled: *Truth Is Always Changing*. Mr. Paradise is an expert on the crime called trademark counterfeiting or product counterfeiting, which the FBI calls the "business crime of the 21st Century." He's written numerous articles and a best-selling non-fiction book.

Mike Tuggle is a writer living and working in Charlotte, North Carolina, publishing under the name M. C. Tuggle. His mystery, science fiction, and literary short stories have been featured in several publications, including *Mystery Weekly Magazine*, *Hexagon*, and *Metaphorosis*. Novel Fox published his novella, *Aztec Midnight*, in December, 2014.

You can find him blogging on all things literary at www.mctuggle.com.

Edward Lodi has written more than 30 books, both fiction and nonfiction, as well as a poetry chapbook. His short fiction and poetry have appeared in numerous magazines and journals, such as *Mystery Weekly Magazine*, and in anthologies published by Cemetery Dance, Main Street Rag, Rock Village Publishing, Superior Shores Press, and others. His story *Charnel House* was featured on Night Terrors Podcast.

Lynn Hesse won the 2015 First Place Winner, Oak Tree Press, *Cop Tales*, for her mystery, *Well of Rage*. Her novel *Another Kind of Hero* was a finalist for the 2018 Silver Falchion Award and won the Readers' Chill Award in 2021. Her short story *Jewel's Hell* was published September 2019 in *Me Too Short Stories: An Anthology* by Level Best Books and edited by Elizabeth Zelvin.

Her short story about a domestic homicide, *Murder: Food For Thought*, published in the anthology *Double Lives, Reinvention & Those We Leave Behind, 2009* by Wising Up Press was adapted in the play, *We Hunt Our Young,* produced at Emory University Field Showcase and Core Studio Luncheon Time

Series, 2011. Excerpts from the play *Unacceptable Truths* was performed on the Atlanta BeltLine in 2013.

An interview concerning Lynn's role as a police officer, *Blue Steel*, is in The Women's Studies Archives, The Second Feminist Movement, Georgia State University. She performs in several dance and theatrical troupes in Atlanta, Georgia. The dandelion is one of her performance personas. Find her at www.lynnhesse.com

Kelly Zimmer read her first Agatha Christie mystery at age thirteen. Since then, she's lived on a steady diet of murder, thrillers, horror, and suspense novels. For most of her adult life, Kelly labored in a stifling corporate atmosphere in the wonderfully bizarre and diverse landscape of Florida, USA.

Visit Kelly on her website at www.kellyzimmerauthor.com or on Instagram at kellyzimmerauthor.

John M. Floyd's work has appeared in more than 300 different publications, including *Alfred Hitchcock's Mystery Magazine, Ellery Queen's Mystery Magazine, Strand Magazine, the Saturday Evening Post*, and three editions of *The Best American Mystery Stories*. A former Air Force captain and IBM systems engineer, John is also an Edgar Award finalist, a four-time Derringer Award winner, and the author of nine books.

His short story – *The Judge's Wife* – appeared in CRIMEUCOPIA – *The Cosy Nostra, Redemption* in CRIMEUCOPIA – *Dead Man's Hand,* and *Saving Mrs Hapwell* in CRIMEUCOPIA – *As In Funny Ha-Ha, Or Just Peculiar.*

A fan of all things fantastical and frightening, **Shannon Lawrence** writes primarily horror and fantasy. Her stories can be found in over forty anthologies and magazines, and her three solo horror short story collections, *Blue Sludge Blues & Other Abominations*, *Bruised Souls & Other Torments*, and *Happy Ghoulidays* are available now. Other appearances include *Ember: A Journal of Luminous Things* and *The Society of Misfit Stories*. You can also find her as a co-host of the true crime podcast *Mysteries, Monsters, & Mayhem*. Find her at www.thewarriormuse.com.

16 stories ranging from the 14th to the 21st Century, all from women authors whose forte is crime.

Featuring *Karen Skinner, Hilary Davidson, Pauline Gostling, Linda Kerr, Kate Miller, Tiffany Lindfield, Lena Ng, Ginny Swart, Sandrine Bergèss, Michelle Ann King, Amanda Steel, Kelly Lewis, Paulene Turner, Claire Leng, Madeleine McDonald and Joan Hall Hovey.*

**Paperback Edition ISBN:
9781909498198
eBook Edition ISBN:
9781909498204**

18 authors take time to look under the skin of the people who sometimes inhabit their heads, and put what they find down on paper.

Featuring John Gerard Fagan, Nick Boldock, Weldon Burge, Chris Phillips, Dan Meyers, Jeff Dosser, Eve Fisher, Emilian Wojnowski, Fabiyas M V, Lamont A. Turner, Edward Ahern, Robert Petyo, Al Hagan, Caroline Tuohey, Steve Carr, Bobby Mathews, Michael Bracken, and June Lorraine Roberts.

Paperback Edition ISBN:
9781909498235
eBook Edition ISBN:
9781909498228

17 writers take us on Cosy journeys - some
more traditional, while others are very much up
to date.

Eve Fisher, Alexander Frew, Tom Johnstone,
John M.Floyd, Andrew Humphrey, Joan Leotta,
Gary Thomson, Eamonn Murphey,
Matias Travieso-Diaz, Madeline McEwen,
Lyn Fraser, Ella Moon, Gina L. Grandi,
Louise Taylor, Judy Penz Sheluk,
Joan Hall Hovey and Judy Upton.

Paperback Edition ISBN: 9781909498242
eBook Edition ISBN: 9781909498259

CRIMEUCOPIA

As In Funny Ha-Ha

Or Just Peculiar

**Putting the Outré back into
OMG are**

*Jesse Hilson, Gabriel Stevenson,
Maddi Davidson, Brandon Barrows,
Robb T. White, Regina Clarke,
Martin Zeigler, K. G. Anderson,
Andrew Hook, Ed Nobody,
Jody Smith, Michael Grimala,
W. T. Paterson, James Blakey,
Emilian Wojnowski,
Andrew Darlington,
Lawrence Allan, Ricky Sprague,
Bethany Maines, John M. Floyd and
Julie Richards*

**Paperback Edition ISBN:
9781909498266
eBook Edition ISBN:
9781909498273**

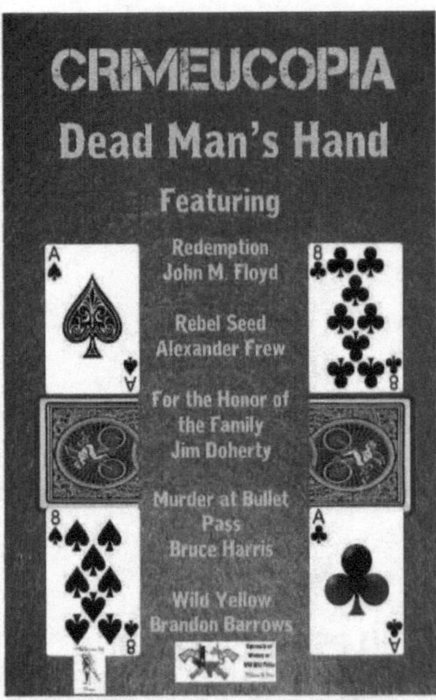

The five writers here have very respectable track records in the Western genre, and are old hands when it comes to telling compelling stories.

So join
John M. Floyd
Alexander Frew
Jim Doherty
Bruce Harris
and
Brandon Barrows

and let them take you back to a time of six-guns an' whiskey, an' wild, wild fiction.

Paperback Edition ISBN:
9781909498266
eBook Edition ISBN:
9781909498273

Oh Baby, Baby, How Was I Supposed To Know…

Is Love ever perfect? Or is it an obsession that remains rather than just a passing phase? And who's to say that Revenge isn't, in fact, a dish best served hot from the flames of passion?

Fifteen writers tell us about affairs of the heart – some with humour, some with a darker intent, and others that are never quite exactly what they seem. Is it all about manipulation? Can there be more than one agenda? And does Love really conquer all, even when it's supposedly blind? Or maybe Love is just an old Devil, looking for mischief?

Steve Sneyd, Ange Morrissey, James Roth, Michael Wiley, Gustavo Bondoni, Matthew Wilson, Peter W. J. Hayes, Wil A. Emerson, Brandon Barrows, Bern Sy Moss, Michael Anthony Dioguardi, Russell Richardson, Robert Petyo, Sam Westcott, Bryn Fortey and *Vicky LaPerso* – all of whom take us on roller coaster rides through a fictional Tunnel of Love.

Paperback Edition ISBN: 9781909498303
eBook Edition ISBN: 9781909498310

www.ingramcontent.com/pod-product-compliance
Lightning Source LLC
Chambersburg PA
CBHW050809190726
48285CB00005B/1850